MAR -- '03

Four for a Boy

Also by Mary Reed and Eric Mayer

One for Sorrow
Two for Joy
Three for a Letter

To receive a free catalog of other Poisoned Pen Press titles, please contact us in one of the following ways:

Phone: 1-800-421-3976
Facsimile: 1-480-949-1707
Email: info@poisonedpenpress.com
Website: www.poisonedpenpress.com

Poisoned Pen Press
6962 E. First Ave. Ste 103
Scottsdale, AZ 85251

Four for a Boy

Mary Reed & Eric Mayer

Poisoned Pen Press

Copyright 2002 by Mary Reed and Eric Mayer

First Edition 2003

10 9 8 7 6 5 4 3 2 1

Library of Congress Catalog Card Number: 2002105066

ISBN: 1-59058-031-1 Hardcover

Poisoned Pen Press
6962 E. First Ave. Ste. 103
Scottsdale, AZ 85251
www.poisonedpenpress.com
info@poisonedpenpress.com

Printed in the United States of America

For D

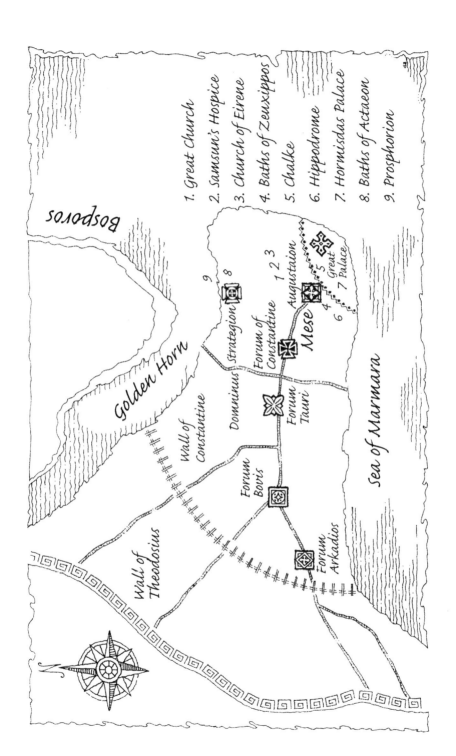

Bosporos

Golden Horn

Wall of Constantine

Wall of Theodosius

Sea of Marmara

Dominius Strategion

Forum of Constantine

Forum Tauri

Forum Bovis

Forum Arkadios

Mese

Augustaion

Great Palace

1 2 3
4
5
6 7

9 8

1. Great Church
2. Samsun's Hospice
3. Church of Eirene
4. Baths of Zeuxippos
5. Chalke
6. Hippodrome
7. Hormisdas Palace
8. Baths of Actaeon
9. Prosphorion

Prologue

June 540 A.D.

Sweet perfume wafted briefly from drifts of rose petals strewn on the marble floor of the Great Church as a procession paced majestically into the sacred building.

The lengthy contingent of court dignitaries and guards passed through a wide doorway constructed of wood the faithful believed to be from Noah's Ark, and came to a halt in front of the Patriarch and a flock of lesser clergy waiting to greet them.

Following a few paces behind the emperor and empress, John glanced rapidly around. Hundreds of lamps filled the vast space with lambent illumination. His gaze skimmed over the huge church's countless columns of green, pink, and white marble topped with lacy carvings and adorned with imperial monograms, the silver, gold, and glittering gems decorating the altar and sacred vessels, and the equally colorful ranks of courtiers dressed in their finest silks and embroidered robes.

It was difficult to believe that this soaring edifice had been completed less than a handful of years before, replacing the former Great Church destroyed by rioting mobs. This glorious, light-filled building seemed more a creation of angels than men.

From above came a faint fluttering of wings. A nesting bird disturbed by the commotion. Or perhaps, John thought wryly as a dove feather drifted down like a lazy snowflake, the Holy Spirit had decided to attend the ceremony.

John had organized the route from the palace and ensured that all participants were in their proper places. Now that the imperial couple and their entourage had entered the Great Church, his task was done for the present. As he took his place among the official observers, he noted the contingent of Ostrogoths standing a few paces from the altar. What did they think about this service of thanksgiving for the fall of Ravenna, a great triumph in Justinian's war to regain Italy from their countrymen?

The Patriarch stepped forward to greet the procession with formal and flowery phrases. Emperor Justinian regarded him with a slight smirk while Empress Theodora maintained a neutral expression, her eyes dark as the black veins in the marble floor.

John glanced down at the petals. He no longer contemplated the political or religious significance of the ceremony. Nor was he recalling the lost glory of the empire Justinian sought to reclaim.

Instead, he remembered a woman.

Had it been fifteen years since he had tutored her? It seemed much longer than that. Then he had been an insignificant palace slave. Now he was commonly referred to as John the Eunuch, or more formally as Lord Chamberlain to Emperor Justinian.

He shifted his feet slightly. Fragrance wafted upward like a wraith from the roses crushed beneath his boots.

Roses always reminded him of Lady Anna.

Chapter One

January 525 A.D.

The swaggering and elegant young thugs who styled themselves the Blues had terrorized Constantinople for months. They had driven their rivals, the Greens, from the streets. Now their target was the populace.

As John escorted Lady Anna along the Mese he kept watch for possible ambush. The well honed alertness of the mercenary he had been in another life had never deserted him. So far, however, the colonnaded thoroughfare that ran from the heart of Constantinople to its defensive walls had revealed no dangers.

The shops crowded along both sides of the wide street boasted only a handful of customers that morning. The purveyors of pottery and glass, cloths both fine and inexpensive, spices, olives, and cooking oils, peered out disconsolately from their emporiums. The smells of their wares were as enticing as ever, John thought. It was hard to say whether the sparse number of pedestrians was due to the civil unrest or the wintry weather.

Two ill dressed boys, breath steaming in the cold, raced recklessly across the Mese.

"Take care, Lady Anna," John murmured. He stepped nimbly into the path of the urchins, deflecting their careening course away from his companion. The boys shouldered him insolently as they went by and ran into an alley. There they paused only long enough to taunt a beggar huddled in a doorway. The unfortunate man clutched closer to his chest the largesse of the state. To the usual loaf of bread the authorities had added a small lump of meat. It was another reason for those dependent on the emperor's generosity to refrain from rioting against their benefactor.

Lady Anna noticed the ragged man crouched in his makeshift shelter and turned her head away. Her shoulders trembled beneath the thick yellow woolen cloak hanging from her angular form. Perhaps, John thought, it was nothing more than a reaction to the frigid wind. There was enough tragedy on public display every day in Constantinople to make even the kindest hearts weary of grieving.

Shouted curses pulled John's attention from the beggar to a gang of workmen laboring to repair a broken column on a colonnade just down the street. The chill lying on the still air served to amplify sounds even as it suppressed the familiar marshy tang of the sea, a smell now overlaid with the sharply acrid scent of smoke from a thousand braziers heating the city's shops and dwellings.

Cold seeped through the leather soles of John's boots. "To the Great Church, lady?" he inquired quietly of his companion.

Lady Anna looked up at him, her plain, thin-lipped face animated by a lively look of interest. Though she was unbecomingly tall for a woman, her lean escort was much taller.

"Yes, indeed. Everyone tells me the new installation there is a wonder, but I intend to judge for myself before the Patriarch is convinced that it should be removed as blasphemous. Or these rampaging mobs father keeps warning me about set the church on fire." They had come to the Augustaion. Anna inclined her head toward a stolid, brick basilica across the nearly deserted square.

"As you order." John glanced keenly around again.

Snow had floured the city overnight. Dark imprints left by booted human feet formed purposeful paths over the faint, meandering trails of foraging seagulls. A few of the large birds squawked noisily and took to the sky as John and Anna intruded on their search for food.

As the couple stepped briskly forward, John remembered crossing frozen fields in Bretania, tilting his head toward their bordering forest, heart racing, listening for the stealthy hiss of steel drawn from scabbards. There was danger in Constantinople too, but of a different sort. The enemies here were alien to John. Not military men. Not Persians or Picts, but fashionably dressed young men, racing fans, more familiar with chariot tactics on the Hippodrome track than battlefield formations. The blades they wielded were as sharp as any Persian weapon, and the factions were ready to defend the honor of their favorite racing teams with all the ferocity of warriors defending a border.

Or to turn their ferocity on the innocent.

Suddenly one of the few other figures visible, a man shrouded in a black cloak, changed direction and walked purposefully toward them.

John's hand fastened on the hilt of his blade, but as the man drew nearer realized he was not a Blue. His gold-trimmed, heavily embroidered cloak was certainly ostentatious enough to please any member of that faction, but he did not sport voluminous sleeves or their Hunnic hairstyle, shaved in front and long in the back.

The man was short but solidly built with a smooth, square jaw and close-cropped black hair. He was also, it turned out, known to Anna.

"Trenico!" she said. "What a surprise! You've been to see the notorious statue, I wager!"

The man stopped an arm's length from John. He contrived to look through him in an insultingly obvious fashion and gave Lady Anna a stiff bow.

"Anna! I thought it was you. Yes, you deduce correctly. I decided to take a stroll to blow the cobwebs away. This is certainly the right weather for that! And what do you think of this? I was just standing outside the Great Church talking to a couple of senators, good friends of mine, and I saw the most amazing thing. There was a commotion around the corner and the several of the Gourd's men went racing past, with swords drawn no less. I wonder what that was all about?"

Lady Anna said she was not surprised. "We're living in an armed encampment these days. We should count ourselves fortunate if we are merely robbed and not murdered for daring to venture out." Her lips curved briefly into an ironic smile.

"As you say. An armed encampment," Trenico agreed. "Even the Greens are afraid to be out on the streets."

"So the Blues have spared us from the depredations of the Greens, at least," Anna observed.

"The cold hasn't frozen your wit! Let's hope the emperor regains his senses and orders some chariot races before long. Then these miserable factions can get back to insulting each other from opposite ends of the Hippodrome and leave the rest of us in peace."

John had occasionally glimpsed Trenico at Lady Anna's home. The man seemed intent on ingratiating himself with her father, Senator Opimius. That was one path to advancement for a soft fop of a courtier who probably knew nothing about armed encampments.

"You can see I'm well protected." Lady Anna gestured at John.

"Well protected? By whom?" For the first time Trenico acknowledged John's presence. "Oh yes, him. But surely this is only the slave your father borrowed from the Keeper of the Plate's office to tutor you? A eunuch, is it not? How can a eunuch tutor protect you from a street gang? Frighten them away by reciting epic verses?"

John struggled to maintain a blank expression. He succeeded, barely. Luckily Trenico did not glance down at John's hand, tightened around the hilt of his dagger until his knuckles were pale. It would be sweet to sink the blade into that jeering fool. He forced himself to look away from Trenico and glance around the Augustaion again. His dark eyes were furious.

It would also be folly indeed to spill aristocratic blood, John's practical side reminded him. He did not consider himself as truly a slave, and would never accept his slavery. Unfortunately, the world saw things differently.

"You don't seem worried about running into any danger in the streets, Trenico," Anna was saying. "Aren't you tempting thieves going about in such finery?"

Trenico's broad shoulders went back. To John he resembled a dove puffing its feathered breast. "Even those murdering Blues won't force me to creep around the city sporting a brass belt buckle. I'd rather die defending my best silver buckle, or the gold one for that matter."

"I would think your life would be worth more than a silver buckle."

Trenico shrugged off her comment. "Don't fret, Anna, I can defend myself. But I fear I must be on my way now. I have an audience at the Hormisdas Palace with Theodora. This is absolutely confidential, you understand."

John glared at Trenico's receding back. A smoky haze was settling, suffusing the city with a gray twilight. In the eerie light the massed buildings, a jumble of tenements crowding up to churches, mansions protected by stout doors, looming warehouses, elegant colonnaded baths, all of them sporting roofs bristling with crosses, appeared to John as nothing more than a fanciful fresco on the wall of an eccentric's villa.

It had been only a handful of years since he had been brought here to labor in metaphorical chains. There were still days when Constantinople and his life within the Great Palace seemed unreal.

Perhaps that notion had helped him to endure the unendurable.

"I wonder what all that fuss Trenico mentioned was about?" Anna mused as they continued on toward the Great Church. "The City Prefect always has armed men running around. It's mostly done to impress citizens, or at least that's what father says."

"That could well be so."

They ascended the steps to the church. When they reached the shelter of its wide, columned portico John almost—unforgivably—relaxed his vigilance. He heard the muffled pounding of approaching footsteps and for a heartbeat imagined they signaled the reappearance of the rambunctious street urchins.

Then two Blues careened out of the building and down the stairs. With a swift sweep of his arm, John pushed Lady Anna into a corner of the portico and placed himself between her and the church door.

Just in time before a third Blue burst out.

This one raised his weapon to strike, saw the blade waiting in John's hand, and instead bolted off toward the Mese.

John registered a fleeting impression. An enormous man with the shoulders of a brick carrier and a squashed and crooked nose. Then two of the Prefect's men rushed out. They halted at the top of the steps, labored breath hanging on the air, as they stared out over the open space before them.

Behind them, in the church, the screaming began.

"The bastards have split up," growled one of the men.

"Where's Septimius?" asked his companion.

"He's trying to stop the doorkeeper's bleeding. One of them slashed the old man on their way out. A clever diversion. They're not all stupid, the Blues."

"What about Hypatius?"

John noticed Lady Anna pale at the mention of the name.

"He's beyond tending," came the reply. "Look, I'll follow the short fellow. See if you can catch the one who ran toward the hospice. Once he's gone through there into the alleys we've lost him. Let the giant go. Someone his size won't be able to hide for long."

John looked across the square. The quarry had already disappeared from sight even as the men finally lumbered off in pursuit. They would be fortunate to catch the fleeing miscreants. He suspected they didn't particularly want to corner them.

He turned toward Anna. "Forgive my impertinence in touching you." He broke off, seeing her expression. Her face looked whiter than the freshest snow shrouding the city.

"Hypatius," she whispered. "Surely not the same Hypatius...."

She spun around and entered the church. John followed.

Just inside the vestibule a man bent over a prone figure, no doubt the wounded doorkeeper. Worshippers milled about in panic. The screaming had stopped, but several women sobbed and a short man with gray hair shook his fist at no one in particular.

"I saw it with my own eyes!" he shouted. "Murder even while the Lord looks on!"

John pushed his way through the crowd, clearing a path for Lady Anna as they advanced toward the life-sized marble sculpture standing on a shoulder-high pedestal in the center of the vestibule. It was an image of the meek god the Christians worshipped, a condemned man as helpless as any slave, hanging from a cross. Wisps of coiling lamp smoke imparted a hint of animation to the dying man's chiseled features, but the groan of anguish was Anna's.

She had knelt beside a crumpled shape lying like a carelessly discarded robe at the foot of the pedestal on which the instrument of execution was displayed. Lamplight glinted on a dark, glassy pool spreading from the motionless form.

"It is Hypatius. My father's friend. They will never discuss philosophy or share wine again."

❊ ❊ ❊

Felix flinched as Emperor Justin's spidery hand unexpectedly dropped onto his shoulder. At first the young German excubitor feared that some loathsome creature had fallen on him from the low roof of the bridge between the church and the Great Palace. When he jerked his helmeted head around and saw instead Justin's veined and palsied hand, his heart jumped. Most of the empire's inhabitants would meet their god without even setting eyes on their emperor. His fleshly touch was profoundly unsettling.

Justin staggered forward a step before steadying himself. Felix felt the man's weight on his shoulder, the ponderous, unexpected weight of the battlefield dead. Then the quaestor Proclus, accompanying Justin as usual, swiftly took charge.

"Caesar, this should have been swept clean before your walk. Someone is certainly going to pay for that slippery spot." His voice was calm and firm.

Felix glanced down at the strip of purple carpeting pointing an imperial finger along the bridge. Snow had drifted in between the marble pillars supporting the roof and melted in the warmth radiated by lamps set in niches along the chest-high wall. To think that such a commonplace occurrence might have caused the emperor, a man with absolute power over all his subjects, to fall like a common drunkard swaying out of an inn!

Proclus glared at the attendants stationed on either side of Justin. They were big muscular fellows, costumed like courtiers. Their embroidered robes brushed the emperor's heavy cloak. From a distance they appeared to be leaning toward Justin, engaged in some privileged conversation. In the confusion of rich fabrics it was not immediately evident that they were firmly gripping the old man's arms. Or rather were gripping them again, thanks to Proclus' silent reprimand. Even so, they continued to look down over the low wall toward the commotion that had distracted them.

"What is it?" asked Justin. "What's going on? You're blocking my view." His voice was querulous.

"Three Blues just ran out of the Great Church," replied Proclus. "Up to no good as usual, I suspect." Justin's advisor had the look of a patrician. The broad, pale brow revealed by his receding hairline appeared waiting for a laurel wreath. Felix would have mistaken him for the emperor, had he not known better.

Justin, by contrast, appeared in old age the peasant he had been. Once a large and impressive man, he was now merely big, stooped and thick necked. His prominent nose had flattened and spread across his red, chafed face. "Why aren't all these troublemakers under control, Proclus? Isn't the Gourd doing his job?"

"Yes, he is. Some of his men are already in pursuit," Proclus offered after a swift glance.

The emperor scowled. "It's only Blues? Nothing worse?"

"Simply a bit of unrest in the street," Proclus reassured him. "But perhaps it might be wiser to visit the church another time? May I suggest we go to our meeting with Justinian instead?"

"My nephew is not so unwell this morning?"

"So I am informed."

Justin laughed. "Even so, doubtless Theodora will be speaking for him as usual."

The attendant next to Felix glanced over at him, raised his eyebrows, and grimaced. Felix ignored him. He had only recently been appointed to the imperial bodyguard, a position of great honor and responsibility. It was not for him to sit in judgment of an emperor, especially one who had risen from the ranks of the military.

"But it is only those troublesome young men, you say? Nothing more?" Justin fretted.

"Nothing more, Caesar." Proclus turned to go back the way they had come.

"Very well. I'm afraid that Euphemia will be sorely disappointed. I promised I would describe this remarkable figure of Christ to her in the most minute detail since she is not well enough to see it herself right now."

Proclus gave no order, but the entourage of guards and attendants turned so that Felix found himself looking at Justin's bent back. He could still feel the weight of the emperor's hand on his shoulder. No, it was not for him to judge his ruler.

Yet he could not help wondering about Justin's words. Empress Euphemia had been dead for months.

Chapter Two

The imperial crown sitting on John's pallet was beautifully constructed, the product of painstaking labor. That was John's immediate reaction as he entered the dormitory of the slaves' quarters in the Great Palace.

His second was blinding anger. On examination, the parchment circlet and its pendulia turned out not to be a model to be delivered to a jeweler for fashioning in gold as he had first supposed. Rather it had been constructed from the missing list of the palace's silver plate John had been searching for only the day before.

All thought of a quiet hour or two following his unexpectedly harrowing excursion to the Great Church vanished. He snatched up the fragile creation and stormed out along the corridor to the dining room where his fellow slaves had already gathered to eat.

The thick gruel of wheat meal, poured out to congeal over a large board set in the center of the table and garnished with meats boiled in inexpensive wine, had already largely been consumed. Several of the eunuchs suppressed sniggers as John strode into the room, the crown in his clenched fist.

Andrew, a large, round-faced man, leaned across the table, trespassing on his neighbor's culinary territory in order to grab a sausage. "John! What's that you've got there? A little gift for Lady Anna perhaps? Oh, but she'll be very cross with you. You've squeezed it too hard and ruined it!"

His fellow conspirator, distinguished by his glossy black hair and pock-marked skin, nudged him in the ribs. "It's tragic," he grinned. "How can a slave compete with that handsome Trenico? Everyone knows he's got designs on Anna. Not for her physical charms, of course...."

"Oh, absolutely not, Sisinnius," Andrew agreed, "but certainly her fortune is very charming, isn't it?"

"While poor John here can offer neither companionship nor wealth."

Andrew shook his head in mock sympathy. "So sad, really, isn't it? You'd think he'd know by now that love is not for him!" He waggled the little sausage he held in his pudgy hand before popping it into his mouth.

John took a pace or two further into the room. His lips were drawn into a taut line of anger.

"But now we get to the truth of the matter," Andrew continued. "It's obvious our John has been spending far too much time daydreaming. No wonder he couldn't find that list he lost. He didn't realize it had turned into an imperial crown. It was all done by magick, you know!"

Laughter crept around the table as John's cheek-bones reddened.

"And see," Sisinnius replied in a casual but too loud tone, "there's the proof of it. The man blushes!"

"As well he should," Andrew said. "You'd think he'd have long since given up lusting after women. Even one as plain as—"

John's fist tightened, crushing the crown into a shapeless mass. He was across the room before Andrew had finished his sentence. John grabbed his neck, yanked him up from the bench and begun to stuff the crumpled parchment into his mouth.

His tormentor's face turned scarlet.

Several slaves leapt up and ran out into the corridor, shouting hysterically. In his rage, John saw nothing except the man flopping fishlike around in his grasp as the creature's hot spittle dribbled on his knuckles.

The physical contact was repellent and he loosened his grip. Andrew jerked away. He spit out the soggy wad of parchment and shrieked, "You miserable Greek bastard!"

Then he sank his teeth into John's wrist.

"That's right," shouted Sisinnius gleefully, "give him what he deserves!"

The words had hardly left his mouth before John had slapped one hand onto the table, sending the remains of the meal flying, and vaulted over it, kicking Sisinnius off the bench. Before the man could gather his scrambled wits, John had knelt on him. He banged Sisinnius' head on the floor and screamed lurid curses, mostly concerning the other's ancestry and tastes in intimate companionship. A red stain began to creep across the tiles.

Sisinnius squirmed and squealed. He finally managed to knee John in the stomach. Andrew ran around the end of the table, grabbed John's arms, and pulled him back. Sisinnius punched and clawed at his attacker's face.

John leapt to his feet. Blood streamed down his cheek.

Andrew and Sisinnius were joined in battle by two of the remaining eunuchs, who danced around, kicking clumsily at John's legs.

"So at the Great Palace bullies fight four to one," John sneered, swiping blood from his face with the sleeve of his tunic. "Good odds for weaklings! Or eunuchs!"

With a roar of rage, Andrew started pummeling him with fists resembling slabs of meat. And almost as soft, John thought. Nevertheless, he stepped back out of reach.

He had overlooked Sisinnius, who remained prone on the floor. The dark-haired slave immediately grasped John's boot and jerked his foot out from under him. John fell sideways. His head cracked painfully against the corner of the table.

Then the familiar black mist descended and again he was a young mercenary, striking out left and right, seeking the best place to land a killing blow.

The pounding of boots in the corridor announced the arrival of an excubitor. A couple of the eunuchs who had fled for help cowered outside the room, peering around the doorpost.

"I order this ended!" the guard shouted.

His command was hardly necessary, for silence had suddenly fallen.

❋ ❋ ❋

His back against a rough stone wall, John sat on a cold flagstone floor and contemplated the rapid change in his fortunes.

In the space of less than an hour he had gone from escorting a senator's daughter to wearing shackles in a cold, underground room that reeked of mold and fear.

"Fortuna, you do not smile on me today!" he muttered, shifting his lean flanks uncomfortably.

"Shut up!" came his answer, not from that fickle goddess Fortuna but rather from Andrew, chained to the opposite wall. "Do you want to bring even more trouble down on our heads?" The big eunuch's voice trembled and tears welled in his eyes.

"You mean it's illegal to invoke pagan deities in a Christian emperor's dungeon?" John asked with a sarcastic grin.

"What I meant was that we're all going to be punished extremely severely for damaging imperial property and you don't need to make it any worse!"

John pointed out that apart from a few broken plates and slight damage to the plaster wall little damage had been done to the slave's dining room.

"No, you fool! The imperial property we've damaged is ourselves! And we'll pay for it dearly!"

"I see." John lapsed into silence.

"Why couldn't you just laugh at our little joke?" Andrew mourned. "Why do you hate us so much when you're the same?" He began to weep, snuffling and wiping his nose on his blood-spattered tunic.

John examined the ragged bite mark on his thin wrist. "Your weapon needs sharpening," he grumbled.

Andrew didn't reply. He was now sitting hunched over, staring at the steady flame of a small lamp burning on the floor by the door. "Do you think it will last long?" he finally asked.

"I suppose it depends on what punishment is meted out to property-destroying slaves." John spit out the final word.

The other shook his head. "No, I meant the oil in the lamp. Do you think it will last long?"

John stared at him. The big man's frame seemed suddenly shrunken, his bruised face pitiful. "You're afraid of the dark!"

Andrew looked at the floor and said nothing.

As the silence stretched out, John contemplated what might soon transpire. That severe punishment that was about to be meted out to all five brawlers was in itself not of much concern. He was familiar with the usual form of justice administered to slaves. Compared to what he had already suffered, a flogging would amount to little. However, he would not like to lose his eyesight and fervently hoped his services were valuable enough to the Keeper of the Plate to forestall anything so drastic. But, then too, he reminded himself, slaves had been summarily put to death for lesser misdemeanors than fighting amongst themselves.

If he lived, he would endure, as he had somehow endured the terrible events that eventually brought him to Constantinople. As to whether he would live, that was in the hands of Fortuna. And she had been filled with black humors for much too long.

The regular tread of military men approached slowly along the corridor. A bolt rattled, and the heavy door of the room swung open and admitted an excubitor who looked down with obvious distaste at the sorry spectacle of two crouching, blood-spattered prisoners.

"You! Eunuch!" He glared at John and bared his teeth in an unpleasant grin. "You've been summoned to an audience with Justinian."

John's shackles were unlocked and he was thrust out into the corridor where two armed guards waited.

The imperial jailer blew out the lamp inside the room John had just left before yanking its door shut. John was not sure if the faint sound he heard was the creak of the closing door or a horrified groan from Andrew inside the suddenly darkened cell.

He had no time to contemplate the question. The excubitor prodded John's back with a sword tip. "What are you waiting for? I'd think you'd be eager to get to a meeting with Justinian."

The man at John's right shoulder only partly suppressed a laugh as both guards grabbed John's arms and forced him forward.

John's feet felt heavy as blocks of stone. He knew little of court life. He did know, however, that prisoners were not usually dragged off to meetings with the second most powerful man in the empire.

At the end of the corridor they were met by a thin, stooped man who carried a lantern suspended on a leather cord. Its need was soon apparent, since instead of emerging into daylight as John had expected, they instead clattered down a flight of narrow stone steps and emerged into another dark hallway.

The lantern's cap had been painstakingly decorated with a swirling pattern of punched holes. The circles of light it cast flowed over the hallway's uneven ceiling, occasionally vanishing up into musty darkness when the men passed through cavernous, seemingly empty rooms whose purpose John could not begin to guess.

John sniffed at the cool air flowing in his face. It smelled of loam.

Since his capture he had wished daily for the earth's final embrace. Although he longed for the destination, something within him feared the journey, however short it might turn out to be. It was easy enough to face death in battle when the mind was fogged by warfare's powerful, black potion of fury and terror. Such a death was honorable. But extermination in some dark corner like a rat in a cellar was not.

Yet if this was the manner in which Mithra had chosen to answer his oft prayed wish, how could he protest?

The procession passed across an unused cistern, where stagnant puddles lay amidst a forest of pillars and small creatures scrabbled in the shadows. Here and there arches in the hallway's sweating walls revealed nothing but utter darkness. Soon they moved along the edge of another cistern where the black mirror of water which had never known wind faintly reflected the lantern's light.

"Almost there," announced the big excubitor, his voice wakening echoes around them.

John wondered what method would be used to extinguish him. He hoped it would be a mercifully speedy thrust of the blade.

Mithra, let it not be strangulation or drowning, he prayed fervently as he stumbled against the first step of a stairway leading upward.

He should lash out at his captors, he thought rapidly. Attempt to escape. Yes, that would ensure a clean death.

But the obstinate creature inside him, the thing that so feared death, refused, greedy for the last few heartbeats of life.

At the top of the stairs, their lantern bearer pulled a narrow door open to admit a blinding flood of light. John blinked as he crossed the threshold into a corridor whose wall depicted the progress of a tiger hunt.

There was no time for comprehension. He was dragged around a corner, another door opened, and he was shoved forward to fall onto a thick rug.

Incredulous, he saw the big excubitor immediately prostrate himself beside him. The other three men had disappeared. Turning his head forward, John found himself staring at a pair of dainty, amethyst-encrusted shoes.

"Get up!"

The voice was a woman's. The tone of the command was a man's.

John stood, half expecting the bite of a blade in his back or the hideous embrace of a garrote.

He faced a woman who would have been mistaken for nothing more than a pretty girl except for the fortune in silk robes and jewels which covered her short frame and the gem-studded crown she wore, a real crown, not a parchment imitation.

"It is a sad thing indeed when Justinian is forced to deal with such sorry specimens as you two," said the woman.

John realized that as impossible as it seemed he must indeed have been summoned to meet with Justinian. The woman could only be the powerful man's notorious concubine, the former actress Theodora.

John was engulfed in Theodora's musky scent. It held a suggestion of a spice-seller's shop and a spring meadow as well. Nothing, not the perfume, the incense smoldering in gold pots, not even the oily smoke curling from glass lamps set atop silver tripods, could quite mask the foetor of disease.

"Justinian is very ill," Theodora continued. "It is no secret. He has obviously been poisoned by some stealthy enemy. Yet deception must be met by deception. Those who would fight like slaves, slipping potions into the master's food, must be opposed by slaves."

"Yes, highness," the excubitor beside John muttered, unable to stop himself from replying to her tirade.

Theodora glared venomously at him, her eyes as fathomless as polished jet. "You need not speak. Emulate the silence of your friend here. He understands his place." She glanced at John as her lips formed a red sickle of a smile.

"Justinian has the interest of all citizens at heart," she went on, "and naturally the citizens are outraged by the murder of Hypatius, a pious and generous man. A murder in broad daylight in the Great Church itself! And what's more, Hypatius was one of those who contributed toward the Christ figure!"

She paused, as if to give John and Felix time to grasp what she was saying. "Ironic, isn't it? A man enters a holy place to view the beautiful work of art he has arranged to have placed there and he is rewarded in such an unthinkable fashion. More than ironic, I would say. This was a murder designed to catch the citizens' attention. Justinian naturally shares the public outrage. Yet it has already been whispered abroad that certain of the Blues were responsible and worse yet, that Justinian, well known as one of their supporters, condones their act. Those who spread this filthy rumor would not dare to do so were their future emperor not confined to his bed."

Theodora's embroidered robes rustled as she turned away. For the first time, released from the rabbit snare of her gaze and voice, John became aware of the wide bed set in an alcove framed by draperies.

"Justinian wishes to address you," Theodora said. "Step forward."

The men did as she ordered.

The unprepossessing figure propped up in bed, a purple coverlet pulled up to his neck, did not resemble the usual notion of a future emperor. His face was bland and round with a strong familial resemblance to Justin's, especially the small eyes.

Justinian smiled weakly.

"Felix. It's Felix, isn't it? One of my uncle Justin's favorite bodyguards. 'Reminds me of myself in my excubitor days,' he told me. In fact, he insisted on volunteering your services when he heard I planned to have the matter of Hypatius' murder investigated."

Felix opened his mouth to reply, but shut it without saying anything. He looked shocked.

"And you are John," Justinian went on. "A highly intelligent man, or so I am reliably informed. The palace is a small place. Those with quick wits are soon noticed and rewarded. Are you surprised I should call upon a slave? I was not born to the palace and neither was our emperor. Both of us might have been farmers. I would as soon be served by those of similar humble origins. Adversity is a better teacher than luxury."

John glanced at Felix. The excubitor's expression remained one of stunned amazement.

"Now as to why you're both here," Justinian continued. "I'm enlisting you in the defense of the empire. You will report to Theodotus, the City Prefect, and assist him for the time being. He'll have orders for you. When he has none, you will continue with your usual duties. The fact that you are working for him can hardly be kept secret, but you will say nothing about this meeting and who assigned you to the Prefect's office. I do not have to tell you the consequences of disobedience." Justinian's voice faded abruptly and his head fell back against his pillow.

Just that quickly, their audience was ended.

"You have tired him out," snapped Theodora. "Leave."

The men began to back toward the door.

Fortuna had arranged for something momentous to take place soon, John thought. She must have, for he and the excubitor Felix had just been addressed by the man who would almost certainly be the next emperor. Indeed, many said he had been the de facto ruler for years.

Where was the drama, he wondered. Where the magnificence? The sickly and unimpressive man lying in bed had sounded like a petty bureaucrat instructing his clerks to undertake some minor task or other.

John suddenly felt dizzy. Was it caused by the room's smoke or its cloying heat? Or was it relief?

He had expected to be dead and his feet set firmly on the seven-runged ladder to Mithra by now.

Chapter Three

"Careful where you're treading with those filthy boots!"

John glanced down at the puddle of icy water forming on the kitchen floor. When he looked up, the servant who'd scolded him gaped in alarm and hurried off.

The cold blast of air that had swirled in through the servants' entrance of Senator Opimius' house clung to the folds of John's cloak. A pair of cook's assistants, laboring over a long table standing under the kitchen's steam-fogged window, peeked around at him, exchanged excited whispers, and then went back to expertly jointing a pile of freshly plucked chicken carcasses.

John noticed their surreptitious stares as he made his way to the kitchen brazier. No one offered a greeting. He found himself shivering. The heat rising from the glowing charcoal seemed to hold no warmth.

A pair of girls strolled into the room, carrying baskets filled with olives and cheese. They giggled as they chatted.

"So I went and got myself a love charm. Cost me a lot, too. But has it worked? Ha!" one complained.

"I keep telling you it's all nonsense!" her companion replied. "The only people who get any satisfaction out of them are the ones making a fortune selling the wretched things!"

"I have an idea," offered the other, evidently inspired by the activity going on at the table. "We could sell some of the master's spare chickens to folk needing them for magick rites and make our own fortunes!"

Then they belatedly spotted John, set their baskets down quickly and fled.

John frowned.

"Why do you look so puzzled? Wouldn't you be frightened if a shade suddenly appeared in your kitchen?"

Opimius' ancient house steward, who had been looking over a pile of vegetables spread out on the other end of the table, came up to John and patted his shoulder. It was a gesture John disliked intensely.

"You feel solid enough," Dorotheus continued with a wide smile. "Nonetheless, everyone in the household heard you'd been dragged off to the imperial cells. Usually that means you're as good as dead."

John nodded. He should have realized how startling his reappearance must be. His death had seemed a foregone conclusion to them, just as it had to him. He did not offer Dorotheus an explanation for his salvation and the old man did not ask.

John moved his hands closer to the fire. They were almost colorless and numb with cold. The hands of a shade. "I was instructed to resume my duties here, Dorotheus, although occasionally I shall be required elsewhere. I thought I'd warm up a little before seeking Lady Anna."

"You won't find her at home, John. She and the master are both out." The steward's face was the same brown as the leaves that clung to trees all winter in the northern climes where John had fought long ago. "You look barely alive. What did they do to you?"

John said he had not been mistreated.

Dorotheus looked unconvinced. He puffed his cheeks out in a manner that, coupled with his brown face and small beak of a nose, gave him a distinct resemblance to a plump pheasant.

"You were extremely fortunate. The trouble with you is you don't know when you're well off. Just back from the dead, and there you stand, looking as sour as spoiled milk."

"Alive or dead, my fate has nothing to do with my own efforts. It was Fortuna spared me and nothing more than that."

"I should say it was the Lord that spared you," Dorotheus replied with a quick scowl. "If you want to call Him Fortuna, I doubt He cares. But having Him on your side is better than having all the emperor's armies at your back."

John said nothing and gloomily continued to warm his hands.

Dorotheus sighed. Cheerful by nature, he was a man who could have consulted the oracle of Trophonius and still emerged with a smile on his face, but John's mood was almost bleak enough to chill even his perpetually sunny demeanor.

He requested John to step out of the kitchen so that they could have a few private words.

There was a sudden exclamation as one of the kitchen workers sliced into her thumb. Perhaps she had been more intent on her eavesdropping than her work.

John murmured agreement. Could he properly refuse a request from Dorotheus, who was a slave like himself, but as steward ruled in his master's absence? John had been at the palace for several years and every change in his work still brought new uncertainties. He had only recently grown accustomed to laboring in the office of the Keeper of the Plate and had just begun to enjoy it when he was thrust into new duties tutoring Lady Anna.

Now his situation was different again, although for the present he preferred not to think of the mysterious new assignment set before him.

Given his years of military employment, the prospect of taking orders from the Prefect Theodotus was not unappealing in itself, although, for all he knew, he might only be handling written work for him. Justinian had said something about an investigation into the death of Hypatius the philanthropist, the murder the whole city had been talking about. Perhaps he expected John to organize reports and evidence as he would marshal the Keeper of the Plate's valuable dinnerware for a banquet.

Dorotheus led John from the kitchen and along a hallway whose windows looked out into an inner courtyard. Its fountain was coated with rivulets of ice resembling meandering streams of wax from a melting candle. A few brown leaves drifted down from the branches of a skeletal tree. The sky was leaden.

"I am expecting more snow. It's most unnatural, if you ask me," the steward observed. "In all my years I can't remember such winter weather. Thank the Lord we have warm beds to sleep in and good food to eat. Many are not as fortunate."

"That's true enough." Troubled as he was, John couldn't help thinking of the shivering beggar he and Anna had seen huddled in a doorway not that far from this well-appointed household. He mentioned the incident to Dorotheus and wondered aloud if the unfortunate man had managed to find better shelter for what would certainly turn into a bitterly cold night. Dorotheus observed confidently that the Lord looked after His flock and made the sign of his religion.

John did not like cold weather and never had. He was thin. Any chill in the air found its way into his bones too easily. One of the few things he liked about living in the empire's capital was that it was not often as frigid as it had been the past few days.

"Yes," Dorotheus took up his previous observation, "there's plenty who would envy us. We may not be free men, John, yet we have a better life than many who are proud to so call themselves. Free to freeze or starve, more like it!"

They climbed the staircase at the end of the hallway and entered Dorotheus' room, a cramped space cluttered with a pallet, a pair of stools and two chests. A bronze brazier warmed the air with a few smoldering embers.

"Sit down, John." Dorotheus stirred up the fire, pushed a stool toward its warmth, and seated himself on the edge of his pallet.

"I've been waiting for an opportunity to talk with you ever since you began tutoring Lady Anna.

She's very fond of you and so we all are. There's nothing more important here than her happiness. Apart from the master's, of course, but as his depends on hers, it amounts to the same thing."

John did not reply. Glancing out of the room's tiny window, he saw that snow flurries had begun to lazily bedaub the sky.

Taking his silence for attentiveness, his companion plunged ahead enthusiastically. "You see, I realized immediately that you're one of those headstrong young men who are dissatisfied with the place assigned him. Don't deny it! You are more discreet in your speech than most, but I can see it in your eyes."

Dorotheus hesitated, collecting his thoughts. "Now, I've been with the senator's household since I was purchased as a mere boy. Never in all that time have I wanted for anything. A kinder master than Opimius you could scarcely find. On the whole ours is not a bad life, wouldn't you say?"

"Do you think so?"

"You have a quick temper, John," Dorotheus said sorrowfully. "But what man is not a slave in some way or another? We are all slaves to time and age. And we all must serve the Lord, even the emperor. Eunuchs like us are less enchained than many a free man, since we're not slaves to our passions."

Was rage then not a passion? John said nothing. He did not want to hurt Dorotheus' feelings. He would never have chosen the life Dorotheus found so natural. He could only hope he would not have to endure it for as long as the old steward already had.

"Nor do any of us need question what befalls us, for it is all the will of heaven," Dorotheus said, as if reading what John was thinking. "Now, you know the tale of John Chrysostom and the eunuch Eutropius?"

John nodded. Who had not heard the story of how the paths of the Christian Chrysostom, he of the golden tongue, and of Eutropius had crossed more than a century earlier in this very city?

"Then consider this," Dorotheus said. "Eutropius originally worked in a minor position in the palace administration. It's said he came to imperial attention through his wit and piety, but whatever the reason in due course he was elevated to chamberlain and consul."

"You're saying I should not despair, that I might shed my chains one day?"

Dorotheus smiled. "John, you're being deliberately obstinate, I fear. Surely you recall that Eutropius grew greedy and corrupt and was eventually executed? Obviously what we should learn from his sorry tale is we ought not to seek to rise beyond the position in which we are placed. Especially when ours is such a comfortable one."

John made no reply. He could scarcely reveal that his position had suddenly become much less comfortable than Dorotheus innocently supposed.

"Now, John, your life isn't really such a nightmare, is it? You have not flung yourself over the seawall in despair."

John paused before replying. After his capture and castration, he no longer suffered nightmares. When he could not avoid thinking about it, this seemed to him a natural result of his maiming. By that unthinkable act in the Persian camp, the night exhausted its forces. The formless terror that lurked just out of sight around sleep's darkest corners had presented itself all too clearly. The heart-stopping fall had ended, not in waking but with crippling impact. As for death, the bottomless dread upon which all other fears play like ripples, John would gladly have plunged into its depths if he had not felt even more strongly that his duty, as a soldier of Mithra, was to endure.

When he replied to Dorotheus, John chose his words carefully. "It's true I have not thrown myself over the seawall. That is because heaven has ordered that I exist in this world. It's an order renewed each time I awake. I cannot imagine the purpose of it, but one should not question heaven."

Dorotheus gazed at him sorrowfully. John remained silent. How could he explain to this cheerful old man, a man who had never known anything but slavery, how it was to be free, to chart one's course in the world, to make one's own way?

And having done so how then to convey the stark horror of being captured and offered for sale to anyone with enough coins to buy a man, a woman, or a child and with that purchase the right of absolute power over their bodies and their fates?

It was not possible to even begin to describe it, he thought, nor did he wish to attempt it. His past life was gone. The man he had been had died under a bloodstained blade.

✸✸✸

"What's he up to? That's what I'd like to know! He's burdened me with an excubitor and a slave. It's a certain wager they've been told to keep an eye on what I'm doing. I won't have it!"

Theodotus had stamped into Proclus' office without announcement. Not that he needed any. There were few in Constantinople who would not have recognized the rough-hewn City Prefect. Though he dressed like a peasant in leather breeches and a rough wool shirt, no one could have mistaken the broad-chested figure, shambling along as if weighed down by the enormous and asymmetrical head set between wide shoulders without apparent benefit of a neck.

Some whispered he'd been kicked in the head by a horse as a youngster. Others said the misshapen head was a result of his mother easing her pregnancy with demonic potions. No one, however, said anything at all about the matter when within earshot of the man nicknamed the Gourd.

"You're speaking of your two new assistants?" Proclus was seated behind a cluttered desk beside Emperor Justin. He had been helping the emperor sign new legislation when Proclus barged in. Justin didn't bother to look up from the papers he labored over. "I'd heard about them. By direct order of Justinian, wasn't it? And the emperor, of course."

Theodotus ran stubby fingers through hair consisting of a few frazzled strands. "How can I possibly fail to keep order in the city with so much help thrust upon me?" His voice was heavy with sarcasm.

"The murder of Hypatius has dangerous political overtones. There are plenty who might use it for their own ends." Proclus spoke so quietly he might have been sharing a confidence with the Prefect rather than pointing out something so obvious.

"What he means is my nephew's let his precious Blues run amuck and now they've killed someone important. Not just common beggars and shop keepers. Interesting, isn't it? With the public outrage it's caused, he might not get his wish to push me aside before my carcass is cold. Ah! Look. I've blotched this one too." Justin yanked the wooden stencil he'd been tracing off the parchment.

Proclus plucked the sheet up and examined it. "It is perfectly acceptable, Caesar."

"So you say, but no one ever tells the emperor he's got a boil on the end of his nose," Justin growled.

"Why should they? Boil or not, he is the emperor."

"Few would dare to talk to their ruler like that," Justin observed. "That's why I value your advice so much. And Theodotus' also. He doesn't care how he speaks in my presence either. What is this document about anyway? My eyes seem particularly blurred today."

"It's a list of regulations regarding warehouse fees."

"Then it's all right. Business owners have better things to worry about than blotched signatures."

Theodotus emitted a loud grunt. "But what about all this additional help I suddenly have, Caesar? Do you suppose I'm not already on the trail of the villain who killed Hypatius? Why would I need a fuzzy-cheeked excubitor and a slave to assist me with my investigations?"

"I agree with Justinian. It's in everyone's interest that Hypatius' murder is solved quickly," Justin replied. "This business of a murder in the church. And Hypatius being a church patron. It's got everyone's attention. We have to be sure it's solved in a manner that we can all be certain is, let us say, impartial."

"Impartial? What does solved impartially mean? Solved is solved," Theodotus said impatiently.

Proclus looked thoughtful. "Sometimes, however—"

The emperor slammed his kalamos down on the desk. "We all need eyes everywhere. You have plenty of spies around the city, Theodotus. They don't seem to have helped you catch the culprits."

"I see your point," Theodotus admitted. "I will have a letter of introduction drawn up for these men, to facilitate their investigations, allow them to interview people. I just hope they don't interfere with the real investigation. I am holding a dinner party tonight. I'll set them to guard my guests. Theodora will be there so doubtless that will please her. She can report to Justinian that his slave is already keeping an eye on me."

The emperor slumped back in his chair, as if tracing a signature on a few documents had exhausted him. "I had high ambitions for my nephew once, until that little whore got hold of him," he said. "Euphemia hates her. Theodora wants me out of the way so Justinian can rule, and what Theodora wants, my nephew wants. He never paid attention to these street brawlers until she came along. Just because the Blues aided the woman's family when the Greens wouldn't, is that a reason to put the whole empire into turmoil? Is this what it's come to, that Roman citizens should be ruled by the daughter of a bearkeeper for one of the factions? Well, I'm not dead yet. And I don't intend to die for some time."

Proclus removed the wooden stencil. Justin had obviously finished his labors although a stack of documents remained unsigned.

"Don't let this matter of Hypatius keep you from your work restoring order in the streets, Theodotus," Justin went on. "Street riots threaten the empire as much as any conspiracy."

"I'll skin everyone in the city alive if that's what it takes to make the streets safe."

"It's not the beatings and robberies and assaults that scare people, it's all the counting and scribbling it down," Justin observed. "If a clerk with a kalamos hadn't recorded it, you wouldn't have someone like Senator Balbinus railing about how there were two murders near the Strategion and fifteen assaults on the Mese overnight. Not to mention a grocer had three bunches of leeks snatched. Citizens wouldn't be so fearful if we didn't keep count." Justin's teeth clenched as he came to an abrupt halt and reached a trembling hand down to his leg.

Theodotus reached into the pouch at his belt, took a few awkward steps forward and set a terracotta pot down on the desk in front of Justin. "Your medication for that old wound, excellency. A fresh batch. I made it only this morning."

The emperor drew the tiny container toward him. "You have served me well, Theodotus, and I trust you will continue to do so. Now off you go to prepare for your banquet. What entertainments do you plan? It's a pity you can't ask Theodora to perform some of her specialties for your guests! However, I'm sure you will think of something almost as diverting."

Chapter Four

Theodotus stationed his pair of unwanted assistants beside the gilded door of his dining room with instructions to look lively in the event of any trouble, but otherwise to remain as unobtrusive as possible.

The spacious room where the City Prefect held the lavish banquets the court expected from such high-ranking officials looked out on an inner garden. Its orderly statuary and rigorously pruned bushes and trees were now little more than silhouettes beneath a cloudless and star-sprinkled sky. In the streets, beggars were already seeking sheltered corners, preferring an empty belly and a good place to sleep to the unlikely possibility of charitable donations from those hurrying home to hot meals and warm beds.

"I don't know about being unobtrusive." Felix stepped back to allow two slaves carrying wine jugs to get by. "We don't exactly blend in with the Gourd's decorations. Well, perhaps I do, but as for you…."

He cast a quick glance behind him. The painting decorating the length of the plastered wall depicted several stalwarts engaged in fighting assorted desperate citizens of Troy. A large wooden horse stood with its belly agape, giving birth to the doom of the ancient city.

John ignored the other's barb. It was almost preferable to the angry silence the man had maintained. He looked around the large room. How could remaining unobtrusively beside a doorway aid Justinian? What could it have to do with the death of Hypatius?

The cloying scent of exotic flowers mingled with the sweet tang of pine. Conifer branches looped in garlands around columns were echoed by ropes of greenery hung along the edges of the tables.

On the opposite side of the room, a hunting scene was depicted in full cry. A wild-eyed stag crashed through shrubbery, its pursuers so intent on its capture that they did not see the beautiful, pale figure of Diana, goddess of the chase, standing in front of a dark grove of trees in the background.

The scenes would not have been John's choice to decorate a room devoted to pleasures of the stomach. They made an interesting combination of subjects, though. John wondered whether he and his military companion should consider themselves as belonging among the hidden warriors in the Trojan horse or among the hunted prey, or both.

Felix would probably not appreciate being considered a colleague of John, a slave and a eunuch at that. He had made his dislike for John bluntly clear during their swift walk from the Great Palace.

Felix had also made it plain that he supposed their real job at the banquet, whatever the Gourd told them, would be to act as spies on behalf of Justinian and the emperor. What could they expect to learn? It wasn't likely that plotters would discuss their plans over dinner in this house, where walls had ears. The slaves serving Theodotus' guests might also be selling information to certain parties whom the Prefect would have welcomed into the dungeons sooner than into his home.

John's morose chain of thought was interrupted by the return of Theodotus. Immaculately smooth of chin and dressed in green robes, he accompanied his first guest into the torchlit room.

Trenico appeared startled to see John standing next to Felix.

"What's he doing here?" His tone was injured and loud as if John were as deaf as the dead of Troy.

"I wish I knew!" Theodotus skewered John with a pointed stare. "Perhaps he's keeping an eye on you for Lady Anna. But don't worry, Trenico. A certain lady friend of yours will not be here tonight. Just as well too. You won't be tempted to go and inspect the topiary bushes again! It's too cold this evening."

Trenico frowned as Felix smirked at the innuendo.

"I think you'll enjoy my cook's offerings, however," his host went on. "I selected some elaborate dishes. A bit too elaborate for my tastes, but you know how it is. The court likes its streets policed by a man with good taste. If it's chicken stuffed with chestnuts and fried veal garnished with asparagus they want, then it's veal and chicken they'll get. Not to mention fig cakes gilded with gold leaf. Have some wine." He gestured toward jugs on the nearest table. "In fact, I order you to drink. You'll be glad you've fortified yourself when you see the entertainments I've got planned."

Trenico spoke through a mouthful of honeyed almonds he'd scooped up from a silver dish. "Surely not that abominable dwarf mime Theodora is so fond of? Or the dancers from that other low woman's establishment you keep telling me about. What is her name? Nefertiti? Something Egyptian, anyhow. They're all too risqué for a public dinner party."

Theodotus emitted a coarse laugh. "You sounded hopeful when you said that. Don't you have enough ladies without me having to show you some more? Or are the rumors wrong?"

"I was thinking of your own welfare, Theodotus. What if Justinian heard about such diversions?"

"He will. Theodora is attending." A swift glance at John and Felix conveyed Theodotus' thoughts on others who kept Justinian informed. "It was his suggestion that I invite her. A suggestion from Justinian isn't much different than an order from the emperor."

Trenico gulped down the last of the almonds and expressed surprise in a slightly choked voice.

"Oh yes," Theodotus continued amiably. "Yes, I've had a lot of help with my guest list. Add a slave here, a future empress there, and how about an excubitor while you're at it? Is this my own house or not? And you never know what sort of twisted report Theodora will carry back to Justinian. So watch your manners and keep a guard on your tongue. You, my friend, are a guest I chose myself. I would hate it if I were ordered to haul you off to the dungeons. Or if it were suggested I do so." He laughed.

Felix gave John a meaningful look as a servant dressed in blue hurried in to inform his master that more guests had arrived.

"I must go and greet them," Theodotus said. "Remember now. Fortify yourself! By direct order of the City Prefect!"

Trenico's expression remained carefully neutral as he watched his host lumber off. Turning then to the men standing by the door he gave a sly grin.

"Well, John, we seem to keep running into each other. Not surprising, though, is it? Although we are of different worlds, we occupy the same world. There's an epigram in there somewhere. And who will you be reporting to, I wonder? The mistress I am aware of? A master I don't know about? Both?"

John bowed slightly. "I attend here under orders of Theodotus to stand guard along with this excubitor."

"Of course! The head of the city policing force is in great need of eunuchs to protect him in his own home, as the world and his brother knows. I would not have taken you for a military man, but then you are a man of many talents. Or so my dear Anna tells me. Very well, I am certain someone of your abilities will be able to fetch some wine for a superior."

John felt heat rising in his face and struggled to control his expression as he followed Trenico's order. He did not want to allow the man the satisfaction of seeing the anger he had aroused.

As Trenico wandered off to converse with other guests who were now filing in, John glanced toward Felix. Now his lips did narrow and his jaw clamped reflexively, almost painfully. The big German was grinning. He obviously enjoyed John's discomfiture.

"Laugh at me all you want, Felix," John said in a low, furious voice. "But you would have had to obey that perfumed fop too if he'd ordered you to pour his wine."

Felix's expression darkened immediately. He had no opportunity to respond, however, since a cluster of guests was now entering the room, led by Theodora. Resplendent in white silk, she wore an ornamental gold circlet that very much resembled a crown.

⁂

As the dinner party progressed, John kept as close an eye, and ear, on the guests as his appointed station allowed. Scraps of conversation drifted over to him. The talk grew louder as more of the City Prefect's fine wine was consumed.

Occasionally Felix vanished to patrol the garden. Or so he said. John wondered briefly if the excubitor had received orders about which he knew nothing or simply wanted to get away from his undesired companion for a while and had seized upon a fine excuse to do so.

John had to admit that Theodotus kept a fine table. Because of his work in the office of the Master of the Plate, his attention was drawn less to the culinary dainties offered than to the coruscating array of silver, gold, and glass tableware on which they arrived. He would not have given these ostentatious treasures a second glance in the past. Now, however, since his survival at the palace depended on successfully performing the duties he had been assigned, he had taken a close and prudent interest in such things.

He had eventually come to enjoy the work. Plates, jugs, cups, table settings, and banquets were more easily ordered than life. Especially life in the corridors of the Great Palace.

The evening wore on. John glanced repeatedly into the bowl of the large clock set in a corner. The level marking the hours fell so slowly the water might have been frozen.

The conversation surged and ebbed like the murmur of the sea. Every so often a few distinguishable words floated to where John stood.

A guest who had emptied his wine cup more times than was wise remarked how odd it was that Theodotus had tactlessly chosen to outfit his servants in blue. After all, wasn't it the Blues who were terrorizing the city?

"Why do you think he's called the Gourd?" replied his neighbor. "He's not exactly the brightest man in the empire, you know."

"Ah! I thought he got the nickname from the monstrous shape of his head," a third man chimed in.

The origin of the City Prefect's nickname launched a lively debate.

John turned his attention elsewhere. He heard little of consequence.

Someone worried about Justinian's illness. Two matrons, seated near enough for John to overhear their lowered voices, argued over the merit of the controversial sculpture in the Great Church. If they mentioned the man who had died at its base, John missed their comments.

As the guests ate and chatted, two girls serenaded them with flute music. Now and then they accompanied an older woman whose voice was a light, sweet soprano. The sound reminded John of his youth, when those working in the fields would sing as evening drew near, to honor the land and its bounty and celebrate their impending freedom from toil for a few hours. The recollection made him unexpectedly homesick. He reminded himself that he had no home now.

Here, those who never toiled complained to one another that the suckling pigs had been boiled too long, the fish not smoked long enough, and that the fruit soaked in wine was overripe. However, John noticed, they consumed it all readily.

The sighing trill of flutes ended and, in the sudden silence, heads turned toward the far end of the room as Theodotus rose to his feet. His splendid green robes were a contrast to the rough shirts and tunics he normally wore.

"The entertainment I promised is about to begin," he announced. "But first a very special culinary treat will be brought in. Which reminds me. I believe you'll have noticed that my servants are all dressed in blue. This is to remind you that although the streets are infested by Blues today, before long you'll be as safe outside as you are among my blue-garbed slaves."

Felix, who had resumed his post after one of his excursions around the garden, gave a soft grunt of contempt. He and John watched curiously as covered salvers were set in front of the diners.

"Please feel free to enjoy this unusual delicacy, my friends," Theodotus smiled.

A rustle of movement filled the room as the guests lifted lids from salvers, followed by audible gasps and the rattle of lids being set hastily down. No one spoke.

John leaned forward slightly, looking over the shoulder of the nearest diner.

Steaming on the salver in front of the man was half a large, baked gourd.

"Now it is commonly said these things are inedible." Theodotus sounded almost gleeful. "They are bitter and tough, not to mention misshapen. People make fun of those who grow them. Why bother to nurture such an ugly vegetable, they ask. My cook protested at the very notion of cooking them. But you know me. When I order a thing done, I expect it done."

A single, sharp caw of laughter cut through the ensuing silence. It was Theodora.

"Eat," Theodotus said. "Enjoy yourselves. I order it."

Cowed, the diners dutifully ate their unexpected course. John imagined that no matter how the concoction tasted, most of the guests were having a hard time swallowing the insult with which it was seasoned.

Before long, Theodotus clapped his hands sharply. Instantly two burly attendants entered the room, carrying between them a glowing brazier. They placed it in front of Theodotus and departed.

"As you'll see, I also ordered my cook to prepare another surprise for you."

The pair of attendants reappeared, this time bearing an iron cauldron hanging from a stout pole. They began to circle the dining room, displaying its contents to the guests. A few diners shifted in their seats to move away, as if alarmed. As it passed by, John could see that the mixture in the cauldron was still bubbling.

"Done to perfection!" Theodotus' enormous head bobbed with satisfaction. "Not that it takes much skill to boil pitch."

An acrid smell overpowered the delicate scent of the room's now wilting flowers. Guests leaned this way and that to obtain a better view. A careless elbow knocked over a wine cup. Its dark contents ruined silk robes worth half of a laborer's lifetime earnings.

Finally the cauldron, its circuit complete, was hefted onto the burning brazier.

Theodotus looked down at the roiling, viscous substance in the cauldron. "Good. Let's be certain it stays hot. Now, perhaps, it is time to prepare another dish. I am indeed a man of many talents, as I believe I have overheard some of you kindly remark." He rolled up his sleeves, revealing short, brawny arms.

"Honored guests, friends, and Theodora, I promised entertainment and I am a man of my word. You have all seen the pitch bubbling. Can you imagine its effect on living flesh? And how delicate would be the flavor of something so freshly cooked?"

A murmur ran through the crowd as a servant appeared with a caged dove. Theodotus grasped the short chain fastened to the top of the cage and swung it out over the boiling pitch.

There were scattered cries of alarm.

"What? So squeamish? Haven't you just partaken of the delicate cooked flesh of creatures similar to this bird? Or perhaps even its family?" He let a short length of chain play out and the cage dropped toward the cauldron, stopping short of its rim.

The agitated bird flapped its wings against the bars of its prison.

More protests filled the air.

"Theodotus, perhaps you could spare the sensibilities of the ladies?" Trenico called out.

Theodotus paused, as if to mull over the suggestion. Then he yanked the cage away from the bubbling brew. "You're right." He beckoned Felix to him. "Take the creature outside and give it its freedom." He handed the cage to the excubitor.

John remembered the cold outside. He thought of Dorotheus' observation that freedom often meant freedom to starve—or freeze.

Theodotus gazed down into the cauldron again. "It would be a shame to waste such a fine pot of boiling pitch. No, my friends, you will still have your entertainment except that rather than our poor winged friend I will instead plunge a hand into this cauldron."

A buzz of surprise and speculation rose around the table.

Theodora's eyes glittered with delight. "I shall be interested to see that, Theodotus. The hand will certainly be maimed. Or do you intend to make it whole again?"

"There will be no need to make it whole. Therein is the magick. Indeed, I intend to demonstrate my powers. Would I really cook a live dove? How could you think such a thing of me?"

"Whose hand do you propose to use?" Theodora asked with an alacrity that made John wonder if she'd played magician's assistant during her former career.

Theodotus flexed his stubby fingers. "Whose hand? Why, it will be my own!"

Suiting action to word, he plunged his bared arm wrist deep into the bubbling mixture.

A high-pitched babble of alarm and shock surged around the room. More than one guest looked hastily away.

John looked away also, but toward the window. His keen hearing had caught the sound of someone running across the garden.

A collective gasp drew his attention back to Theodotus. The Prefect had withdrawn his arm from the boiling mix and was waving his apparently uninjured hand triumphantly. He formed a fist and hammered at the air.

"This is the indestructible hand that reaches into the darkest alleys to choke the life from the murderous bastards who lurk there! Why do you think they whisper my name with such dread? They know my powers. They fear me. And rightly so!" He glared at his guests.

Theodora jumped to her feet. "You have amazed me!" she said in excitement, her face flushed. "I would not have believed it had I not seen it with my own eyes! You must visit Justinian when he has recovered and perform this amazing piece of magick for him."

John had no time to ponder what he had just seen because Felix was suddenly at his side.

"Trouble," the excubitor loudly announced without preamble. "A messenger's just arrived. Says there's a riot brewing."

Chapter Five

The iron-banded door of the Prefect's house crashed open. Torchlit smoke spilled into the street along with Theodotus and the noisy crowd of excited guests, accompanied by a number of confused and frightened servants.

Theodotus and the messenger galloped off. Many of his guests followed in close pursuit although a few, more cautious, took their opportunity to depart in the opposite direction.

Felix cursed. "The fools! They've drunk so much wine they probably think this is part of the entertainment. There's nothing courtiers enjoy more than seeing blood spilled. Until a drop of it gets on their clothing. We're supposed to be working for the Gourd. Remember? We'd better follow him and be quick about it."

Felix took off at a run. John followed.

As he loped along, it occurred to John how easy it would be to slip away down an alley and make a dash for freedom. He had considered flight more than once. But the very idea was impossible. Educated and capable slaves of John's sort were too valuable. The Keeper of the Plate would be as determined to recover John as a charioteer would be to retrieve a champion horse.

John and Felix arrived at the crest of a steep street. Several of the Gourd's men blocked further progress. Felix conferred quickly with one and then returned to John's side without offering an explanation.

John stared down the sloping, colonnaded street into the Strategion. Indistinct figures moved around the Egyptian obelisk where blunt finger pointed heavenward. More of the Gourd's men, no doubt. Beyond the seawall where warehouses clustered like conspirators, a slight glow was cast upward by the lights of ships in the Prosphorion harbor. Away from the water, torches set outside shops embroidered the city with glittering lines of fire that did little to dispel its darkness.

"What a beautiful night for a riot," remarked the man who had appeared at John's shoulder. It was Trenico.

"Theodotus' guests are going to be disappointed," Felix told him. "I've learned that the Blues are already surrounded in that small forum off the Strategion."

"I heard they intended to set fire to the oil warehouses. Sheer lunacy, of course," Trenico replied. "Who can say where the wind would take a conflagration like that?"

The forum where the Blues had gathered could not be seen from where they stood, but above its location a faintly luminescent cloud of mist, like steam rising from penned cattle at a winter market, hung in the clear, cold sky.

"I wouldn't be surprised if our host has more tricks up his peasant's sleeves." Trenico turned at the clatter of hooves and the creak of heavy wheels. A carriage ornamented with bronze and ivory and drawn by four horses rumbled through the throng. It stopped near their vantage point. Heavy curtains obscured its passenger. John noted the flash of jeweled rings on the delicate hand that parted the rich fabrics just enough for its occupant to peer out.

Trenico chuckled. "Trust Theodora to want the best view possible! Now the Gourd has no choice but to come up with further entertainment."

"Take your seat then," Felix growled. "We're supposed to be actors in this performance." He started down the street toward the Strategion.

The wide square was nearly deserted.

"It's one thing to meet the enemy on a battlefield, but riots, well, you can't depend on skill or strategy in those." Felix might have been muttering to himself. He snapped at John, "We'd better make certain we're seen to be here. Be careful, though. Don't do anything you're not given a direct order to do."

Felix trotted past the decorative obelisk and hailed a man he apparently knew, stationed with others near the archway leading to the adjacent forum. John looked through the pillared opening. He could see a crowd of Blues clustered in the space beyond. It struck him that they were milling about like bewildered market visitors rather than organizing themselves for arson and rioting.

Theodotus burst into sight. He bellowed at his brawny companion, evidently one of his captains. John caught the barked words.

"All the escape routes sealed off? Good! I gather their plan was to put the oil warehouses to the torch? A pretty scene that would be! The whole city'd be ablaze before dawn. Yes, I shall certainly have to make an example of them."

He lumbered past. From a distance John saw him gesture emphatically as he spoke to the leader of a large armed company that had just clattered into view.

A look of incredulity crossed Felix' face. "The Gourd's called out half the army of the East to fight a handful of trouble makers!"

There was no time for a reply.

Several stones came flying out of the darkness. John glimpsed one tumbling down, half illuminated in torchlight.

"They're attacking!" someone shouted.

Then orders were given and the Prefect's men advanced swiftly under the archway, into the forum, and toward the Blues.

"It's started," Felix observed grimly. "It wasn't a Blue who tossed those stones, I'll wager, but one of the Gourd's men. It's always best to have even a miserable excuse when you intend to murder the innocent."

Felix's fingers dug into John's arm. The excubitor's shaggy hair brushed his face as he shouted into John's ear, in order to be heard above the din now rending the air with the thunderous clatter of hoofs and nail-studded boot soles and echoing screams of terror and agony.

"Come with me!" Felix ordered. "I'm not going to see you killed and be blamed for not protecting you. We'll lie low in a shop until things quiet down. The Gourd doesn't need my assistance in a slaughterhouse, anyway." The disgust in his tone was withering.

They quickly slipped into the small forum, where men were already dying, ducked under the nearest portico, and leapt into the first alcove of a shop. Peering from its shield of darkness, they could pick out little detail from the frenzy of shadows and struggling men. Already, here and there, dark shapes lay crumpled.

A running figure erupted from the melee. From its dress and hairstyle it was obviously a Blue. Three men gave chase. The first to catch up with the fleeing man grabbed the victim's long hair, yanked his head back, and cut his throat. The second completed the job by putting his sword into their victim's back. The straggler had to content himself with kicking a corpse.

The massacre was soon over. The tumult faded. Finally there was only an occasional high-pitched shriek as the wounded were dispatched to oblivion. The Gourd was nothing if not thorough, John acknowledged to himself.

He stepped back from the doorway and was suddenly prodded on his shoulder from behind. He whirled, startled, as Felix stifled a bitter laugh.

Then John saw the cause of his companion's strange humor.

What had nudged his back dangled from a iron hook in the ceiling. It was the skinned carcass of a monstrous pig, the biggest John had ever seen. They had taken refuge in a butcher's shop. He pushed the corpse away. It swung ponderously to and fro from its hook.

"A strange place to find shelter from a slaughter," observed Felix.

"Fortuna is said to have a cruel sense of humor." John turned back to the door.

The continuing search for survivors was a terrible sight. Several men strolled around the forum, casually thrusting blades into motionless bodies. Others had begun to search the surrounding shops, vanishing into darkened cavities to emerge in one instance with a struggling figure which was soon stilled, but increasingly with shadowy handfuls of whatever goods had taken their fancy.

"It's one thing for a soldier to take the reward he's earned from honorably defeating an enemy, but only a thief robs his fellow citizens!" Felix averted his head and spit sideways in disgust.

"Ugh!"

It was a reflexive cry of distress.

John bent down and looked behind the pile of baskets sitting under the butcher's scarred chopping table. A young boy crouched there, wiping his face. He looked up in terror but made no attempt to escape, frozen in fear like a rabbit. Felix dragged him out.

The boy couldn't have been more than eleven or twelve and small for his age at that. Nonetheless he was dressed as a Blue, with a splendid cloak and his hair shaved high in the front.

"Stole your father's razor, didn't you?" Felix gave the boy a rough shake. "Not for that beardless face but to shave your hair. You did a good job, boy. Too good. You look enough like a Blue to get your belly sliced open."

The boy began to sob. "My tutor said I had to memorize Homer. I thought fighting would be more heroic! I was going to write verse about it. We weren't hurting anybody. Don't let them kill me!"

Felix muttered words that weren't fit for the boy's ears, not as a response to the lad's confession, but rather because he had just seen several men working their way down the line of shops.

From what could already be seen and heard, their search was extremely thorough. Furniture was knocked over, crates smashed, sacks torn open and their contents tossed out into the forum.

"He looks enough like a Blue to get all our bellies sliced open if we're caught hiding him," John pointed out. "There's only one solution. Give me your sword!"

Felix regarded John with a sneer. "What, is it anything to save your own skin?" The boy in his grip squirmed convulsively, but had the presence of mind not to begin yelling for help.

"Don't worry, I'm not going to hurt him. Just don't forget the lesson you learned tonight, young man. Life's rarely poetic."

From much too close by came the sound of shattering pottery.

"Give me your sword, Felix. Quickly!" John demanded again.

Felix hesitated for a heartbeat, then complied. John ducked behind the enormous hanging pig carcass and swiftly hacked at the opening made by the butcher to extract its offal.

Raised voices could be heard from a shop only an alcove or two away. Amphorae smashed on the ground, followed by raucous laughter.

Understanding dawned and Felix picked up the boy and thrust him inside the huge bloody carcass. "Don't make a sound!" he cautioned.

Two men appeared at the shop's doorway.

John kicked a stool savagely against a wall. "You ignorant fool! You're stupider than a fish that's been lying on the dock for days! We're wasting our time! There's no one in here!" he shouted at Felix.

The men outside were featureless shadows. Their heads moved in John's direction. He was obviously not one they sought, not to mention ordering about a man immediately identifiable as an excubitor by his clothing.

The pair set to work to finish the search John had feigned beginning.

They looked under the chopping table, opened a chest and scattered its contents on the floor. Felix helped the searchers overturn a large vat filled with layers of salted meat.

Apparently satisfied, the two men turned to go. One paused suddenly. He looked up at the huge gutted pig hanging from its hook.

His companion let out a bark of laughter. "Forget taking that as well! You can't hide it under your tunic!"

"That wasn't what I was thinking." The man raised his sword and took a step toward the carcass.

His blade descended swiftly and in an instant a hefty slice of pig flesh was clutched in his fist.

"Dinner!" he announced, shoving it into his tunic. "And speaking of dinner, as a little thank you I'll give the butcher's customers some sauce for theirs...."

He urinated on the pig and then the pair left, laughing.

The dead swine swung wildly as the boy emerged, speckled in gore and scraps of offal. He was shaking. John removed his cloak, folded it, and draped it across the boy's narrow shoulders.

Felix peered out. "They're dragging bodies away now. We'll be able to leave shortly. And where do you live, boy?"

Too busy wiping pig's blood from his face, the would-be Blue didn't answer.

"No point in setting you loose to get yourself killed now." Felix smiled grimly. "Don't worry. We'll get you safely home."

"I can get home by myself!" The boy darted forward.

Felix casually stuck out his foot, sending the lad sprawling.

"Let me go home!" the boy pleaded.

"Do you even have a proper home to go to? Maybe we should turn you over to the Prefect?"

Tears welled up in the boy's eyes and ran down his face, leaving meandering streaks on his dirty, blood-smeared cheeks.

"Anatolius," he said. "That's my name. But please don't tell my father what I did!"

Felix snorted. "Afraid of the thrashing you deserve? And what will your mother say to see your curls sacrificed for such a stupid reason? They'll realize what you've been up to as soon as they see your new hairstyle. Unless you propose to wear a wig for a while?"

Anatolius snuffled miserably, wiping his nose on his sleeve.

The trio made their way through the darkness.

The Prefect's men had turned their attention elsewhere.

A small mound of bodies had been piled at the bottom of the street that ran into the Strategion. Theodotus' guests, their ranks no doubt swelled by the curious, had been permitted to come closer and now stood not far off.

The unmistakable figure of Theodotus strode toward the pile of corpses. A rising murmur came from the onlookers as he kicked at the bodies. He raised his arms over his head and thundered to his audience or perhaps to the heavens.

"Let this be a lesson to the vermin who would terrorize our streets! They can expect no mercy!"

John took hold of Anatolius' hand and tried to pull him away. The boy resisted. He stared back at the obelisk in the middle of the Strategion.

A man had been bound to its base. He was illuminated by a ring of lamps set on the ground around him.

Theodotus paced back and forth as he continued his diatribe.

John tugged at Anatolius' hand.

"No, let him watch if he wants," Felix said quietly. "Sometimes a lesson needs repeating."

Theodotus' voice boomed through the cold air. "That was their plot, to set fire to the oil warehouses. The flames would spread quickly. By sunrise the city would be ashes with no one's property spared. This is why I have eyes and ears everywhere. My own, those of my men, and many belonging to other, unseen, helpers. Before you think to harm this sacred seven-hilled city, remember, I have ways of knowing your thoughts almost before you form them."

The bound man squirmed as Theodotus grasped a large clay pot sitting beside the obelisk and hefted it up as easily as if it were a small cup.

"Your plan failed," he told the man tied to the obelisk. "But since you were looking forward to a fire, I don't want to disappoint."

Upending the pot he doused the Blue with lamp oil. The man began to struggle frantically as the viscous liquid soaked into his clothing and trickled down, forming a puddle.

Theodotus stepped away and casually kicked one of the lamps illuminating the scene toward the obelisk. The lamp skittered on its side, rolling in a tiny wheel of flames to come to rest against the man's oil-sodden cloak. A thin line of red snaked slowly along it and began climbing up the man's chest.

Then the oil exploded into a ball of flame, inside which a dark figure writhed and screamed.

His agonized cries were drowned out almost immediately by a roar of approval from the onlookers.

※ ※ ※

Felix, John, and Anatolius had placed many streets between themselves and the Strategion before any of them spoke.

It was Felix who finally broke the silence. "Do you really have a home, Anatolius, or are you just playing games and leading us all over the city?"

Anatolius looked around the forum they were crossing. In its center a statue of an emperor, or some lesser, forgotten luminary, appeared to be wading in a fountain basin.

"We're almost there," he replied.

"I'll wager a nummus your father's a shopkeeper," said Felix.

Anatolius ignored him. He turned down what appeared at first glance to be an alley, but whose narrow way ended at an enormous gate set in a wall protecting a massive villa. Orange lamp light poured from a window.

Anatolius sprinted forward and the gate swung open as if someone had been awaiting his return. For an instant his slight frame was silhouetted in the gateway, then he was inside the grounds and the gate had banged shut.

John's ruined cloak lay in front of the gate and as he retrieved it, Felix gazed at the villa beyond, amazement plain on his face.

Chapter Six

Felix squinted down the Mese where wan morning light slanted into the colonnades. He spoke without looking at John.

"That boy we rescued last night...he's the son of Senator Aurelius. A couple of my colleagues knew the villa immediately when I described it to them. They'd escorted Quaestor Proclus there for some meeting or other a few weeks ago. The senator's known to be a staunch supporter of Justinian. It appears you've done your master a service. Maybe we can work together after all without you getting either of us killed."

"I appreciate your confidence."

"Yes, well, in such a situation as last night I would have expected you to be more...shall we say... excitable."

Excitable? Like a woman? Because he was a eunuch? John's cheekbones darkened with a flush of anger. He pulled his cloak closer around his lean frame and quickened his steps to match the excubitor's steady pace. He managed to remain silent.

"There may be riots in the streets and murders in churches," Felix continued, "but it seems that commerce carries on regardless. And begging." He inclined his head in the direction of a man squatting against a wall. The man extended a dirty hand toward them as a biting wind came rushing down the wide street like icy water through an aqueduct.

"Neither enterprise appears to be receiving much custom," John observed. He wished he had a coin to give. The beggar pulled his hand back into the scant protection of his threadbare tunic as the two men strode past.

They had not had much sleep after the previous night's hectic events. When they met the Gourd in his office that morning, he seemed perfectly fresh, even invigorated. The orders he gave them were vague. They were to investigate Hypatius' murder, as the emperor and his nephew desired. Talk to people living or working near the Great Church and so forth. His men had already covered the ground, but since the emperor had so ordered, it must be done again.

It wasn't clear to what extent the orders were Justin's or Justinian's, or for that matter which were the Gourd's interpretation of whatever had been said to him. At any rate, investigating the area near the scene of the crime seemed a sensible start.

Thus most of the morning had been spent interviewing those residents and merchants whose homes and commercial premises clustered along the Mese. In particular, they had questioned those near its intersection with the Augustaion on which stood the Great Church where Hypatius had died.

"So what have we learnt these past few hours?" Felix grumbled irritably. "That merchants keep a close eye on their goods. Those indoors keep their windows shut against the cold. Naturally no one sees or hears anything. All of which we could have easily guessed while sitting in a warm tavern with a cup of wine instead of tramping about in the cold."

"Nevertheless, you can't solve a murder just sitting in a warm corner. You have to go out and gather information."

Felix said nothing.

Each interview had followed the same pattern, suggested by John and accepted, grudgingly, but accepted nevertheless, by Felix. First they inquired whether the person to whom they were speaking had noticed anything on the day Hypatius was killed. Next, whether he might have seen something unusual. Finally if he had observed a very large, broad-shouldered Blue running by. It seemed to John that even if someone had noticed nothing else, he could not have missed a man of that size in full flight.

But that was indeed the case. At least if all those to whom they spoke were to be believed. He remarked on this to his companion.

Felix smiled. "These people wouldn't have noticed if Emperor Constantine had leaped down off his column, jumped on a horse, and galloped up the Mese. Not if a pair from the palace was asking about it. Perhaps—" Felix broke off. "You!" he shouted at a figure emerging from a shop in front of them. "Wait!"

The young man he addressed began to run. Felix caught up to him in a few strides and grabbed a skinny arm. It was the hair hanging down the back of the tunic that had caught Felix's eye, but when he spun his captive around John saw no evidence of the shaved hair so many Blues had adopted.

"You're a faction member, aren't you?" Felix barked anyway.

The youngster looked confused. "Yes, sir. Not the Blues though. And not when I'm on the street."

Felix gave the arm a shake. "Explain."

"I...I'm a Green, sir. Or rather I used to be. We don't dare venture out any more. The Blues would kill a Green as soon as look at him. I was sent to buy a few things for my employer."

Felix sent the young man on his way. He and John stood in front of a grocer's emporium, identified as such by a brass plaque engraved with a steelyard.

"We might as well ask in this shop, just like all the rest," said Felix. "Or maybe we should find a large stone to roll up a hill instead."

Stepping inside, they found an impressive array of household necessaries including pottery and glassware displayed amid barrels of salted fish. Baskets of vegetables and bowls of honeycombs leaned conspiratorially cheek by jowl on shelves attached to roughly plastered walls. The atmosphere was redolent of cheese, vinegar, and sawdust. Beside the door stacked amphorae held wine and the various types of oils needed for cooking or lighting. They reminded John uncomfortably of the very recent attempt to set the oil warehouses on fire.

"And how may I assist you, masters?" A short, thin man emerged from behind a stack of crates piled near the back of the cramped, rectangular room. He bowed very low while simultaneously contriving to examine his visitors from under a fringe of lank, black hair.

It would be difficult to steal anything from under this man's narrow, pinched nose, John thought, as Felix began his questioning.

Unlike earlier interviewees, the man looked neither impressed nor terrified by their quest. "I regret that the owner of this establishment is temporarily absent," he said smoothly, "but I will naturally be glad to help you as best I can."

"We'll talk to him later," Felix replied curtly. "First, his name and yours?"

"The master is Timothy and I am Alkabaides. I am his assistant."

Felix looked around the well-stocked interior. "Your master's trade appears to prosper."

"Indeed it does, sir. We charge a fair price for what we sell, unlike many others in this street." A jocular smile crossed the man's face. "While our competitors fill our ears with complaints about taxes and the high costs of doing business, we ourselves have just opened another shop. It sells nothing but the finest perfumes. Being situated near the booksellers' quarter and very close to court, we're privileged to count many of the great among our clients. I think we can guarantee you're certain to find something there to please your ladies, should you favor us with your custom."

Felix looked nonplussed, as if he couldn't decide whether the man was jesting or not. "I shall bear that in mind." He proceeded to question Alkabaides closely, not about fragrances or vegetables, but about whether he had noticed anything the day Hypatius died? Nothing at all? Nothing unusual? What about a large young man affecting the sartorial style of the Blues?

The assistant screwed up his face in thought but, like everyone else to whom they had spoken that morning, was unable to offer any information.

"If I'd actually seen such a man as you describe, I'm certain I would have remembered him. However, I must admit that a company of demons could have been racing each other right past the door and I wouldn't have seen them. I don't go out into the street when I'm working. Those poor unfortunates living in the gutter would be in and out behind my back in the wink of an eye and a wheel of cheese or a handful of fish gone with them."

"In which case for a day at least they would not be quite so unfortunate."

Alkabaides looked offended. "The master often gives them coins. He is a kind man despite losing a wife to a fever and his son in an accident. Never mind that in my opinion such charity just encourages beggars to further boldness. They repay kindness with trouble, fighting and keeping decent citizens awake half the night with their running around screaming at all hours. Not that I am criticizing my master, sirs, he is a good Christian."

"Sounds like some of those wild palace banquets one hears about. Does your master ever provide delicacies for any of those?"

The grocer's assistant shook his head. "I doubt that courtiers would care to dine on salt fish, although our vegetables are much remarked upon."

It appeared that Alkabaides had more to tell John and Felix about the grocery business than about the business that interested them. They left the shop.

As they retraced their footsteps along the Mese, John noticed that the beggar who had unsuccessfully asked them for alms had now moved to the other side of the street. John was suddenly struck by a thought.

"Felix, with respect, since none of the merchants have seen anything or anyone even remotely suspicious, may I suggest that those that nobody sees might possibly be more forthcoming?"

The other regarded him with a tired frown. "What do you mean?"

"The people who live on the streets. They're so much part of the scenery that most of the time we don't see them unless they hold a hand out. However, they always see us. And since they see us, who else might they have seen?"

"Not a bad idea, I suppose. You think well on your feet." He gave John an appraising look. "I noticed that last night. And when you borrowed my sword, I could swear you handled it as if you'd used a blade to better purpose than slicing a bit of pork off a haunch. You're in excellent condition too. Visit the gymnasium much?"

John did not take Felix's interest as a sign of friendliness. That the other was trying to draw him out about his past was obvious.

"I exercise daily at the baths." He didn't mention that he found such bodily exertion helped still the furies that bedeviled him and thus enabled him to present at least a nominally calm face to the world.

"And a cautious man too. You occasionally have an almost military look about you. If I didn't know what sort of man you were…." Felix appeared hopeful of further revelations.

John said nothing, but instead pointed to the beggar in the doorway. "I saw that man sitting right there the day Hypatius was murdered."

"I don't know how you can tell one bag of rags from the next. But if you saw him in the same place he might know something. There's a good view of the Augustaion from this part of the street." Felix started across the Mese. "He must at least have seen where that enormous Blue went."

The beggar appeared to be less a bag of rags than a disorganized pile of them with a pair of incongruously newish boots protruding from it. Strangely, he did not jump up and run off, as most did when they realized they were about to become the objects of official attention. On the contrary, the eyes set in a web of wrinkles brightened with anticipation. As John and Felix approached, he held out a dirty, three-fingered hand.

Felix ignored it. Anxious to get back indoors, he began to question the mendicant brusquely.

The man looked up, his face fixed in a grimace that mixed a vacant smile with an expression of bafflement. Again he waved his open hand at Felix and then at John.

Felix roughly slapped the hand down. "We're looking into a death! You will answer me or answer for it!"

The beggar shook his head, grunted and pointed to his throat and finally extended his hand hopefully again.

Felix looked puzzled. "What do you mean? You're hungry? So are we. And cold. So for the final time...."

The man grunted even more loudly. A panic-stricken note entered his strangled noises.

John stepped to Felix's side. "Your questions are fruitless. The man cannot speak."

With an oath, Felix turned away. "Naturally! How can I be surprised when everyone else around here is blind and deaf?"

"There is one person we can be sure saw something."

"Is that so? Who would that be?"

"The church doorkeeper who was stabbed just after Hypatius was murdered."

Chapter Seven

The brick-built Hospice of Samsun crouched
like a squat, homely beggar in the shadow
of the Hagia Eirene. Devoted to healing the
sick and broken bodies of the city's poor, the hospice's low-ceilinged rooms were inevitably crowded
past capacity.

"It's the doorkeeper of the Great Church I wish
to talk to, Gaius," Felix informed a ruddy-faced,
harried-looking man in a bloodstained tunic. "Is
he in fit shape to be questioned?"

They were standing in the entrance to Gaius'
surgery. The physician, an acquaintance of Felix's,
set a pottery bowl down with a thud on the long
wooden table against one wall.

"Why bother to ask? Even if the poor man were
at death's door, you'd still insist on grilling him
like St Lawrence. Doesn't the Gourd have better
things to do than pester my patients? And what's

this about you working for him anyway? Is it better than serving that doddering emperor of ours, or worse?"

John glimpsed Felix's grin, hastily banished by a frown.

"My position in the Prefect's office is temporary, I hope," Felix replied. "As for Justin, he may be old and ill now, but he was once a mere excubitor like myself. He rose to his position by his own abilities. He deserves to be spoken about with respect for that if for nothing else."

Gaius looked unconvinced. "A nice speech. Looking to rise yourself, are you? Justin may have been a man of some ability once, but he's fading away by all accounts. Can't even find his own boots in the morning, or so they say. I suppose it won't be long before you'll be coming around asking me where the emperor's boots are!"

John, standing by the door, glanced down the corridor behind him. A hum of conversation, interrupted now and then by muted cries of pain, wafted along between its narrow plastered walls.

The hospice smelt of crowded humanity, sickness, and herbs, overlaid with the acrid, metallic tang emanating from the brazier at the far end of the corridor. He wondered if it was used to heat cauterizing irons.

The thought turned his attention to the surgery. Bare, whitewashed walls reflected such light as filtered in through a single window from a sky the color of a fresh bruise. Apart from the table and a low stool it was unfurnished. Scattered dark patches on the table told their own tale, as did the bloodied bronze scalpels in the bowl Gaius had just set down.

"What's more, Felix," the physician was saying, "it would be very helpful if next time you're guarding Justin you could suggest that he occasionally authorize funds be diverted from paying for dancing girls for all those palace banquets or some such frippery into our meager coffers. We're full to the very doors and still people arrive for help."

Felix snorted. "Do I look like the quaestor to you? Or perhaps a Lord Chamberlain, that I would venture to speak to the emperor in such a fashion? Why would you think Justin takes financial advice from his guards?"

"They'd give better counsel than his dead wife, for a start! Oh yes, it's no good scowling, it's all over the city that the emperor talks to her shade. She should counsel him about stopping the street violence. It was bad enough when the Blues and Greens fought each other. At least the Greens could give a good account of themselves and so kept the Blues in check. Now they maim and murder at will."

"Not if the Prefect can help it."

"He puts on a good show. He can't burn every Blue in the city though. You think the judges won't release any he arrests? There isn't a magistrate who hasn't been bought by Justinian. But it isn't just the damned Blues keeping us busy. Most days we can depend on someone arriving with his scalp hanging half off. Hair caught in a winch at the docks or some other bizarre mishap you'd wager was impossible if you hadn't seen the results. Others break their heads open brawling in the gutters. It never ends. We send one patient out, more or less patched up, and two more are sitting on the doorstep waiting to come in."

Gaius took a breath and glanced curiously at John. "You haven't introduced your friend."

"Not a friend. A slave who's working with me. John is his name."

"I see."

Looking at the physician John noticed his eyes seemed fever bright. He'd had an extra cup of wine, he guessed, and no wonder, given his work.

"Mind you, it's not just beggars coughing up blood," Gaius was saying, "or needing broken bones set or some such common repairs. No, the entire city is on edge. We're seeing a lot more patients with knife wounds of late and that's a sure sign of it, in my experience. People start drinking too so their humors are worse. Then they get argumentative and soon the blades come out. You should have been here a week or so ago. A man was brought in with the worst case of mortification I've ever seen. It was a miracle he wasn't dead already. I had to take his leg off."

"Very inconvenient for you, I'd imagine."

Gaius sighed. "You military men have it easy. One clean thrust is all your job requires. Try sawing through a femur as fast as you can, before your patient wakes up and starts screaming. And how do you suppose he came to be in such a state?"

Felix admitted he had no notion.

"Got into a fight over a girl. He'll certainly be a bit less hot-headed after he hops out of here, if he survives. Not that he'll be fighting over women. They like their men with all their members. He claimed he was a soldier, but he must have been incompetent to lose a knife fight to a civilian. No more military campaigns for him."

"He'll leave well equipped to succeed as a beggar," Felix pointed out. "A missing leg's much more effective for getting sympathy and a coin or two than any amount of rubbing dirt into sores or borrowing malformed babies or cutting chunks of flesh out of the face."

Gaius stared at the instruments in the bowl. "You'd have more sympathy if you had my job, Felix. We see innumerable children. Not that long ago we had one poor child brought in whose head was crushed in a cart accident. Often there's nothing you can do but watch them die, wash them down, and send them home for burial. At least Hypatius saw a few years!"

"Yes, yes, I do see your point," Felix replied. "But, as I said, we need to speak to the doorkeeper."

Gaius finally fell silent and led them down corridors as difficult to navigate as the Bosporos, thanks to the patients lining them, some leaning against the walls and others stretched out on the floor. They crossed a bare courtyard where untainted air swirled briefly around their faces. Then they plunged back into the warm, malodorous atmosphere of the far wing.

John glanced into the doorless cell-like rooms they passed. Each contained three or four patients lying on thin pallets under threadbare blankets. Even so, he reflected, many must be in better quarters than wherever they lived outside the hospice.

In one room, a cluster of solemn children stood around an emaciated, white-bearded man who lay comatose, his face covered in sores. Stentorian breathing rattled in his throat. In his mercenary days, John had heard the sound often from the lips of the dying. The man was not long for the world.

Gaius showed the two men into a room no different from the rest except that it was so narrow that it had space for only two pallets. Only one was currently occupied. Perhaps, John mused, the doorkeeper's roommate had just been discharged, either from the hospice or from earthly pain, and that very recently. After ascertaining that the room's sole occupant was awake and lucid, Gaius left.

"Come by when you have a free hour or so," he told Felix on his way out. "We'll resume our tour of the city's taverns."

John had only glimpsed the wounded doorkeeper in the Great Church. There the old man had been nothing more than a pile of discarded robes in the shadows. Here, swathed in a coverlet, he appeared not much different. His thin, leathery face reminded John of a preserved holy relic.

"Who are you, good sirs?" The doorkeeper's eyes were bloodshot. His gaze darted back and forth between his visitors in terrified fashion.

Felix made his usual introduction. His mention of the Prefect elicited a peep of horror. "And what is your name?"

"Demetrios."

"You were one of the doorkeepers on duty the day that the man Hypatius was murdered in the Great Church?"

"My job was to guard the door. Not the vestibule. The villains stabbed me too." The man pulled himself up into a sitting position, revealing wrists as thin as a kalamos. He was shaking.

"I'm sure you're not responsible in any way for Hypatius' death, Demetrios. We just need to know if you saw anything that might help us find the men who committed the crime. You are attentive, I'm sure."

Demetrios seemed to relax a bit. "Certainly. Doorkeepers always have to be alert. I regret to say that not all our visitors are pious. Some of them, and you will scarcely credit this, even seek to steal whatever they can conceal about their persons. So we keep a close watch on all who come into the church and also aid worshippers as needed. The old and the feeble, for example, sometimes need help. All are welcome in the house of the Lord but some need extra assistance getting into it."

"No doubt that's true. But did you witness the murder?"

"I did." Demetrios sat up straighter. "It was not long after Hypatius arrived. A sad loss, sir. He was a most pious gentleman, very generous to the church and full of charitable works. He always gave us doorkeepers a coin or two. We'll miss him. But as to that terrible event—it was bitterly cold that day and not much better inside the church. The archdeacon does not allow much funding for charcoal, you see."

The old man shivered as if memories of the cold had chilled him anew. "Yet even so, a fair number of people came, mostly to see the sculpture. It offends some, sirs. Others, sadly more superstitious than devout, consider such representations to be magickal. I've had to tell more than one not to soil the marble with their grubby hands. There was even a fellow we had to pull down off the pedestal because he was convinced his wife would be cured of her fever if he touched Christ's face. The sculpture is so lifelike that, well, sometimes, and especially when the light was dim, it gave me pause. Yet if such a pious gentleman as Hypatius thought to glorify the church with it, then who is a simple doorkeeper to say otherwise?"

Felix removed his helmet and ran a hand through his thick hair. Despite the seriousness of their investigation, John had to suppress a smile. Between

Gaius and Demetrios one might guess the main affliction besetting Constantinople was a mysterious disease which refused to allow the lips to stop moving.

Felix broke into the doorkeeper's ramblings to ask when the Blues had arrived on the scene.

"Oh, there was already a crowd of them in the church," was the surprising reply. "All are welcome, as I said, without exception. Now as it happened, I was standing inside by the main door. I'd just come in for a short time to get out of the bitter wind, you understand, when it happened. It was all very confusing, between the number of people in the vestibule and the fact that it's not as well lit as the rest of the church. Anyhow, the trouble broke out among the crowd gathered around the sculpture."

"These were Blues?" put in Felix hopefully.

"Some certainly were, but most of them were regular visitors. I knew many of them by sight. Hypatius was standing looking up at the sculpture, when one of the Blues shouted."

"What was it he shouted?"

"Let's just say it was a blasphemy and leave it at that. Hypatius took him to task for using such words in a holy place. The others immediately started yelling even worse. A few of our regular worshippers tried to shout them down. Then Hypatius attempted to calm everyone. It was no good. Things had gone too far."

Felix shook his head. "And this in a holy place!"

"As you say, sir. It turned into chaos. Women were getting hysterical. Men ran outside to escape. Wisely so. Damage was done to the church...yet really it all happened in less time than it takes to tell you. Within a few heartbeats fighting began."

Demetrios' voice rose incredulously as he continued. "Including among the faithful! Suddenly Hypatius fell, mortally wounded as it turned out. It was as if he had been struck by the hand of God. But why a man of such piety? And he hadn't even started the argument. That is how blood was spilled in the house of the Lord, sirs!"

To John's surprise, the doorkeeper began to cry feebly. "Yes, blood was spilled in the house of the Lord," Demetrios repeated forlornly.

"And it was then that you were wounded?" Felix asked after a brief silence.

The doorkeeper's head bobbed in agreement. "I tried to go to Hypatius' aid. The Blues were running away and a couple shoved me aside, but not before one turned back and sunk his blade into my shoulder. Why would they do that? Killing one man, wounding another, and for what reason? Is there nothing they won't stoop to? We're not safe in our beds!" The thought brought fear back to his face.

"The city will be calm now," Felix reassured him. "Look at the way the Prefect put down those rioters just the other night. They'll think twice about starting anything now."

"Those young troublemakers aren't averse to murder. They'll be very hard to convince."

John had the fleeting impression that the doorkeeper was about to leap off his pallet. The man raised a stick-like arm and waved it in feeble agitation. "Decent citizens never know whether or when they'll be assaulted. Prudent men go about their business well guarded and it's best for women to stay at home. Except for attending church, that is." He slumped down, looking suddenly exhausted.

Felix asked the doorkeeper if he had related all that he had seen.

"That's all, sir."

There was an outburst of screaming in the corridor. Looking out, John saw a young woman, her head covered with a soiled veil, carted shrieking into a nearby room. Gaius raced into view.

Felix stepped out of the sickroom and laid a hand on the physician's arm before he could pass. "What's happened?"

Gaius wrenched his arm free. "It's a street whore. A dissatisfied customer threw a lamp full of burning oil into her face." He vanished into the room where the woman's continued screams now had a raw, rasping quality. Evidently the tortured cries had been going on for a long time.

"Gaius was right, John," Felix said as they departed the hospice. "Tempers are short. There'll be worse before long, I'd wager my sword on it. Anyone who's not prepared to fight should stay off the streets."

Chapter Eight

John followed Lady Anna as she stepped hastily into the bookseller's shop just off the Augustaion. Her quick step resulted not so much from eagerness to discover what new offerings might be found in the brightly lit emporium as from her desire to take shelter against the feathery snow beginning to drift from a sullen sky.

"Ah, my lady." The bookseller greeted her with a low bow. He appeared not to have noticed John at all. "It is good to see you again. And how is your father the senator?"

"Well indeed, Scipio."

The bold odors of spice, perfume and freshly baked bread had streamed from the doorways of other establishments John and Anna had passed. The air here was scented more subtly by dusty parchment. Scipio's scrolls and codices were arranged neatly on shelves and tables and in wall niches, as if in a library.

Anna began to warm her hands at the brazier set by the far wall. It stood as far away from the flammable wares as possible.

"And yourself, my lady?" The bookseller was a slightly built man with a shaved head. Quite young, John thought, to be the owner of such an establishment.

"I am well also, at least now that I can feel my fingers again. Have you anything to show me today?"

Scipio nodded his bald head. "Only a single item, but one that I think you'll find most intriguing."

He took down an ornamented box from a shelf and opened it to display a codex with an unadorned leather cover.

"It was sent to me by my brother, who often finds such treasures. An aristocrat, whom I will not name, was selling off a few valuables to satisfy the tax collector's latest outrageous demand. Alas, the libraries always go first. Knowing your interest in gardens, I have not shown this to anyone yet."

Anna took the proffered item. John saw it was a selection of Pliny the Younger's letters, the first of which was devoted to describing his gardens.

She scanned it eagerly. "John, is this not beautiful?"

John agreed it was.

"This is certainly of great interest, Scipio," she said, "but I should like to consider the matter overnight. I could send a message tomorrow, if you would be willing to wait."

The bookseller assured her that he would be more than happy to do so and politely ushered them out. A thin veil of snow had begun to whiten everything in the street, bits of broken pottery, animal dung, straw, scraps of rotted fruit, and even a scrap of parchment escaped from Scipio's shop.

"Do you think it's worth the price?" Anna wondered as their steps turned homeward.

"Not to a collector. The cover was plain to begin with and looks badly worn. I noticed that a few of the pages are stained. But since the subject matter interests you...if you think it has value, then it does."

"True indeed."

They proceeded at a brisk pace. John kept a cautious watch on the doorways and narrow alleys they passed. While he felt he should be pursuing the investigation into Hypatius' death, Justinian's orders, however odd, had been very clear; he was to continue with his other duties so far as possible. It had happened, for one reason or another, that his tutoring of Lady Anna had also come to include escorting her about the city on occasion.

"What value can you put on a person, John?" Anna said. "I'm not talking about slaves. Pardon me if I offended you."

John softly pointed out that slaves were unoffendable and that no apology was therefore necessary.

Anna smiled, her plain face suddenly beautiful from its sweetness. "I spoke without thought, John. It's hard to think of you as what...as who...you are. And now what is it that makes you look so solemn?"

How could he tell her that it was her inappropriate tone that distressed him? "I find myself wondering about Hypatius. A man of great worth, it seems."

"If Hypatius were a book, his cover would be of carved ivory but his verses wouldn't scan." Anna pulled her cloak closer around her angular frame as they turned into the street on which stood her father's house. "While we should not speak in ill fashion of the departed, the reason I say this is that he had been paying romantic attention to me for some time. Frankly, I had become very tired of it."

John observed that was entirely understandable. A servant girl opened the house door for them and took their snow-damp cloaks.

He noticed that the atrium was darker than usual. Because of the cold weather, several folding wooden panels had been shut, closing the senator's office off from both the garden beyond and the rest of the house.

"Some spiced wine, please," Anna instructed the servant. "And two cups. And ask Dorotheus to send someone to light the brazier in my study. We'll be in father's office."

Suppressing a surprised giggle, the girl vanished toward the kitchen.

"Father won't mind if we wait in here until my study's warmed up." Anna led John into the office and motioned him to take a seat. "He's attending a church service. Tiresome, perhaps, but necessary for a senator."

John made no reply. Although never spoken of, it was obvious to him that Opimius was a pagan. Like a handful of other senators who remained loyal to the gods of their ancestors, Anna's father made a show of observing the state religion. He had no other choice. However, it was exceedingly improper, not to say unwise, for Anna to refer to the matter even obliquely.

The office's rich wall hangings and carpet seemed to hold the heat from its lamps. Anna went immediately to the brazier.

"Why don't you warm your hands, John? You suffer from the cold just as I do. You think I haven't noticed?"

John assured Anna he was warm enough. It made him uneasy that she should notice such a thing, or mention it. Anna sat down on an upholstered couch next to John's chair.

"Hypatius was a friend of my father's," she continued. "Naturally he often visited. He was a pious man, but a man who was pious in an obvious way. He attended services daily, funded charitable works, gave the church ostentatious gifts, and so on."

The servant entered to place a wine jug on the table beside the couch. She looked John over with obvious curiosity before she was dismissed.

John took a sip from his wine cup. Orange lamp light flickered around the rim. He suggested that Hypatius' activities were not unworthy.

"As you say." Anna drained her cup. "However, there are those who do good deeds for the sake of the doing and those who do them for the sake of being known for their charity."

"Still, charity is charity."

Anna smiled at him again and John looked down into his wine.

"I suppose you are right, John. Perhaps I do him a disservice. He was a regular visitor here for years. I never felt that I got to know him very well or much about him except that he was very wealthy and his business interests were many and varied. And, as I said, he pawed at me when father wasn't looking."

"You did not want to know him well?"

"Father would have been happier if I had. In fact, he would have been positively ecstatic if I had become that old hypocrite's wife. Fortunately for me, Hypatius did not have the opportunity to propose I be thus honored."

"Did you think he intended to?" John finished his wine. Before he realized it, Lady Anna had picked up the jug and began to refill his cup.

John felt his chest constrict. He could hardly draw his cup back and allow the wine to spill onto the senator's fine carpet. He looked at Anna, questioningly, and she fixed her gaze on him. Her eyes were unremarkable yet he could not look away. His cheeks prickled as if all the lamps in the room had suddenly flared up into raging bonfires.

Anna poured the wine slowly until his cup had been filled. She was not very adept at such duties. A trickle ran down the side of the vessel and puddled on the table top.

"Hypatius intended to hold a banquet next month, and hinted he intended to make an announcement of some import during it. I thought it might have to do with me, I admit, and had been dreading it." She sighed. "I am not certain. He was, after all, a wealthy man. He did not need my attractive dowry. He could have bought himself some woman as beautiful as a sculpture of Helen."

"But he was paying you unwanted attentions," John managed to say.

She pursed her lips. "Perhaps he thought he was being kind. No, a rich man like him would not wish to take as wife someone plain as I am. I'm sorry if I sound cross, John, but everyone seems to believe they know what is best for me. Or, rather, what father has told them is best for me. Everyone wishes to please father. He has convinced a widow of his acquaintance, a redoubtable woman indeed, to counsel me on how a single woman of wealth conducts her affairs. I suppose this would be in case I remain obdurately single should father die. A few months ago Dominica, that's her name, suddenly began visiting more frequently. At first I thought she had her eye on father! Then she started taking me aside for little talks."

"I am familiar with such well-meant lectures," John said. He couldn't help but remember the advice Dorotheus had insisted on giving. It was not proper for a lady to converse in such manner with a slave. Yet how could a slave properly tell a lady that? To his dismay Anna plunged ahead.

"And now there is the matter of Trenico."

John scowled, but remained silent.

"His wealth is, it seems, not unlike the Christian's Lord, something one must take on faith. Lately there are fewer believers amongst his creditors. Father tells me that Trenico's dropping broad hints about marriage and dowries. That's as far as it's gone."

"You will be hoping then that he does not mention any upcoming banquets of great import."

"I trust not. I know Trenico well enough to realize that marriage would not put an end to his romantic liaisons with ladies of the court, not to mention those in lower strata of society. Not that I would criticize his being attracted to a woman of a humbler class. We are all of the same flesh, after all."

John was saved from finding a reply by the hollow sound of the stout front door being banged shut, closely followed by raised voices in the atrium. Quick steps sounded and Senator Opimius stamped into his office, brushing snow from his hair.

Anna's father was as plain as his daughter. Of average height, his pale features seemed rather too small and crowded together. He could have been mistaken for one of the hundreds of minor functionaries populating the palace's administrative offices.

"Anna. Always at the lessons, I see. John, fetch me wine." His voice trembled.

Anna handed her cup to the senator. "Here, father, take mine. There's more wine in the jug. I can see something terrible has happened. What was it?"

Senator Opimius took the wine and sat heavily in the chair John had hurriedly vacated.

"Please remain, John," Opimius told him. "This concerns you also. By great good fortune, you brought Anna home without mishap, but she will not be venturing out again without at least three bodyguards. Do you hear that, Anna? I just escaped grave injury myself."

"Injury…?"

Opimius took a gulp of wine before speaking. "We were attacked by a ruffian. Or a demon. In that narrow way that runs between the Church of Eirene and Samsun's Hospice… Yes, yes, I know it was foolish to cut through there, but I was anxious to be home. This man, this demon, appeared from thin air and flew at us like a wild beast. I've never seen such rage on a human face…. The slave escorting me fought him off but—"

"There's blood on your sleeve," Anna interrupted, panic in her voice. "Let me—"

Opimius shook his head. "It's not my blood, Anna. Dorotheus defended me."

"Dorotheus?" Ann's voice was a barely audible whisper.

Opimius looked at his daughter and John saw that the senator's eyes were glistening. "Anna, if only your mother were alive. She would know how to tell you, how to make it..." He shook his head, almost imperceptibly. The gesture was terrible nevertheless. "Dorotheus is dead."

In the ensuing silence John could hear excited voices from somewhere deep inside the house and the faint sizzling of oil burning low in one of the office lamps.

Anna let out a hoarse sob and John stiffened with horror.

Unseen by her father, Anna had clasped John's hand.

Chapter Nine

"Surely the attack on Senator Opimius was nothing more than an attempt at robbery?" Felix squinted across the cobbled square and up toward the sun just now rising over the roof tops. A few of the big German's fellow excubitors, on their way out of the barracks where he and John had agreed to meet, barked brief greetings at their colleague and cast curious backward glances at the tall man by his side.

"Going by Opimius' description, his attacker wasn't a member of a faction. There's nothing unusual about street violence these days, sad to say, and if one chooses to go out in public without an adequate guard…. He regrets his mistake now. Not to mention the grief it has caused his daughter." As he spoke John seemed to feel again the pressure of Anna's hand on his own. He shivered, as at the touch of a phantom.

"You wouldn't think a senator would be so foolish as to be going about the city with only an elderly servant as a guard. But, I understand, this particular senator has a history of making foolish decisions. I've made some inquiries, and—"

"You've been investigating Senator Opimius?"

"Don't look so shocked. I've been ordered to work with his daughter's tutor. It pays to know as much as possible about the man you're working with, including anyone connected with him. Actually, I happened on certain information while trying to ascertain why, in particular, Opimius had engaged you for the job. Apparently the senator made enemies at the palace when he backed Vitalian so strongly five years ago."

Seabirds swooped in to fight raucously over a chunk of stale bread lying not far away. John hoped it had been dropped by someone who could afford the loss and not by a beggar who would go hungry for the day. Then again, he reasoned, how many beggars could be wandering the grounds of the Great Palace?

"Vitalian? Didn't the emperor invite him to Constantinople to appoint him consul? A reward for his defense of orthodoxy, wasn't it? So why would Opimius' support of Vitalian make him enemies in the palace? Not that a man doesn't make some enemies no matter what he chooses to do or say or think."

"Let's walk while we discuss this matter. We shouldn't be seen standing around looking idle. It wouldn't be good for our careers!"

Felix set off across the square, scattering the seabirds, which retreated noisily to the roof of the house across from the barracks.

"The senator's real problem," he continued, "or so rumor has it, is that he truly did support Vitalian. You'll recall that imperial hospitality extended to a banquet at which Vitalian was stabbed to death. Seventeen wounds the man had. Now where were the guards while seventeen blows were being struck? A dining hall may be large, but try putting a blade into someone that many times without being noticed!"

They turned down a path which funneled a stiff breeze, redolent of the unglimpsed sea, into their faces.

"I've heard about that. Justinian's opponents claim to this day that he arranged Vitalian's murder, and, over time, the murders of half the aristocracy to boot. But where is the proof?"

"Where's the proof of anything in this city? Right here!" Felix slapped the hilt of the sword at his belt.

"Even so, that was years ago. Justinian could have relieved Opimius of his head long since if he wanted it. Why now? I've never heard a word breathed against Opimius' loyalties. And he's a good friend of Senator Aurelius, one of Justinian's strongest supporters."

They climbed a wide set of stairs and entered a cavernous hall. Light filtering from a row of windows set high up in the gaudily frescoed walls fell on a whirlpool of humanity where those hastening away from the palace on imperial business converged and swirled with those leaving to go to their day's labors inside the vast complex.

"It's my opinion that all this street violence is an excellent cover for people with scores to settle," Felix remarked, "but what makes me wonder about the attack on the senator is that it happened not long after Justinian recruited us both."

John stopped walking, forcing Felix to do the same. "What do you mean?"

The crowd surged around them, jostling and casting ill-tempered looks at the two unexpected rocks dividing their current. The clatter of boots, the sound of voices reverberating in the vaulted ceiling overhead, rang in their ears.

Felix shook his head with disgust. "I'm not stupid. You know as well as I do that it is very peculiar Justinian insisted that you continue your tutoring. What is it to him if Lady Anna can speak Persian when there are far weightier matters demanding immediate attention? Do you suppose he has his eye on that dowdy woman when he's already got a famous actress in his bed? And if he's looking for an emissary to send to Persia he wouldn't choose a woman. Clearly, he wants someone in there, keeping an eye on Opimius' household. Why do you think Justinian chose you, in particular, to investigate the murder? Simply because you are clever? How many clever slaves are there at the palace? Now, ask yourself, how many clever slaves from the palace work in Opimius' household?"

He was right, John admitted to himself. Felix might be just an ordinary military man, but he was far shrewder than most. It wasn't so easy, as he'd already discovered, for a slave in the lower echelons of the palace bureaucracy to discover anything and it must be almost as difficult for an excubitor, even if he did belong to the emperor's bodyguard.

They continued on, past a small army of guards and through the Chalke, the palace's massive bronze gate. The sun seemed much brighter now by contrast to the dim interior from which they had just emerged. From nearby perfume shops the sweet scent of flowers mingled with the pungent odor of animal dung in the street, a remnant of early morning deliveries.

"And what about this attack on Opimius?" John mused. "If someone wanted Opimius dead because he was suspected of opposing Justinian years ago, that would surely be meant to benefit Justinian."

"Whatever the reason, if someone is in fact out to kill Senator Opimius then everyone near him is in danger as well. Including you. And perhaps myself, since we are working together."

And, thought John, Anna also. "So far we've been asking whether anyone saw anything. Perhaps we should instead direct our investigations toward those who might be responsible."

"But you saw those responsible. Blues. That's who we're looking for."

"They, or one of them at least, are certainly the killers. Did someone hire them? If Justinian's enemies wanted to implicate him, would they wait for a convenient murder?"

"They might not have had it in mind, just seized the opportunity."

"On the other hand, as Theodora said, it's almost as if Hypatius' murder was designed to outrage the public."

"That's obvious enough, but our job is only to find the man who actually wielded the blade. We're in no position to do more. At least the sun's out for once. Why the look of gloom?"

John said nothing. He wished the demons that tortured him could be driven off by a few rays of sunlight.

"It always feels as if someone's staring at my back in this city." Felix glanced back at the palace entrance. "Perhaps it's that." He gestured toward the Chalke. The huge icon of Christ set on it appeared to be gazing up the Mese. "He must've seen something," Felix went on. "If only we could ask. If He's looking for sinners to grieve over, He should be gazing into the Great Palace instead of away from it."

"What now? We've already questioned every shopkeeper in the street."

"There are apartments above some of the shops," Felix suggested.

"Yes, but not much can be seen from them except the roof of the colonnade. Unless our quarry ran down the middle of the street?"

Felix grunted. "I suppose that's true. He probably cut away from the Mese as soon as he could. We'll try some more of the nearby streets."

Only a few paces down the first thoroughfare, their progress became blocked by a knot of people. Drawing nearer they saw the crowd had gathered at the entrance of a small semi-circular plaza giving access to a few shops, all of which were currently unoccupied.

John tensed. Lately crowds meant trouble. He was surprised to hear laughter from this group.

"What's going on?" Felix demanded of a tall man who stood near the back of the throng, craning his neck to see.

"It's a troupe of actors drumming up business. Not that they can perform this piece in the theater. It's the life of Theodora. Exceedingly scurrilous and indecent!"

"Indecent?" Felix began to shove his way unceremoniously through the crowd. "If they were on the street at the time of Hypatius' murder, it's possible they noticed something useful."

To John, the actors were nearly indistinguishable from beggars. The rags they sported may have been slightly more colorful than those mendicants generally wore. He supposed it was a bad time for actors. Street violence didn't put the public in a mood for light entertainment.

A man wearing a voluminous old-fashioned toga and an equally oversized and obviously false beard declaimed stridently at the spectators.

"Though she had already learned to sate their bestial lusts in a fashion so unnatural we would not dare to speak of it in public, young Theodora's career had only begun," he declared. "No longer was she content to carry the stool of her older sister from engagement to engagement. Soon she developed certain specialties of her own. Specialties as fiendishly clever as they were vile. Parts which the Lord gave us were put to uses even He could not have imagined, for if He had, He would surely have created Adam and Eve quite differently."

A figure wrapped in garish red robes and sporting a preposterous wig with coils of hair as big as beehives swayed out from the doorway of one of the vacant shops. The gaudy, ersatz crown balanced on the wobbly hairpiece proclaimed the figure to be Theodora. The stubble beneath the rouge revealed the future empress to be male.

Felix chuckled. "An empress like that would put the whole Persian army to flight."

The white-bearded narrator leaned toward the crowd and spoke in a stage whisper. "Friends, our troupe is privileged to have among us one who lately occupied the same stage as Theodora and was thus intimately acquainted with her act, if not with the woman herself."

He paused to leer and to allow a few onlookers to add their own coarse wit to the script. "Thus, for your enlightenment, we are able to present, not a poor simulation, but an exact recreation of the famous performance many talk about, but few actually witnessed. Some may call what you are about to see vulgar, salacious, unfit for the eyes of decent Christians, or even an abomination. But, as Thucydides so aptly put it, history is comprised of examples taught by philosophy."

John caught Felix's eye and nodded in the direction of several actors who stood unobtrusively to one side. They had already played their parts or were waiting to do so. "I thought you intended to question these people?"

"And miss seeing the example he mentioned? Have some respect for philosophy!"

The painted, hirsute empress strutted back and forth in front of the crowd, puckering her red-smeared lips. Without warning, she flopped onto the ground like a bird that had taken an arrow, and slowly began to disrobe.

Or, John thought, it would be more proper to say dis-rag, to judge by the scraps of cloth that fell to the ground.

"Stop! Stop!" The narrator rushed over to the fallen empress and waved his arms frantically.

"Oh good sir, I cannot stop," the empress wailed in a hideous falsetto. "I am but a poor actress and must earn my crust, or preferably a few coins, any way I can."

From the crowd came a cry of "It's a disgrace!"

Ignoring the comment, a lanky fellow carrying a bag of grain over his shoulder approached the prone figure. The straw in his hair revealed that he was acting the part of a farmer.

The narrator again addressed the audience. "What's this chickpea up to? Can it be? Was Theodora's performance really just as common gossip has it?"

Several in the crowd honked like geese.

The narrator screwed his face up in mock offense. "Some may find it humorous that a future empress was forced to support herself by stripping and allowing geese to gobble grain from her naked body." He paused and raised his eyebrows. "Although I'll wager the Patriarch isn't one of them!"

The farmer opened his bag and sprinkled a few grains onto the prone empress. The crowd hooted. He daintily sprinkled a few more. The crowd grew noisier. Finally, he raised the bag, and dumped its entire contents on his fellow thespian.

The exaggerated choking noises made by the half-buried Theodora were drowned out by raucous honking of a much more professional and convincing nature than the audience's hootings. Three goose impersonators burst out from behind the troupe of actors. Each manipulated the long, flaccid neck of a plucked and rather desiccated fowl.

"Ah, but philosophy is a merciless teacher," cried the narrator. "I would rather pluck my eyes out like Oedipus than witness this sorry example, this spectacle of degradation. Is there not a Roman citizen among you who would spare our future empress this indignity? A coin or two. I beg of you. Feed the starving actress before she is further befowled."

A few bits of copper flew out from the onlookers. The narrator called for more contributions, but the scanty rain soon abated. He paused and then whirled around, directing attention to one of the darker shop doorways.

A misty shape materialized in the dimness and then a stocky, dwarfish figure rushed out. It was totally white and wore a crown. The figure ran toward the recumbent empress, leaving a faint trail of the flour that covered it.

"May heaven preserve us," thundered the narrator. "It is the shade of the Empress Euphemia!"

The diminutive phantom leapt acrobatically into the air and came crashing down on Theodora in an explosion of grain and flour. The two men dressed as women began a hissing, mewling battle, much to the crowd's delight.

Felix laughed until he had to wipe his eyes. Despite John's urgings he refused to budge until the epic had been finished, with the doughty Euphemia ousting the terrified Theodora, and then delivering a bombastic homily on morality.

"A good morning's work," John muttered as the crowd finally began to disperse. He and Felix approached the narrator as he counted a handful of coins, and made the usual inquiries.

The actor tugged at his beard, pulling it down around his neck, and scratched his chin. "A Blue, you say, but an enormous fellow? A regular Hercules?"

Felix confirmed that they were searching for such a man.

"Did he have an oddly crushed sort of nose?"

"Yes, that's him!"

The actor shook his head. "Sorry, sirs, I haven't seen him."

Felix's eyes blazed, but as he opened his mouth to retort, the actor held up a hand and smiled. "Forgive my jest. I have seen him, but not lately and not around here. He was in our audience once. We were working up near the northern harbor at the time. Or was it the southern? I can't recall. I just remember seeing this huge man looming in the crowd. Such a man could have an excellent career in the theater, you know. He'd be perfect for a giant or Zeus. Any hero for that matter, even the emperor."

Chapter Ten

The broad-shouldered and highly perfumed man who answered Felix's rap at Madame Isis' door took the excubitor's sword and the short blade that John carried before allowing them inside.

The day had been long and fruitless. Felix had finally suggested they come here. "There's more information to be found at Isis' place than there is marble on Proconnesus," he'd said.

The atrium's floor, with its intricate scenes of entwined carnality, left no doubt as to what sort of establishment they had just entered. It was equally obvious by his accent, curly beard, and long, wavy hair that its doorkeeper was Persian. For John, the Persian and the erotic mosaic created a painful juxtaposition.

"We're here for some wine and conversation, Darius." As Felix spoke a girl dressed in white, hair crowned with a chaplet of interwoven flowers, rose gracefully from a gilded couch that sat beside a statue of Venus in the embrace of Mars. She padded toward them on bare feet.

Felix frowned. "I don't have the coins for more right now, I fear. They're right when they say if you don't have a nummus for a sausage it's better not to be hungry!"

"Well, Darius, it seems we have been favored by a visit of two gentlemen from court." The girl smiled sweetly at John and Felix, and then raked them with a shrewd, appraising glance.

"In this instance I fear we have arrived to see Madam Isis, not you, Hunila."

The girl pouted. "Oh, Felix, it's been ages since I entertained you. When are they going to raise your wages?"

The girl looked down to the floor and following her gaze John saw she was expertly caressing one of the mosaic's naked figures there with her bare toe. She looked up expectantly at John. "And who's this handsome friend of yours?"

"John. He's a slave. Assisting me."

"I will ask madam if she can see you." Darius moved away quietly. John saw he was wearing soft yellow slippers.

"As far as that goes," Hunila said, "we make no distinctions here, although I can think of a few of my clients who would be horrified to learn I've also occasionally entertained their servants. There again, who's going to tell them?"

Felix observed that they would certainly not reveal anything. "I'm certain we can trust your professional discretion as well. Even though I'm sure there are plenty of interesting stories you could tell."

Hunila's face suffused with such anger that the flush on her cheeks showed through her fashionable white makeup. "Interesting? Ugly, more like it! If it hadn't been for Darius we would have had a very bad incident the other night. Three boys from one of those idiotic factions showed up in the small hours. Not that madam minds since she just charges them extra for keeping us up late."

Felix guffawed at such business acumen.

The girl glared at him. "Unfortunately they objected to paying a little extra for the inconvenience. You know how they are, dressed so richly but generally with about as much wealth as starving dogs. And the manners of starving dogs. Anyway, they decided to take what they wanted for nothing. Just as they'd probably stolen their fine clothing. Darius tossed them out. I thought madam would be annoyed to lose clients, but she just patted him on his shoulder and thanked him for his efforts."

Felix turned to John. "Darius has been with Isis ever since she set up this house. Beautiful place, isn't it?"

"It's certainly very well appointed." John didn't add that the dizzyingly detailed floors, plush wall hangings, decorative columns, and the gilt glittering from every nook and cranny did not match his Spartan tastes. He studied the statue of Venus and Mars, who, in contrast to the white-faced girl, had been painted in warmly realistic flesh tones.

"Would you like to see my room? I have a very interesting fresco." Hunila favored John with a sly smile that he guessed was as contrived as the expressions on the statue a few paces away.

"He's no use to you," Felix cut in. "Here's Darius to take us to see Isis. I'll try and visit you soon, Hunila."

Isis was perched on an ivory stool in front of the window of her private sitting room. Sunlight delineated the delicate features of an olive-skinned young woman arranging her employer's long, glossy black hair.

To John's chagrin the Persian doorkeeper formally announced them as the excubitor Felix and the slave John.

Isis welcomed them warmly. As she spoke, her hairdresser swept the last stray, raven locks into a tight coil and deftly secured them with a jeweled hair pin. She handed Isis a mirror.

"It is done, madam," the girl said softly in Egyptian, Isis' native language.

Isis complimented the woman on her efforts. "Take a few sweetmeats and share them with the other girls."

The servant took the proffered bowl, gave a small bow and departed.

"Isn't she a treasure? Not only wonderful at arranging my hair, but an excellent cook. I was lucky to be able to buy both her and her mother at a reduced price."

It was the sort of comment John heard every day. It reminded him he was a chattel that could be purchased by even a well-to-do whore. His jaw clenched. Their sharp-eyed hostess noticed the tiny movement.

"John, let me tell you that I was once a slave myself. There's no shame in it. And it's not too long since I scraped up enough to buy my freedom although it took a year or two longer to be able to set myself up in business. Who knows what Hemsut has in store for any of us? Until you find out, sit down and have some wine. In my house all are equal."

Felix dropped onto an overstuffed couch and helped himself to wine from an intricately engraved silver vessel that would not have looked out of place on the emperor's table. "I'll wager you're wondering how I know Isis, beyond the obvious. She keeps me informed of what's going on behind the emperor's back. I make sure her establishment isn't overlooked by interested parties at court who might like some female companionship."

"And when you succeed in sending me clients with heavy coin purses who also happen to know what's going on behind the emperor's back, the better for both of us!" Isis commented. "Information is a valuable commodity in this city, John. As you are learning. Here, have a splash of wine." John accepted a cup and sat next to Felix.

Isis poured herself a libation. "And now, my friends, a toast. To the health of Emperor Justin and to his nephew Justinian."

"I shall drink to half of that!" Felix replied.

Isis smiled at Felix and then cursed him for his stupidity with a string of Egyptian epithets that would have burned the ears off the Sphinx.

"Is that another of those melodious poems from your native land, Isis?" Felix inquired.

John's eyes had widened at the unexpected phrases. Isis pointed a ring-encircled finger at him. "You understood what I said! You speak Egyptian, don't you?"

John admitted it was so in Isis' native language.

"You have a passable accent. How long is it since you were there?" Isis began chattering away happily.

Felix looked at his companions in confusion. "Isis, you amaze me. We've been here a very short time and already you've found out something about this man's mysterious background. You certainly take a keen interest in the lives of your visitors as well as your clients!"

"That's because my clients and visitors have such interesting lives, Felix," Isis laughed. She was an attractive woman, John thought, although in that soft, rounded way that had never much appealed to him. "Now John, when were you last in Egypt?"

"It is some years since I left, madam."

"And you lived where?"

"Alexandria."

"Oh, but Hemsut has been kind today." Isis clasped her hands in front of her ample bosom. "I too lived there before I came to Constantinople. I hope to see Alexandria again when I am able to retire. That will be few more years yet. Yes, it will be good to live there again. Do you not long for those bottomless skies? Soft nights with stars as bright as the gems on an empress' robes. The Nile flooding in the spring until nothing remains of the land but the cities, rising above the water like islands in the Sea of Marmara."

John gave a thin smile. "I think of Egypt often, madam. Unfortunately my master requires my constant attendance at court."

"Yes. How thoughtless of me. I apologize." She reached over and patted John's knee. "What does your friend Felix want to know?"

Felix frowned at the two whose conversation, in Egyptian, had been indecipherable to him. "I hope you're not busy plotting, Isis. If you're going to talk about me, can't you speak in Greek?"

"Of course." Isis refilled his cup and pushed a tray of dried apples toward him. "What do you seek?"

Felix took a hearty swallow of wine. His eyes looked unfocussed. "We're interested in anything you might have heard from your girls about the Blues." He described the distinctive young man John had observed fleeing after Hypatius' death.

Isis shook her head. "Nobody like that has been here, Felix. It sounds as if even Darius would have had his hands full if such a man had visited."

"He was larger even than your doorkeeper," said John. "But we hear you've had problems with other Blues?"

Isis muttered a ripe curse under her breath. "Yes, we have. I am contemplating barring them from my house since lately they have been more trouble than their money is worth. It's my opinion that Justinian lets them get away with murder because of Theodora's affection for them. Not that I can blame her."

John asked Isis if she had a particular reason for her opinion.

"You've probably heard that her father was a bearkeeper for the Greens and that when he died, her mother remarried. Theodora's stepfather hoped to keep the bearkeeper's job in the family, but the Greens turned him out. They condemned the whole family to poverty, because the father's fate is the family's fate. It was a terrible act. Unforgivable. Theodora and her two sisters were very young. Luckily the Blues were willing to employ the man and so her family was saved. I can appreciate Theodora's feelings perfectly. If for some reason someone had to step in and save my girls, I would be eternally grateful to them as well."

"Few in this city share Theodora's gratitude toward the Blues," put in Felix.

"True enough. But while none of us wants a blade in the ribs, I'd say the empire has more to fear from the Gourd than dim-witted young men parading around in outlandish clothing."

Felix squeezed his eyes shut. John wondered if he was thinking hard or trying to conquer an impression that the room was spinning. Isis had already refilled the excubitor's cup more than once.

"John was treated to a fascinating spectacle the night of the last riot," the excubitor finally said. "I was keeping the statuary in the Gourd's garden in line so I missed the show. From what John told me I begin to wonder if the Gourd really does practice magick, as many say."

"They say it in whispers, surely?" was Isis' tart reply. "And what was this astonishing spectacle?"

John quickly related the scene he had witnessed at the Gourd's dinner party. Isis, chewing on a segment of dried apple, considered the information, then ventured the comment that nothing would surprise her with the Gourd. More importantly, what dishes had he served to his guests?

Mystified, John described the various courses he had seen.

"I am always looking for something new in the culinary line to offer my clients. I don't think those baked gourds you described would do. However, I've had an inspired idea. What do you think of this? I shall redecorate my house in the style of Sobek, the crocodile god!"

"Sounds very exotic to me." Felix's speech was slurred. "Though when visiting a girl, how much notice does anyone take of the surroundings? What did you say? Crocodile god? That might keep the Blues away and everyone else as well!"

"Oh, Felix, it would all be in jest!"

"A toast to whatshisname then, the god of Egypt." Felix spoke too loudly. He helped himself to yet more wine.

John set his own cup down. It was always wise to keep a clear head. He wondered if he'd have to carry the burly excubitor back to his barracks.

✳ ✳ ✳

On their way out, Felix fumbled his sword as Darius returned it. The sun's early promise had proved to be as reliable as that of a man of law. The wind was sweeping in from sea, swirling around corners and throwing dust into pedestrians' eyes. John hoped its chilly fingers would revive his companion.

As the two men stood outside Isis' house several others hurried up, paused as they drew abreast, and then quickened their pace to go by, faces averted. John suggested it would be better if they moved away from Isis' door since their presence there was obviously affecting possible clients.

Felix, however, planted his boots stolidly, leaned against the wall and contemplated the sky, evidently seeking inspiration.

"I'm not certain where we should inquire next," he finally announced, scratching his chin.

He appeared to John to be in no condition to make further inquiries. "As I suggested earlier, we should try to establish who might have an interest in engaging someone to do away with Hypatius."

"And what authority have we been granted to question the sort of people who can hire others to do such murderous tasks?"

"None, strangely enough given the circumstances," John admitted. "However, I think it would be the best—"

"And who are you to be giving orders?"

"I am trying to cooperate as ordered."

"Well, I'm willing to listen to sensible suggestions." Felix spoke thickly.

"We certainly can't find the culprits by sitting around and drinking."

Felix took a lurching step forward. "Watch your tongue, slave, or I'll give you a thrashing you won't soon forget!"

Slave! The insult was a spark to the anger that permeated John's being like oil in a lamp wick. A raven's wing of darkness beat across his eyes and a roaring akin to breaking waves filled his ears.

Felix seemed unaware of his companion's anger. "You dare to insult one of the emperor's body-guard?" he went on. "You. A slave! And a eunuch at that!"

John's fists clenched. The muscles in his arms tightened.

With an effort he stopped himself from lashing out.

A terrible heat rushed up around him as he looked at the excubitor, swaying, splay legged and glassy eyed. An easy target.

John reminded himself he was not free to defend honor he did not possess. Were he to strike Felix, he would be destroyed like a defective tool.

Not that that possibility concerned him, for it would mean a merciful end to the undesired, phantom existence into which he had been cast.

But how then could he find those shadowy enemies who seemed to be menacing Senator Opimius and his daughter, Lady Anna?

"What, you're not going to fight? At least pretend to be a man." Felix took a unsteady step toward John and fell forward.

John caught him. "Come on, Felix," he said. "Perhaps we can get you into the barracks without your captain noticing."

Chapter Eleven

"Do you know, Proclus, I sometimes wish I were still Captain of the Excubitors. It's a more straight-forward job than this emperor business. I should have refused the crown, especially since the Master of Offices was eager enough to wear it."

Justin shifted uncomfortably on the marble bench in an instinctive but vain attempt to relieve the ever-present pain of his wound. He did not look at his quaestor. Instead, he stared out into the night, across the sunken garden he had insisted they visit.

"It was you for whom the crowds in the Hippodrome roared, Caesar," Proclus replied smoothly, "and the empire would have been the poorer had you not acceded to the public will."

"The empire got on perfectly adequately without me for several centuries. It will manage just as well when I'm gone. Each journey I take is more difficult.

I wonder if this will be the last time I see this place?"

"You mused about the same thing only two weeks ago, Caesar," Proclus pointed out.

They had descended several terraces in the palace grounds, down precipitous staircases and along twisting paths meandering between groves of dark cypresses.

Their winding way took them to a long colonnade whose pillars were embraced by climbing plants, leafless in this dead season. The sylvan retreat was fitted with benches and faced a marble fountain whose wind-blown jet dared sprinkle droplets on the ruler of the empire as the small procession passed by.

Justin produced a key, opened a low door in the far corner of the colonnade, and thus they had come at last to this concealed garden.

Hemmed in by the blank back of the colonnade and two tall brick retaining walls, the narrow, enclosed space held its secrets fast among the cascading vines and trailing bushes spilling down in thick profusion from plantings on the terrace towering above its fourth side. The trees faintly silhouetted on the level above them might have been floating in the starry sky.

Justin's attendants, breathing as heavily as the emperor, had lowered him to the bench and, on his curt order, departed to the other side of the colonnade door.

"This garden was Euphemia's notion," Justin said. "A private place kept only for us, away from prying eyes and ears. We often came here at night. It's a good place to talk, and sometimes even...yes...."
A reminiscent smile lightened his broad, ruddy face.

Proclus observed that the imperial living quarters offered more warmth, not to mention comfort, on this cold night and pointedly suggested that Justin might be more comfortable there rather than sitting in a cold, dark garden.

"Would I? Even the most trusted guards have ears, Proclus. Yes, on reflection, I should have allowed someone else to take the throne. My life would have been simpler."

"The Master of Offices was incompetent. As for your other rival, Amantius...he was a villain, to say the least. A treacherous eunuch. Would you have allowed him to place his own man on the throne?"

"There are those who think I am more treacherous still," Justin replied. "My nephew, to name but one. He believes I condemned Amantius for no other reason than to serve my own ambition. Naturally, he fears I intend to employ the same strategy with him, which is to say executing him for the murder of Hypatius. My own nephew, a man I have educated and nurtured and made my heir, believes this vile lie! How do I know, you wonder? Let's just say that, like my guards, the walls of the Hormisdas have ears. Perhaps, after all, I am not a foolish old man to wish to speak to you privately here."

His voice was so low that Proclus could barely make out his words over the sound of water reverberating around the rectangular space. At the base of the waterfall tumbling from the terrace above an alabaster Diana stood poised on a marble outcrop in the middle of a pool whose edges were lost in thick undergrowth.

The moon had risen. As his eyes grew accustomed to its stark, blue light, Proclus could see other alabaster forms, a deer, a goat, a boar, half concealed amid rampant bushes. The pale animals looked alive and made him uneasy, although less so than when he looked up at the rectangle of sky. Then he felt as if he was standing at the bottom of a freshly dug grave.

"Your humors are troubling you this evening, Caesar, and naturally your nephew's illness worries you, as it does everyone," he offered. "All these ridiculous plots people gossip about are no more real than that hare by your foot."

Justin let out a wheezing cough. The long walk down to the garden had taxed his strength. "I have placed my trust in you, Proclus. I want to make certain you know exactly what is going on so you can take appropriate measures should anything happen to me."

"Happen? What do you mean?"

"If I knew what might happen, I could prevent it," Justin snapped back. "When the streets are on fire who can predict where the wind will carry sparks? You must be prepared for all eventualities."

"The City Prefect is bringing the troublemakers firmly under control, exactly as you ordered," Proclus assured him.

"Is he? How can a man who dabbles in magick and potions be trusted?"

"I thought you placed great faith in that pain-killing concoction he brings you?"

"To relieve this agony, Proclus, I would deal with Satan. I am not saying that the Gourd does not serve me, but that he is most unreliable. He has strange notions. The other day he told me he knows a man who has unlocked the secret of flight. The Gourd was very excited. He envisions his men soaring above the city, spying out malefactors, swooping down upon them. How can you trust a man with such delusions?"

"Nevertheless, he is making the streets safer, by all accounts."

"Would this be for my benefit, or to further his own ambitions?"

"You think that he has designs on the throne, Caesar?"

"He has accumulated quite a large force to keep order in the city," Justin pointed out, "and whereas my excubitors may be better trained and armed, their numbers are far fewer."

Proclus hastily assured him of the Prefect's loyalty.

"Justinian trusts him even less than I do," Justin replied. "He claims that is why he initiated his investigation into Hypatius' death. On the contrary, I believe it was launched because he's afraid I've ordered the Gourd to produce evidence implicating him."

"You would never do such a thing." Proclus sounded shocked.

"Of course not! However, Justinian has a certain someone whispering poisonous thoughts in his ear all hours of the day and night, doesn't he?"

From the darkness came the faint mournful call of some nocturnal bird Proclus did not recognize. The quaestor had never taken an interest in the outdoors. To him, night meant neatly scrivened sheets of laws softly glowing in lamplight, and perhaps a splash of wine at the end of his labors.

"Surely Justinian is as interested in finding out the truth about Hypatius' death as you are," he finally ventured.

Justin laughed. "How do you suppose a slave and an excubitor are going to solve such a mystery? Justinian is simply giving a less than subtle warning, telling me he is aware of my supposed conspiracy against him. As if the emperor needs to conspire to remain in power! All I need to do that is order an execution and it is done. That, of course, is what my nephew fears."

He sighed. "Doubtless, the slave is also there to keep an eye on the Gourd, just as Felix has been instructed, except of course the one reports to me and the other to Justinian. Why do you imagine the Gourd's so angry about those two? Frankly, it makes me suspect he's up to something he doesn't want me to know about. And naturally Felix is also keeping watch on Justinian's slave for me. Oh, my nephew and I have had a long conversation about all this, dancing about the subject without ever once coming right out and saying what we meant. It's all very tiresome, Proclus. All of us at court have to deceive endlessly in order to keep each other honest."

His companion's brow wrinkled as he considered the matter. "A pair of informers, known to be such not only to each other but also to the person both are supposed to be informing on....that would appear to create an impasse. If they do manage to find out who murdered Hypatius, so much the better. A most intelligent strategy, Caesar. My compliments." He bowed.

"You don't need to flatter me, Proclus," Justin replied, sounding pleased. "Now tell me this. How do you know I didn't order you to accompany me to this secluded place so you could be strangled?"

"Caesar?" The garden, frosted by moonlight and populated by indistinctly seen creatures lurking in thick vegetation, suddenly appeared sinister and unwelcoming.

"Don't tell me you harbor no ambitions! Yet as I said, I do trust you, and so I will tell you a secret. Ah, you look distressed. It isn't healthy to know an emperor's secrets, is it? Nevertheless, be warned, I have no intention of replacing Justinian with another heir. He is my blood kin, my sister's son, and I promised her when I adopted him that I would raise him up to succeed me. He is like the son Euphemia and I could not have."

Proclus murmured a few words of sympathy.

"Besides which, it's the actress who's the cause of most of the trouble between Justinian and me." Justin sighed. "She's the one who keeps urging him to take action. Why the haste? My nephew's only just in his forties. A young man compared to me. He has plenty of time left to rule. First, though, he must realize that he has to dispose of that vile woman. It might be that this rift between us will help him see his folly, along with the inevitable cooling off of passion. Or so Euphemia has advised me." The emperor moved stiffly on the bench, again shifting his weight, but not the pain from his leg.

Proclus briefly wondered how successful Justin would be in having Justinian removed from the succession in the absence of an excellent pretext, given his nephew's popularity. He didn't voice those thoughts, however. "I assure you I have no designs on the throne, Caesar," he repeated, still expecting to hear stealthy movement behind him at any instant.

"You don't want to be emperor, believe me. I was ambitious and what has it come to? As a young man I left Dardania with two companions. We had nothing but the clothes on our backs and a crust or two of bread for provisions. You know the saying that something that happened long ago might have occurred only yesterday? Well, our journey might have begun just this morning. I'm not old and sick, really, merely tired and footsore from a long day's walk."

Justin closed his eyes, the better to view his memories. "I recall crossing a stone bridge as we left," he said. "The stream was low. Then a little way past the bridge there was the small cemetery where all our kinfolk are buried. Yes, we left both the living and the dead behind to come to Constantinople, seeking a better life."

Proclus listened intently as the ailing man described his long-ago odyssey.

"The three of us walked that dusty, rutted road," Justin recalled. "Sometimes we sang, sometimes we marched along in silence. At night we slept wherever we could find shelter. And we kept walking for many days. I wasn't expecting a great future. The thought of rising to be Captain of Excubitors never crossed my mind, and as for one day ruling the empire, well.... No, all we looked forward to each dawn was the end of the day when we could rest and eat whatever we had managed to find. I achieved more than any man could hope to accomplish, yet what does any of it matter now? It's all behind me."

"I pray that is not so, Caesar."

Justin opened his eyes, but turned his head to look toward the far corner of the garden rather than at Proclus. "It is all as nothing. I might have dreamt being emperor. Memories have no more substance than dreams, and in the end all our lives will become only memories. I've led men into battle, seen kings kneel before me. I've raised great churches to the glory of the Lord, heard the accolades of thousands in the Hippodrome. Yet if I had only an hour of my life to live again, it would be the first time I shared the bed of the girl I married. So much for all our ambitions, my loyal quaestor."

Proclus said nothing.

Justin leaned forward and peered attentively into the shadows clustered around the cascade of trailing vines at the far end of the garden. "Ah, Euphemia, my dear, there you are. I have been waiting for you. Leave us alone for a while now, Proclus."

Proclus followed the emperor's gaze. Back there, partially obscured by a black filigree of tree limbs, something pale caught the moonlight. It was nothing more than an unhealthy mist rising, he thought uneasily. Yet the shape was vaguely that of a woman. A statue, then. One he had not noticed before. He bowed and backed away from Justin's presence.

Proclus did not stop until he was a few paces from the guards who waited just outside the door to the concealed garden. He did not want to risk overhearing the emperor's conversation.

Chaper Twelve

Sitting in Lady Anna's study the next morning, John could still feel Felix's weight. It was as if the excubitor were perched on his shoulders like a demon which had arrived during a nightmare and refused to depart with the morning light.

"You look pained, John. Is my work so poor?" Lady Anna's unpainted lips were set in a line of concern.

"It's well done, Lady Anna." John set aside the copying exercise he had been correcting and managed a smile. Anna's answering smile blossomed.

Anna might not have been considered a beauty by court standards. There was nothing striking about her features and she did not use cosmetics to paint herself a new face. John, however, found her intelligence attractive. It was a pity that her intelligence did not extend to an understanding of more worldly concerns, or, more precisely, other peoples' concerns involving herself.

John made an effort to banish the excubitor's phantom weight. His memories of dark streets and recent events, so inappropriate here, drew back a step.

In this room, painted roses bloomed on walls and climbed over arbors formed by arched niches holding the scrolls and codices Anna collected as other women might hoard jewelry.

"Am I progressing well with this strange language?" Anna sounded anxious.

John smiled again. "In a few more months you will be speaking Persian like a native." His expression clouded for a heartbeat and then cleared again. Not quickly enough to escape the notice of his aristocratic pupil.

"You hate the Persians." It was a statement rather than a question.

"Many hate them. With good reason."

"Why then did you learn their language?"

"Of necessity."

Lady Anna picked a scroll from the neat pile on her writing desk. "I've been trying to translate this romantic tale, John. It is really quite beautiful. The man has not seen the woman since childhood. One day her litter goes past and the wind disturbs its curtain. When he sees her, he is so overcome that he faints and falls off his horse!"

"Unfortunately, the Persians who formed my opinions weren't prone to swooning in their saddles."

"But aren't they just like us? Most of us aren't violent, grasping after power and wealth. Should Persians judge all Romans by the actions of a ruthless man such as the Gourd?"

"If they are prudent, they will." John broke off, appalled not only at his own words but the tone. "I am sorry, Lady Anna. I spoke out of turn."

"But in this perhaps you can learn from me? You are not a man filled with hatred, like so many at the palace. Why do you then hate the Persians so?"

"With respect, slaves should not burden others with their pasts."

Anna toyed with her still furled scroll. She tapped it against her lips, then stared out over it at John. "I could order you to tell me...."

"Lady Anna...."

"I would not do that. The positions we occupy in society are not of our choosing, but our loyalties certainly are." Anna laid her scroll back on the pile. "When I'm somewhat more fluent and have accomplished my translation I shall show it to you. The story concerns love between a man and the wife of his brother. A most improper love, yet I can understand it."

"I shall report your continued progress to your father," John said, changing the subject.

Anna sighed. "Yes, I'm sure father will be pleased by my achievements. I wonder why so many don't realize there are greater enemies closer to home than at the border?"

Hardly a surprising comment, John thought, given the recent attempt on her father's life. Seizing his opportunity, he asked her hesitantly if she had any thoughts on who might wish to harm the senator.

"When men become powerful, they have as many enemies as a ship has barnacles," Anna replied. "Then, too often, men have long memories. They nurse grudges for years until their chance for revenge arrives. Or they have one too many burdens to carry, or some other reason, trifling perhaps in itself, but one that causes them to finally strike."

She paused. "Isn't it said that the best revenge is one that has been contemplated for some time?"

"Certainly many hold it to be so. But as to that, although many thought very highly of Hypatius surely he too had enemies?"

Lady Anna shook her head. "You would have to ask those who knew him best, I suppose." She paused. From further back in the house came the sound of a loud argument. The shrill voices of two women could be heard; they obscenely taunted each other, apparently having fallen out over a man whom one claimed was her lover, a claim hotly disputed with lascivious details by the other.

Anna looked neither shocked nor surprised. "Those two are always fighting. I shall have to quench this outburst before father returns. He doesn't need strife breaking out in his kitchen as well as on the doorstep. If I have to warn them again they will have to go. This seems to be a good time to end my lessons for today, John, so I will say goodbye for now."

John remained in Anna's study and finished correcting her work before going into the corridor. He did not care to witness women's squabbles nor to extend his increasingly uncomfortable visit, so rather then passing through the kitchen to the servants' entrance, he decided he could be forgiven for leaving by the front door for once. Especially if nobody saw him.

Just as he crossed the atrium, however, voices and the stamping of feet at the entrance announced the arrival of Senator Opimius and a companion.

"Ah, John, are you leaving?" the senator said. "Remain for now, please. I want to speak to you about my daughter's progress." Turning to his companion he added, "This is the man I mentioned to you, Aurelius, the one I borrowed from the palace to tutor Anna."

"And what are you teaching her, John?" The visitor arched an imperious eyebrow. His features had the look of the classical busts Justinian had imported and placed all around the Hormisdas Palace, although a tactful sculptor would certainly have chiseled away the nascent, middle-aged jowls. He could be nothing but a senator. A sharp contrast to Opimius, who resembled an assistant to the overseer of an obscure administrative department.

"I am helping her to learn Persian, sir."

Aurelius ran his hand through black curls. Once, they might have been unruly, but they were now thinning and beginning to silver. "An interesting choice of languages. I suppose it's prudent to know your enemies."

"What is more important," put in Opimius, "is knowing which of our acquaintances are also enemies. Anna chose the subject of her lessons herself. She wanted to try to learn something challenging, she said."

"And what will she decide to study next? If I were you, I would be happier if the next subject she takes an interest in is one of Justin's subjects. An unmarried one."

"A thought that has crossed my mind more than once, Aurelius. But then you are a father yourself."

"Yes, it won't be long before Penelope and I will have to start considering matrimonial alliances for Anatolius. Not to mention placing him in a good post at court. Now, if only your Anna were younger or my son was older."

The conversation was interrupted by two laborers in dirt encrusted breeches. The men strolled across

the atrium, paused to give Opimius vague, defer-
ential bows and continued on their way.

Aurelius raised his eyebrow again.

"The bath house hypocaust is not working,"
Opimius explained. "Of all times to fail. Naturally
just when I'd prefer not to be obliged to venture
out to the public baths."

"A problem with the flues perhaps?"

"Possibly. Fate can be unkind even to senators,"
Opimius replied, going on to suggest they repair
to his office. One glance was all John needed to
know that his attendance was required there also.
He could not help thinking that if Opimius' greatest worry was a malfunctioning hypocaust, then
perhaps Fate treated senators very lightly indeed.

As soon as the men were settled John poured
them wine from the glass flask on Opimius' desk.

"Opimius, if you will forgive me for saying so,
with the state the city's currently in, it is not a
wise idea to allow unknown workmen to wander
through your house. I've mentioned this before and
I wish you'd heed my warnings."

"Of course, you are right," Opimius muttered
absently. "You know, Aurelius, the view from this
office is much more pleasant when the garden is
in full bloom." He scowled at the closed panels.
"Anna has been talking about new plantings a lot
lately although spring still seems very far away."

Aurelius sipped his wine. "Yes, she loves her gar-
dening, does Anna. At times I wish I had only a
daughter to look after. Anatolius is a difficult boy,
I fear. Headstrong and yet given to scribbling poetry.
Oh, you can laugh, but believe it or not the other
night he shaved the front of his head and ran off
to play with a bunch of Blues. This was the same

night the Gourd put on his little exhibition. The boy nearly got himself killed."

"Just as well Justin didn't hear about him being involved in that escapade."

Aurelius waved his hand. "Oh, Justin no doubt knows all about it. It would have reached his ears before dawn that the son of one of his senators was involved in that frightful business. He'd realize the boy's too young to have meant any harm. I'm more worried about the Gourd taking it on himself to investigate. You can't tell what the man is liable to do." He held out his wine cup for John to refill.

John did so, maintaining a carefully neutral expression. Even after some years laboring at the palace, he still found it strange that men would blithely speak of the most secret matters in front of their servants, or anyone else's servants for that matter. It was obvious they considered them no more than furniture, and furniture could not hear. Even so, judging from Aurelius' slighting remarks about the Gourd, it was evident that John's new assignment had not yet become common knowledge. No doubt it would be soon enough.

"But what really angered me," Aurelius was saying, "was that when he arrived back home in the middle of the night, the boy had the temerity to tell me some ridiculous tale about hiding in a huge pig and being rescued by an excubitor and a tall fellow with a strange look in his eyes."

Opimius smiled. "Sounds like a budding Homer to me."

"I see you are as amused as I was! Or as amused as I was after I punished him. It's one thing to go out and risk life and limb. We all did that when we were young. Nonetheless, I will not have him lying to me. I sent him off to stay with his uncle Zeno for a while. Away from the city. That'll keep him out of mischief!"

"Zeno? Is that wise? Isn't he the fellow who aspires to launch himself from a tower and fly across the Golden Horn?"

"You're thinking of the man who calls himself Avis. Zeno has some eccentric interests, but he's harmless. The gods forbid that Anatolius should ever make the acquaintance of Avis."

"I wish they hadn't seen fit to allow Anna to meet Avis." Opimius sounded rueful. "Luckily she has sense enough not to try out these wings he's said to be working on. Or at least I hope not. Unfortunately she insists on contributing to his expenses on a regular basis. I fear her fancies sometimes run away with her reason. Penelope must have been frantic over your son's adventure."

"Indeed she was. She's already upset about our impending move. She doesn't want to live closer to the palace, and I don't blame her. I think she'll grow fond of the new house in due course, especially since she has a free hand with its decoration."

"When are you moving?"

"Next month. By the time Anatolius returns from his little holiday at the seaside, we'll be settled in."

"He does know you're moving to a new house?" Opimius asked with a twinkle in his eye. "I mean, he won't get back and find the old one shuttered and deserted?"

"What? Oh, yes, I see. Very good jest, Opimius!" Aurelius laughed.

John came to a sudden decision. "If I may speak, Senator Opimius?"

He had spoken quietly, but Opimius' expression could not have been more startled if his desk had begun to recite Ovid. The tone in which he granted permission clearly indicated there would be a price to be paid later for the impudence. John forged ahead anyway.

"Senator Aurelius, your son told you nothing but the truth concerning his odyssey the other night."

Aurelius' classical features twisted into a most unclassical scowl. He looked John up and down. "And how would you know?" he barked. "You're obviously not a Blue and they were the only ones there at the time, apart from the Gourd's men."

"My apologies, senator, but I was there also." John rapidly described what had transpired after he and Felix had discovered the boy in the butcher's shop. He was careful to say nothing of the nature of his assignment beyond a brief mention that it had placed Felix and himself into temporary service with the Gourd.

Aurelius' expression softened as the details John gave proved the truth of his claim. "So, you are working for the Prefect, whom I have just jestingly been referring to by his nickname...and you are the tall man my son spoke about? I hear that your cloak was torn to shreds?"

"It was ruined by pig's blood, senator."

"Certainly. I was just testing the veracity of your statements," Aurelius admitted. "If Senator Opimius will permit you to come to my house later today, I will be happy to reward you for your swift action. I'll also reimburse you for your cloak. And the excubitor's name?"

"It was the German, Felix. He is one of Justin's bodyguards. But if I may...." John paused and then, taking heart from the fact that given his task he was surely under Justinian's protection, plunged on, ignoring the darkening expression on Opimius' face. "I would wish to ask for something different as a reward."

Aurelius waved his hand airily once more. It had the studied look of a much-practiced gesture. "And this would be?"

"I wish to ask you a couple of questions."

"I see! This is a shrewd fellow indeed, Opimius. He values a senator's knowledge more highly than gold. Proceed! I am not promising I will answer, mark you."

"Senator, you know most of the court and many landowners and wealthy citizens. Are you aware of any who harbor ill will toward the emperor's nephew, Justinian?"

The two senators looked alike in their surprise.

"Not only a shrewd fellow, but courageous as well, to ask such a question," Aurelius remarked. "This man is on the path to great things."

"Unfortunately," observed Opimius, "that particular path passes by more than one early grave."

"This is entirely irregular," Aurelius said after a gulp of wine. "But then, since you are out and about with one of Justin's bodyguards, I must assume that perhaps you seek this information for another." He stopped speaking and looked expectant, but John did not take the opportunity to respond.

"I have as much as admitted my son owes his life to you and Felix, so I can hardly refuse," Aurelius finally said. "I trust I do not need to remind you that I speak in confidence or that a slave's word against a senator's isn't worth a half-nummus. I note you have not revealed the details surrounding this assignment of yours so you are obviously a man of discretion."

John nodded silently.

Opimius set his cup down on his desk. "This is quite absurd, Aurelius. I must apologize."

Aurelius shook his head. "No, I find it rather interesting. I would not be surprised if John here plans to pose equally impertinent questions to whomever I name. Besides, we should all welcome any opportunity to assist our next emperor, no matter the odd guise in which it may present itself. So I believe I can suggest a couple of appropriate avenues of inquiry."

"It's all Anna's doing," Opimius replied. "She's never stern enough with the servants. She gets too fond of them, you see. I'll send him off immediately."

"That would be an error, I think. After all, he and I seem to be working to the same end. John, I will give you two names, and no more than that. However, I would not be accused of saying anything slanderous nor do I care to be asked how I know this or that. Let's say I am basing what I tell you on nothing more than a feeling that I have. Or to put it another way I am playing at being the oracle. And my pronouncement, based on the direction of the wind, is that you should seek out Tryphon, whose mansion overlooks the Golden Horn. The other person is someone you may have seen here on occasion. Trenico."

"Trenico? One of two upon whom you'd cast suspicion?" Opimius' face reddened. "Aurelius, I hope you're not implying that I...."

"I'm implying nothing, Opimius. Your friends are all well aware of Trenico's interest in your daughter. But people who are not familiar with your domestic situation, well, they may draw entirely the wrong conclusions."

"But Trenico is a confidante of Theodora's!"

"So he says. Heed the oracle, my friend." Aurelius smiled, but there was a chill in his eyes. "Now, we should get on with our business and John here can proceed with his." He pursed his lips and stared at John. "Yes, my son is more perceptive than I at times. There is definitely something strange in those eyes. As for getting any information out of the two men I've named, I wish you luck."

Chapter Thirteen

Trenico's eyelids narrowed when he read the introductory letter he had accepted from Felix. Then he stuck out his prominent chin and did his best to look down on John and Felix, both of whom towered over him.

"Since the City Prefect requests it, I suppose I have no choice but to speak to you. We must all assist him in his efforts to make our streets safe. Even when it involves inviting slaves into our homes."

He dismissed the servant who had admitted them and led his unwelcome visitors across the atrium and along a short hallway to an office whose lone window was shuttered.

Felix proceeded with his inquiries.

The excubitor had recovered from his drinking bout and possibly, John thought, had had time to reflect for he seemed to be making some effort to conceal his distaste for the companion with whom he had been temporarily yoked. Perhaps he was also embarrassed by recollections of his behavior.

John glanced around Trenico's office. Its painted walls displayed a fantastical cityscape of impossible spires and domed towers. Lamps sat in niches cleverly aligned with the painted architecture so as to form an impression of illuminated windows. It was easy to imagine he was standing in the street at the evening hour when shadowless twilight flattens reality. He could not help thinking, ruefully, that Lady Anna would be enchanted by the artful effect.

"I have no disagreements with the emperor's nephew, any more than I do with the emperor. Even if I did, why would I admit it to you?" Trenico sniffed and folded brawny arms across his chest, displaying sculpted muscles.

"Senator Aurelius harbors bitter feelings concerning certain business dealings we had," he went on. "The fact of it is that although a man may be born to wealth and privilege it does not make him a good businessman. Perhaps he should employ better advisors."

He stepped toward the window. "We need fresh air in here," he continued, yanking open the shutter. Thin sunlight spilled into the room, reducing the twilight city to mere pigments.

"A year ago," Trenico continued, "Aurelius renovated one of his country estates. I introduced him to an acquaintance, who knew an importer able to secure the senator an excellent price on a shipment of marble. I received a small remuneration from the importer. A mere courtesy on his part. Aurelius, however, did not appreciate either the quality of the goods or the price he was charged for them."

"So that would account for his animosity toward you? He thinks your introduction indirectly led him to pay too much for inferior material?" Felix asked.

Trenico stared into his withered garden, where a single crow perched atop an eroded obelisk. "Yes, I do. Men hold the biggest grudges for the smallest of reasons. As to those who may oppose Justinian, many disapprove not of Justinian personally but of his intended marriage to Theodora."

"A view which you hold yourself?" Felix inquired.

"Not at all. While it is not a common conviction, I believe one should marry for love and nothing else." Trenico clapped his hands together, startling the crow into flight. "Nasty creatures, those birds. I'm proud to say that I'm a confidante of Theodora's. She's called upon me for advice on more than one occasion. So if you must be putting your noses where they don't belong, start looking in the right places. Question those who oppose our future empress."

"And they would be?"

"You might try interviewing Archdeacon Palamos. He has been particularly outspoken, as anyone who moves in palace circles knows. Perhaps he'll also take your interest as a warning. Now, I have nothing more to say so you can leave or I will have you ejected."

As John turned to go, he noticed that twined around the columns framing the office door was a freshly painted, luxuriant bush of roses, so perfect in their beauty that he could almost smell their sweet perfume.

❊ ❊ ❊

"A surly fellow, that Trenico," Felix remarked as he and John traversed the slush-covered Augustaion.

"Did you notice his arms? Impressive at first glance, I admit, but they're the sort of showy muscles gained from the exercise ball, not from using a plow or a pickax, let alone a sword. He'd probably be completely useless in a fight."

They were now approaching a confusion of buildings. The Great Church and the Church of Eirene, Samsun's Hospice, a small monastery and the patriarch's palace clustered together like holy conspirators.

"The palace gossips have it that Emperor Justin also heartily disapproves of his nephew's plans to marry Theodora," John observed. He had no particular desire to pursue a conversation with the excubitor, but realized they could achieve nothing without some degree of cooperation.

"Euphemia was bitterly opposed to it," Felix replied, "and the emperor still talks of her as if she were alive. Sometimes her shade seems to wield more power over her husband than the living woman did. There have been times when I'm on duty when I could practically feel her breath on the back of my neck."

"What about this Archdeacon Palamos? Do you think he is one who is against the marriage, or did he just run afoul of Trenico at some point?"

Felix kicked at the cold slurry underfoot. "The possibility has occurred to me. Aurelius points to Trenico and Trenico points to this Palamos. They're trying more to use us than to reveal anything useful. The bigger question is how are the emperor and his nephew using us?"

They were approaching the Great Church. Piles of dirty snow at the foot of the stairs leading to its portico suggested heavenly clouds tainted by contact with the secular world.

Before John could reply a white blur smacked Felix on the chest. The excubitor staggered slightly in surprise.

A second snowball exploded near John's feet. Looking up at the portico he glimpsed a couple of street urchins peering from behind its columns.

"We've been ambushed," roared Felix. He grinned as he scooped a fistful of dirty snow and sent his icy missile flying upward.

Excited shrieks greeted his counterattack, followed by a flurry of snowballs.

"Reminds me of when I was a boy. In Germania we had real snowfalls." Felix charged forward. For his size he was surprisingly swift as he pounded up the steps.

The urchins dodged from column to column with shrill screams of delight. What could be better than to be fighting one whose helmet and cuirass identified him as a real military man?

Then, without warning, Felix was uttering a string of curses barely acceptable in a military encampment, let alone at the door of a church. His anger wasn't feigned.

When John reached him he saw that the excubitor's jaw was scarlet with blood.

"Treacherous little bastards!" Felix shouted. "They stuck a stone in that last snowball. I should've remembered that trick. We did just the same. It just shows you can't trust even children in this city."

A plump, white-robed figure emerged from the church. He was dwarfed by its bronze doors, which rose to the height of several men.

"This disturbance will cease at once," he ordered.

"And who are you?" Felix asked curtly.

"I am Archdeacon Palamos."

"Perhaps Fortuna is finally smiling on us," Felix muttered.

When introductions had been made, Palamos led his visitors into the church. The archdeacon had the soft look and extreme pallor of a monk who has not emerged from his cell for years. He was, John judged, barely middle-aged, young to hold sway over this enormous church.

"I would not normally be here," Palamos explained, "but the man in charge of the lamps is ill so I'm temporarily overseeing his duties. Half the job is keeping all the lamps filled."

They passed through the vestibule and stood at the top of the nave. The lamps Palamos referred to were everywhere, hanging from golden chains, sitting in wall niches or on stands or tripods. Lamps of all sizes and shapes, some made of gold, others formed of glass, a few of silver. Every corner that the suffused light pouring in from high-set windows failed to reach was thus illuminated, twinkling with points of orange flame that resembled swarms of fireflies.

Palamos beckoned to a boy waiting nearby. "One of the lamps in the dome has blown out, Arion." He grasped the boy's arm lightly, turned him around and directed his attention upward. "On the ledge under John the Baptist, you see? Would you attend to that one next?"

The boy nodded solemnly.

"That's a good boy," Palamos smiled. "We don't want to leave John in the dark, do we? Especially when he's standing out there in the river." He gave the child a quick pat on the rump as the boy departed to carry out his task.

"I used to scramble up there myself to do the same job when I was younger. Hard to believe, isn't it?" Palamos tapped his large belly. "Too much study."

"Theology can be as treacherous as a narrow ledge," John remarked.

Felix glanced back at the controversial sculpture, looming in the vestibule and just visible from where they stood. "His was a very pretty death, despite it being brought about by the betrayal of a man he thought his follower," he mused.

Palamos asked him what he meant.

"Where's the blood? Where's the pain? If you or I were being crucified we wouldn't have the strength to lift our chins off our chests, let alone look up and, well, almost smile."

"There are those who call the sculpture blasphemous," the archdeacon observed.

Felix looked at him questioningly.

"The gossips have it that the sculptor is an ardent, albeit secret, monophysite. Thus, he chiseled a Christ who is wholly divine and would not know pain."

Palamos placed his fingertips together almost as if he were about to pray. "It is even rumored, although it is ridiculous in my opinion, that this sculptor was personally recommended to Hypatius by Theodora, whose deviation from orthodoxy is only too well known."

Felix shook his head. It amazed him that people could become inflamed over such subtle theological concepts. "Yet Justinian still wishes to marry her."

"True enough. I find myself worrying that when Justinian rules he will be far less tolerant of those holding unorthodox religious views than his uncle has been. It's been said the only heretic Justinian will tolerate is the one in his bed." A smile quirked

Palamos' lips. "What most of my flock seem to object to is Theodora's lurid past."

John broke in. "And what is your opinion of this proposed marriage?"

Palamos pushed his fingertips more tightly together. "Legally speaking, a man in Justinian's position cannot marry an actress. Not even a former actress. It has been proposed that Justin change that law. But why should law be bent to the will of a single person? And in the service of nothing more than carnal appetites."

"It appears Theodora is as widely disliked as Justinian is liked," John noted.

"It's her influence on him that's feared. And rightly so. Women often turn good men into beasts."

Felix changed the subject. "Did you know Hypatius well, archdeacon?"

"Yes, indeed. He was a very pious man and extremely generous to the church. That remarkable sculpture is only one example of his philanthropy. There are other sculptures and mosaics he donated all over the city. He spent half his time attending dedications of buildings he'd helped finance. A new wing to a monastery here, a chapel there."

"He seems to have been famous for public good works."

"He was not one to hide his light under a basket, unlike the sculpture's other sponsors. To be fair, he also spent many hours helping at Samsun's Hospice."

"So he was willing to give of his time?"

"Yes, and indeed I observed him there myself now and then. He'd always make the same jest to patients. 'Now you can tell your friends you've been attended by a man who owns horses worth more than your entire family,' he'd say. On the other hand, he did have a reputation as a ruthless businessman. Furthermore, if you ask me, he was far too fond of women for a man of his age."

Movement drew John's attention away from the conversation.

On the narrow ledge running around the base of the dome overhead, Arion ignited the lamp and shadows dissipated, revealing the bearded, emaciated portrait of a sheepskin-clad John the Baptist.

"Good boy!" Palamos shouted, clasping his pudgy hands together. "They are so helpful at that age, you know. Alas, when they get older they tend to fall prey to the baser urges. Not a few of them are even attracted to pagan practices, especially those connected with the flesh."

"Pagans in Constantinople?" John was sure Felix was concealing a smile.

"Alas, yes. There is no doubt there are respectable aristocrats who worship in this very church and then go straight home and disembowel a chicken in front of some obscene ivory goddess of fertility."

To this remark Felix made no reply, but when he and John again stood outside in the suddenly dazzling sunlight he grinned widely. "Well, it seems that many in this city have a dual nature, not just the Christian's god."

"At least Palamos hasn't set us barking on the trail of some enemy of his. Now presumably we will visit this other man Aurelius mentioned? Tryphon?"

"First I think it's time we looked in on the deceased. He'll probably be as forthcoming as everyone else we've spoken to so far. At least he won't lie to us."

Chapter Fourteen

Hypatius' palatial residence sat at the top of a wide thoroughfare. Its neighbors were a jumble of imposing edifices that appeared to John to be nailed to the steep hillside by the crosses protruding from their roofs. Perhaps, however, that was merely a fancy brought on by the long climb up a seemingly perpendicular street.

"He may have been a great philanthropist, but he certainly never took a vow of poverty." Felix was breathing hard. As they drew nearer they saw that the row of shops the mansion appeared to sit behind were in fact part of the building itself. "I call that good strategy. Hypatius didn't have to send his servants very far to buy more glassware or a new lamp. On top of such a wonderful convenience, think of the income from the sort of rents he must have charged."

Despite the crisp air, several second-floor windows stood open. Joyful singing floated down into the street.

"A strange sound to be coming from a house of bereavement," John remarked as he applied the brass door knocker.

A servant with a face the color of a walnut cracked the door open and peered out suspiciously. The cloying scent of heavily perfumed air swept out over them.

"Your business, good sirs?"

"We are here on orders of the City Prefect."

The man ushered them from the entrance hall into an atrium whose watery light was augmented by a number of blazing torches set in brackets garlanded with ivy. Between these and the perfumed air, the house had the aura of being about to host a celebration rather than being in mourning for a recently deceased master.

The servant led them up a stairway, at the top of which a mosaic cross was set in the wall. Smaller examples decorated the tiles of the second floor corridor.

"There is much excitement today, sirs, as you hear. The master's will is to be read this afternoon." A wide smile revealed the servant's fiery red gums and scanty teeth. Now John understood the reason for the joyful singing. The man's anticipation of manumission was obvious.

The decorative crosses ended at the plain whitewashed room at the end of the corridor. It was as if Hypatius had not wished to be distracted by religion while engaged in business affairs.

A man with close-cropped hair stood at a cluttered desk, directing several servants who were crating furniture as he sorted business papers. There were deep creases in his forehead and at the corners of his eyes. He looked troubled in contrast to the servants around him.

"I am Konstantinos, estate manager for Hypatius. If I may assist...?" His gaze darted nervously back and forth between Felix and John.

The men packing vases and plates into straw-lined crates set under the open window stole curious sidelong looks at the two strangers.

"Perhaps we should step into the corridor?" Konstantinos suggested.

As soon as they had done so, the estate manager scanned their introductory letter from the City Prefect, whose lead seal hung from it by a thin cord.

"I see that this instructs all who see it to give every cooperation to the bearers. You're not from the quaestor's office, are you? Is there a problem with the will? It was properly drawn up by a man of law and appropriately witnessed."

"I'm certain that it was. We have no interest in wills," Felix reassured him.

"I see." The man's relief was so obvious that John found himself wondering why.

Laughter sounded in the room they had just left. "Please forgive the impropriety," Konstantinos said quickly. "They anticipate their freedom. Unfortunately, by sunset they will be shedding tears. I've only just learned that they're not to be manumitted. They've all been left to one of the master's business associates."

Felix said he was surprised to hear it.

"The master did not succeed in business by being too kind hearted. For my part, I believe my years of service will ensure I will be allowed to keep my post. Or so I hope. I am of course a free man."

"Given how much we've heard about the good works and charitable character of your late master...."

"He certainly deserves praise on both counts! But if he wasn't a shrewd business man first there would have been no money for the good works he did. You don't give away assets, and that includes slaves, unless for a good price or to settle a debt."

Felix grunted noncommittally.

"Yes, the master was indeed a shrewd man," Konstantinos repeated. "Most of his wealth was in land holdings, which rarely fail to appreciate in value."

"Had Hypatius acquired much land recently?" John put in.

"Yes. I suppose there's no harm in telling you since it's fairly common knowledge. Of late there have been many cases of land owners who were very careless in making arrangements for the disposition of their estates. Thus there were bargains to be had. My master took advantage of a number of them and reaped the benefits. All perfectly legal."

"It's often to the advantage of people other than the heir if such mistakes are found," John noted, ignoring Felix's frown. "Sometimes those with an interest don't have to look far to find the sort of mistakes that invalidate wills. Not enough witnesses, improperly notarized, that sort of thing."

"Exactly so, and it makes one worry about such mistakes, sir. Hence my initial apprehension when you arrived. The fact is that invalid wills generally allow land to revert to the empire. And to be honest, I am somewhat worried...well...."

"You don't have to fear saying it," John assured him. "Were it to happen to your master's estates, you are also naturally worried that they would eventually find their way into the hands of highly placed parties at court?"

"There you have it."

"And let us suppose that if someone high at court indeed gained ownership of Hypatius' estates, you are naturally worried that their managers would be immediately replaced."

The furrows in Konstantinos' forehead deepened even further. "They are always the first to go. Beyond that, many are anxious about how much worse the situation could be once Justinian becomes emperor."

"Justin is not the man he was," Felix said, "but it will still be some time before Justinian rules. Justin was an excubitor, a military man. As strong as a bull in his youth. Then too sometimes old men surprise us by their tenacity in clinging to life."

"That's exactly what the master said to me only last week! He didn't seem concerned at what might happen once Justin died. Now he doesn't have to worry about it at all since he is dead while Justin is still alive."

Felix asked him if he had any notion why Hypatius had been so confident in his optimism.

"I know exactly why it was. He always confided in me more than many men of wealth and power do in their servants. He told me that he relied upon Senator Opimius."

"Relied upon him? What did he mean by that?" John asked.

Konstantinos started as if struck. He had obviously suddenly realized the implications of what he had been saying to these two strangers.

"My master did not reveal details," he began, panic welling in his eyes. "Senators have great influence. And isn't Senator Opimius a close friend of Senator Aurelius, one of Justinian's greatest champions? I have personally ushered those worthy senators together into the very office we just left. Their friendship vouches for the integrity of my master's affairs and because of that, I suppose, he felt there was no need to fear any difficulties arising."

Felix frowned. "I suppose that's true. What sort of interests did Hypatius have aside from land?"

"My work concerns only the estates."

"What about his charitable work, his donations?" asked John. "Do you know anything about this sculpture, for example?"

Konstantinos shook his head. "No. It's a great irony, isn't it? If he had not been such a pious and generous man, he wouldn't have been visiting the church to see his gift. He would still be alive today."

"And his family?" Felix asked.

"He had none. There was often talk in the kitchen of a possible marriage to this high-born lady or that, but it never came to anything."

"When possible candidates were mentioned I daresay one was Senator Opimius' daughter?" John suggested.

"Yes. How did you guess? But she would be a natural candidate because as I mentioned Senator Opimius was a friend of the master's and his daughter is unmarried."

The servant who had admitted John and Felix reappeared in the company of a wizened man whom he announced as the master's man of law.

The sight of the new arrival appeared to send Konstantinos into a new panic. "If you will excuse me, sirs," he stammered, "it is time for the reading of the will. If you have no more questions…? Very well, show these visitors out."

Hardly had the estate manager and the man of law entered Hypatius' office when the servant turned angrily toward Felix and John.

"So, my deceitful pair, you may have convinced Konstantinos but you haven't misled me!"

Felix stared at him. "And what do you mean by that?" His tone was menacing.

"You're no more from the palace than I am!" the servant jeered.

He turned to John and prodded his chest with a grubby forefinger. "You're thieves! After a death, all sorts of strangers must go in and out of a household. Why not take advantage? One of you distracts the steward while the other slips the silver under his cloak."

The servant gave an onion-scented sneer and went on. "You must think yourselves clever, with the forged letter and that military disguise. Unfortunately I knew I had seen you somewhere before. Just now I remembered where. I've escorted the master to Opimius' house. You're the eunuch that's teaching the homely daughter some foreign language or other. A miserable slave!"

"As are you!" John snapped back.

"But not for much longer! And I can assure you that tonight I shall be celebrating my new freedom in a place you'll never be. Between the legs of a whore!"

John took a quick step forward.

Felix's hand clamped painfully down on his arm. "No! We still have a job to do. Don't pay attention to his insults."

The servant opened the house door and saw them out with an ostentatious bow.

John and Felix started back down the steep street. "Thank you," John finally said. "I almost allowed my personal feelings to interfere with our investigation. That would have been unforgivable."

His gaze met Felix's. The excubitor looked away.

Chapter Fifteen

"What do you make of it, uncle?" Justinian laboriously turned his head toward Justin. Slumped in a wooden chair at Justinian's bedside, the emperor was propped up on each side by his attendants. Quaestor Proclus stood nearby.

"Make of it? I make nothing of it! It was just a dream!" The emperor spat on the floor to emphasize his opinion.

"But it was so vivid! I was walking through the city, alone and unattended, a strange thing in itself. Then I came to Constantine's column. It was as real as this very room!"

"If you were me, nephew," Justin broke in impatiently, "you could tell easily the difference between dreams and reality. When I dream I can't feel this damned gnawing agony in my leg."

"Well, this dream was so real I could actually smell the sea," Justinian pressed on.

"That was just the stink in here. You ought to order the window opened, and get rid of most of these lamps. At least have your servants trim the wicks more often so they don't smoke so much."

It was true that a marshy odor, heavy with decay, suffused the dim room. Only the merest trace of the temporarily banished Theodora's musky perfume lingered.

Justinian ignored his uncle's remark. "I could hear the sound of something dripping," he continued. "Then I noticed streams of a viscous green substance running down the column. So I turned my gaze upward and, as I said before, the statue of Constantine had vanished. Squatting there instead, gazing out over the rooftops, was a monstrous toad, oozing poison."

"If you must make such a fuss about it, what do you make of this ridiculous dream yourself? That's the important thing."

"But isn't it clear? Doesn't the City Prefect Theodotus resemble a toad?"

"No. His head looks like a gourd, just as everyone says. They also say he's about as intelligent as a gourd. I think they're wrong as far as that goes. Even so, how can a gourd possibly look like a toad?"

Throughout the exchange, the emperor's attendants remained as silent, expressionless and still as a pair of ugly caryatids. Proclus was a discreet presence behind the emperor's hunched shoulders.

Justinian coughed. A servant materialized from the shadows to wipe away sweat from his forehead and then vanished again.

"How can you not see its meaning?" Justinian said. "The Gourd is poisoning me. And why? Because he plans to set himself above the city, or in other words to declare himself emperor."

"But I am the emperor, not you!" Justin snapped. "So why isn't he poisoning me? Am I dead? Perhaps that's what I smell. I'm putrefying. Is that it, Proclus? Is your emperor dead and rotting?"

"No, Caesar," came the murmured reply.

"Proclus is the type of man you need to put your faith in, nephew. Even if I was indeed dead and rotting, my quaestor here would have me hauled around the palace until I was a mere pile of bones, if such had been my orders."

The emperor reached out and clamped a big, veined hand on Justinian's forearm. "Does that feel like the hand of a phantom? That actress of yours put this ludicrous idea into your head, didn't she? Perhaps it is the actress who is poisoning you. Have you thought of that? According to Euphemia...."

"We have already discussed Euphemia's opinions." Justinian pulled his arm away from the older man's surprisingly strong grip.

"My dear Euphemia's fond of you, Justinian. She just doesn't consider the actress a proper match."

"But what about this dream? I'm rather surprised you dismiss it so lightly, uncle. Remember thirty or so years ago when you were fighting the Isaurians and got thrown in prison by your commander—"

"Yes, John the Hunchback. I forget now what his reason was supposed to be."

"Whatever the reason, you were to be executed, but then the Hunchback dreamed three nights running of an angel that ordered your release. When he spared your life because of those dreams, did you then dismiss them as nonsense?"

"They weren't dreams, you fool! An angel appeared to the Hunchback in his sleep. Do you think angels just stroll up and knock on your door in broad daylight? How could the Gourd be poisoning you, anyway? Do you have him working in the kitchen boiling your eggs? Euphemia says—"

"Caesar," Proclus put in abruptly, "if I may offer an opinion, the Gourd has been doing a remarkable job in rectifying a situation that has gone unattended far too long. His pretense of being a magician is shrewd. Since no one can be everywhere at once, observing every street and alleyway, the next best thing is to appear to be doing just that. Now potential criminals imagine that they are being scrutinized by magickal means, so they watch themselves."

Apparently Proclus made a subtle gesture or uttered a prearranged word, for the emperor and his attendants prepared to leave. Observed from a distance, Justin might have appeared to merely stand, so unobtrusively did his assistants grasp his arms and lift him.

"I agree it is time to go, excellency. Justinian must get his rest," Proclus said tactfully before turning his attention to Justinian. "Might I suggest that this dream will not seem so portentous when your illness has run its course? No one opposes the Prefect's methods except those who would prefer to live in terror while the Blues run wild. I can assure you no man of good will has anything to fear."

❋❋❋

The emperor and his small entourage had hardly left the room before Theodora returned. "Has the old fool been slandering me again?"

"It isn't Justin who slanders you, but his dead wife. He constantly talks about her. I noticed he sometimes called her Lupicina. I really don't think he realized he had."

"I wonder if he used her slave name in private? Perhaps even in bed...."

"Ignore any mention of Euphemia, Theodora. She can't oppose you any longer now she's dead."

"To everyone but the emperor."

Justinian let his head fall back and stared into the smoky haze obscuring the gilded ceiling. "Don't be so certain that Justin believes everything he says. Assumed weakness can serve as a weapon to those who know how to wield it. On the other hand, if he's really losing his wits, his actions will become totally unpredictable. Those around him must tread all the more warily. Including us. Especially us."

A servant again drifted out of the dimness to wipe Justinian's forehead and then was gone as quickly as a dream.

Theodora leaned over Justinian. "So you suppose Justin might be exaggerating his frailty? He did come to visit you today, after all."

"Yes, and it was an unannounced visit at that. I suspect it was really to see if I'd been exaggerating my own illness."

"I know you aren't, but he would hardly take my word for it." Theodora placed her scarlet lips briefly against Justinian's forehead. "Soon you will be well, my love, and then I will take you often to that place where things are not so complicated."

Justinian smiled weakly. "If the empire was wrenched from my grasp, I would still have what I treasure most."

Theodora dropped to her knees, bringing her face level with her consort's. With her eyes blazing, her lips slightly parted, and shadows stroking the smooth concavities of her cheeks, she briefly took on the aspect of some pagan love goddess. Then her eyes narrowed and her features turned harder, almost masculine. "But we will not let anyone wrench the empire away from us, will we?"

"No, of course not! We've both worked too hard to allow that."

"This plot you fear, Justinian. Are you certain it hasn't been spawned by your fever rather than Justin? The man's a peasant. Subtle intrigue isn't his way."

Justinian let out a ragged breath. "Everyone says Justin's a peasant. Why is that, when they can see with their own eyes he's an emperor? And a ruthless one, peasant or not. Don't you recall Amantius, the chamberlain who plotted to put his own man on the throne when Anastasius died? He gave money to Justin to buy support for his candidate. Justin used it for his own ambitious ends and within two weeks of taking the throne he had had Amantius executed."

"You own many eminent peoples'... admiration," Theodora pointed out.

"Like land holdings, people do not necessarily remain owned by the same person."

"But to accuse you, emperor in all but name, of having a hand in murder! Surely that is impossible? After all, emperors may kill. They cannot commit murder."

"I am not yet emperor and my name is linked to the Blues, some of whom are accused of the murder of Hypatius. More such links will be forged soon. You'll see."

"Justin is a doddering old man. Such a plot is beyond him."

"It is not beyond Proclus. Or many others."

Theodora traced Justinian's lips with her fingertip. "What about that slave you rescued from the dungeon? Has he discovered anything useful?"

"Not yet."

Theodora gave a throaty chuckle. "Amantius. Wasn't he a eunuch like this slave of yours? Would it not be a delightful irony after Justin, having bested a eunuch for the throne, hatched a plot against you that was foiled by another of those creatures? However, you say this slave is not proving to be useful?"

"I said he has discovered nothing yet. He is intelligent and a fighter and I am certain will prove useful even if he never learns a single thing of value to us concerning the current matter. For example, already certain people realize I have my eye on them through him. In fact, I may well have other delicate missions for such a man."

Theodora smiled. "And a slave is expendable!" She brought her face closer to Justinian's. "Do you think Justin actually sees Euphemia?"

Justinian registered surprise at the question.

"Might it not be that two people become so close they cannot be parted, even by death?"

"That's something you'd have to ask a philosopher. Or perhaps the Patriarch."

Theodora stood abruptly. The movement sent her perfume swirling around Justinian. "I will not let anyone steal our empire from us! Soon you will assume your rightful place."

"But first I must recover my strength."

"Are you really so unwell, my love?" Theodora leaned across the bed and pulled one of Justinian's hands up to her breast. "Perhaps you are not quite as ill as you think?"

With the easy grace of the mime she had once been, she was suddenly straddling him. The servant who had advanced to wipe Justinian's forehead yet again could not suppress a gasp. She began to retreat.

Theodora stopped her with a glare.

"Continue to wipe his brow, and mine also, until I tell you to stop."

❋❋❋

"What's my nephew up to, that's what I want to know." Justin had returned to his private quarters and was now reclining on a stained and threadbare couch. The rest of the furnishings, their wood smooth with wear rather than polishing, Justin's own furniture obtained early in his career, matched the well-worn couch. They formed a strange contrast to the heavy purple and gold wall hangings Euphemia had commissioned.

"You have employed others to answer that, Caesar," Proclus replied. "For example, that excubitor whose services you pressed upon the City Prefect. Personally, I do not believe your nephew is even able to walk unaided at present. You may need to choose a new successor before long."

"I wager if I dropped dead right now, he'd be out of that soft bed before my bowels had let go,"

"Why do you question your own judgment of the man? You brought him to Constantinople, educated him and made him your heir, after all. It can't be because of Theodora, surely? Men must satisfy their urges according to their particular desires."

"Whores are to be used, not married. By your remarks, do I take it that you've transferred allegiance to him?"

"No, Caesar. None of us has."

"No? Do you think I don't keep track of his visitors? The list goes from Aurelius to Zeno. Justinian's shared in my wealth and used it to buy the whole Senate and half the aristocracy."

"They support Justinian because you do, Caesar."

The emperor glanced peevishly at his two attendants, now stationed beside the couch. "Look at me, being carted around like an infant. You would think my nephew would have the grace to wait until the Lord calls me instead of plotting to hasten me on my journey."

"It is the fate of all to die one day, leaving others to carry on. No one can be faulted for outliving the dead. We are all guilty of it."

"Do you think I'm angry at Justinian because he's younger than I am?"

"It's easy to arrange matters for our heirs when we're young enough that such planning is likely unnecessary. But when we grow older, when we realize our plans will eventually be carried out, often we may wish to rethink them."

"You are advising me to choose someone else as my successor, are you not, Proclus?"

"I was merely commenting in general terms, Caesar. I apologize most humbly if I offended you."

"You're sorry? I doubt it! You remind me of someone. No, something. Remember that crate-load of busts that arrived from Rome? King Theodoric's gift? All those old marble heads, with chipped noses and blind stares. Senators from the time of the Republic or bakers with money to burn, like as not.

My workmen used them to fill in the hole when they removed that broken fountain in Euphemia's garden. You remind me of those very busts. Just stone, not flesh and blood. You've turned against me too. I can see it in those polished eyes." The emperor's voice had risen to a querulous whine.

"Caesar—"

Justin winced and grabbed at his injured leg. "Where's that numbing ointment the Gourd makes for me? No. Wait, I don't want you getting it. Summon a servant."

Grimacing, Justin twisted around on the couch, to look for his attendants. His moist lower lip began to tremble.

"Wait! I see it all now. That's how it will be, isn't it? How much has he paid you? How much?" he demanded of the two men.

They looked down at the flaccid ruin of the man whom they served. Their faces registered surprise, then confusion, and then, as Justin continued to rant, panic.

"Of course it's you two. It's so clear! Who else is so close to me all the time? Always at my elbows or my back. I see it all now, from eggs to apples. Was it your plan, Proclus, or my nephew's? That one day, rather than helping hands, there'd be the blade? Guards! Guards!"

Before Proclus could respond the excubitors stationed outside the door were at the emperor's side.

"Let this serve as a lesson, my loyal quaestor." Justin turned to the excubitors. "Take these two attendants outside for a little stroll around the garden. Then execute them both."

Chapter Sixteen

A sea breeze ruffled Tryphon's white hair as he received John and Felix at the far end of his garden, set high above the mouth of the Golden Horn. He was an elegant, slim man. The white hair perfectly complimented his lean, patrician face.

Despite constant exposure to raking winds bringing the tang of salt, Tryphon's garden was almost unnaturally lush and green, the result of an artificially created abundance of water.

Here, within sight and sound of its sister sea, sweet water flowed wherever the visitor looked. A dazzling white marble fountain, appropriately topped by a statue of several Nereids riding seahorses, splashed and gurgled at the end of a wide, meticulously raked gravel walk. Narrow pools whose wind-rippled slate gray surfaces were partially clothed in the flat pads of water lilies marked the perimeter of the flowerless garden. Neatly trimmed hedges of cypress formed wind breaks around claw-footed benches or served as a dark background for statues of great men or gods of such weathered antiquity as to be nearly indistinguishable from the mossy boulders that rose from pebbled beds set around willow trees.

The Spartan design of the garden allowed no dainty blossoms that in summer would provide havens for bees. It seemed to John to be the retreat of a man not given to accumulation of the world's luxuries, despite the well appointed rooms they had glimpsed while being ushered through the villa.

The green marble shelter to which they had been led was latticed on four sides, its fifth open to the view. The only furniture was a pair of softly uphol-stered couches.

Tryphon had been reading a scroll when John and Felix arrived.

"Felicitations." He laid his scroll aside, invited them to be seated and inquired as to the reason for their visit.

Felix performed the ritual to which he and John had become accustomed, handing Tryphon their letter of introduction. The excubitor looked uncom-fortable, his heavy bulk sunk too far into the pillows.

"You're fortunate to find me here," Tryphon remarked genially after he had perused the letter. "Many of my fellow citizens have already left for their country estates. I intend to follow soon. Between Justinian's illness, the uncertainty that such illness brings, and the violence in the streets, Constantinople is not a safe place. Your master, the Prefect, is to be commended on his efforts, but these Blues are as numerous and hard to trap as rats in a granary." He returned the now crumpled and smudged letter, handling it carefully with the tips of his fingers.

"Then Fortuna smiled by bringing us here before you departed," Felix replied. "As the pagans would say," he added quickly.

"Indeed." Tryphon gave him a keen look, hooded gray eyes sharp despite the years they had witnessed.

"Speaking of country estates," Felix continued, "it is our understanding that certain landowners are beginning to express fears, in private at least, that Justinian may decide to confiscate properties under color of law. More exactly, through incorrectly executed wills."

Tryphon's heavy eyelids veiled his thoughts as he examined the black and white pebbled floor of his retreat with apparent interest before answering. "It is a bold man indeed who would express such fears in public. In private, wine loosens the tongue and leads to regrettable comments."

"Do you fear such confiscations?"

Tryphon shook his head. "No, and I have a large number of holdings and so much to lose. More perhaps than most of the tongue-waggers you mention. Though even mine pale compared to those that belonged to Hypatius. As many will tell you, he was rapidly accumulating properties at the time of his death. I imagine you already knew that?"

Felix ignored the baited question and threw out one of his own. "Are many estates changing hands of late?"

"Yes. And I anticipate that Hypatius' properties will be next. It was rather a pity, really, that he was not allowed time to enjoy them. The last three he purchased were particularly desirable. Had I heard a day or two earlier that Trenico had them on the auction block, I would have put in a bid myself. However, since Hypatius had already purchased considerable property from him, I suppose we cannot be surprised Trenico would give him the first opportunity to buy more."

Felix, with a swift glance at John, asked why Trenico was disposing of so much land.

"Surely you've heard that his finances are not at all sound at the moment? Hc's now said to be contemplating selling a certain vineyard. If so, I shall be making a bid on it. It produces excellent wines, if the ones I have sampled at his dinner parties are any example."

"His rumored financial circumstances suggest this would be an excellent time to make a reasonable offer." John's tone was dry.

"An even better one to make a modest bid. I cannot be the only one who intends to wait another season before declaring interest. By then his circumstances will make him happy to accept an even lower price than he would right now."

"Your comments suggest you and Trenico are not on the best of terms."

"I wouldn't say that. We are men of business. You might say that we are like two friends who bet against each other at the races. However well I may best Trenico now and then, I still do not see him falling into destitution."

"It's also possible that his finances will have improved by next year. There are rumors of him making a good marriage."

Tryphon laughed. "That's the nature of the Great Palace! Full of whisperers in dark corners and plotting in the bushes. I've heard the same. I don't believe a word of it! Mind you, there are apparently any number of courtiers betting against the success of his suit for the hand of a certain senator's daughter."

"May I ask about Hypatius?" John put in, struggling to keep his voice level. The very thought of Trenico attempting to solve his financial problems by a union with Lady Anna angered him. To a greater extent, he realized, than was reasonable. "Do you have any thoughts on who might have wished Hypatius dead? Someone with whom he had had business dealings, perhaps?"

Tryphon regarded him shrewdly. "Ah, now we come to the point of your visit. You think it is possible he may have been murdered over money matters? That's the cause of many murders, I would imagine, but it's less likely grounds among businessmen."

The landowner gazed out over the restless water. Fixing his stare on a distant sail he went on, choosing his words with care. "Hypatius was known for his piety and charitable works. I can't see that those who benefited from his generous purse would wish to see him dead. Occasionally one heard rumors of less than honorable business transactions. Lately there's been some talk of his mistreatment of his servants. I think it's safe to put all that down to disgruntled rivals and the usual whinings of lazy menials. After all, if you cannot attack a man for his success you can always drop a few poisonous words about his private life, even if you know nothing about it."

"Especially if you know nothing about it," Felix observed.

"Successful and wealthy men always attract envy. Envy breeds anger. Angry men speak without thought and usually, so I have noticed, live to regret it."

"We understand that Hypatius was a close associate of Senator Opimius," put in John.

"Opimius?" Tryphon pursed his lips in thought and looked away from the water. The squat shape of the merchant ship he had been watching could now barely be discerned. Doubtless the vessel was laden with marble slabs or amphorae of wine or oil, but from their vantage point it looked like a toy a child had dropped from the seawall, only to cry over its loss.

"I am not acquainted personally with the senator," Tryphon said. "Only with his reputation. Nothing more than that."

❋ ❋ ❋

As John and Felix walked slowly down the cobbled street on which Tryphon's villa perched, Felix looked thoughtful.

"I noticed that Tryphon might admire wine from Trenico's vineyard, but he didn't offer us anything from his own stock," he grumbled. "We might have found inspiration in a cup of wine. What do you make of it all?"

John shrugged. "It appears that the civic-minded public benefactor Hypatius was not quite what he appeared to be. But we'd begun to suspect that, given the business with his will, for example."

Before he could say more, a pair of splendidly dressed, long-haired young men emerged from an emporium at the foot of the street. There was nothing uncommon about that or even threatening under the circumstances. What caught John's attention was the enormous size of one of them.

Then he noted the oddly crushed nose.

It could only be the man he had seen running from the Great Church after Hypatius' murder.

John did not have the opportunity to discover whether the Blue would have been as quick to recognize him as being the man whom he had raced past a few days earlier because as soon as Felix caught sight of them he bellowed, "Halt! By order of the Prefect!"

The two took to their heels. The smaller scuttled into the narrow passageway behind the establishment they had just left. The other, the big one, cut swiftly across the street and disappeared under an archway leading to a stairway down to the docks.

Felix and John raced downhill and plunged through the archway behind him.

The sound of their fleeing prey's boots hitting worn stone steps echoed back, briefly mirrored by the sound of their own thudding feet. They burst from the stairway's darkness into momentarily dazzling sunlight.

The Blue had vanished along with the sound of his boots, but only for an instant. John spotted his large frame, jutting above the crowd of milling laborers on the docks. He sprinted after him.

Those who saw the three running men stepped quickly back out of the way, leaving a clear path along the docks. John found himself in a footrace for the first time since he had been a callow youth attending Plato's Academy.

His prey ran with enormous, loping strides, but was heavily built and obviously not a practiced runner. John fixed his gaze on his quarry's long tail of flapping hair. He began to draw nearer to the broad back, close enough to make out the geometric pattern stitched on the cloak.

Now he could hear the man's wheezing, labored breathing.

John gauged the distance and then lunged out.

And slammed into an unwary pedestrian. He caught a glimpse of a pudgy fellow whose hair resembled an untidy nest. Then he was looking at the sky before smashing down on one side and spinning, sliding across an icy puddle, to crash shoulder first into a brick wall.

In an instant Felix was looking down at him, gasping, his broad face blazing red. "If I owned you I'd have those wings on your heels clipped," he blurted out.

John scrambled up. "Where did he go?"

Felix pointed to the brick building's wide door, beside which was a chiseled inscription announcing it to be the warehouse of Viator, importer of fine marbles and stones.

A swift glance into the gloomy interior revealed the broad back of a large man who seemed intent on examining the contents of a crate. His cloak, however, was brown and undecorated.

"How could he have changed clothes so quickly?" Felix muttered.

The man turned at the sound. "You! Loiterers! I can hear you whispering! Do I have to summon the Prefect's men and have you arrested or are you leaving now?"

He was not young but middle-aged. Clearly, he was not the man John and Felix had pursued.

*** ***

"The notion that my son murdered Hypatius is so outlandish that were I not a law-abiding citizen I would knock you both immediately into the sea for even suggesting it!"

Viator looked perfectly capable of carrying out his threat. He was of such cyclopean size as to make apparent at a glance that he was the fleeing Blue's father. In addition to his bulk, he shared with his offspring the same sort of crushed and crooked nose, evidently an accident of birth rather than the result of fighting.

The marble importer led John and Felix through his warehouse. There was no sign of his son, Victor by name. He could easily have been hiding among the wilderness of marble blocks and huge pieces of stone piled in orderly rows in the dimness. Or perhaps he had slipped out a side door to the docks, from there to disappear into the city.

As they passed along corridors formed by the orderly ranks of stone, the importer reached out ham-like hands to touch here orange-veined yellow marble, there a slab of purple and white, just as a fond father might absentmindedly pat the heads of his children.

"Yes, gentlemen," Viator went on, "I can assure you that the very idea is absurd, despite your eyewitness account." His gaze rested briefly on John. "Oh, Victor's been known to get into mischief now and then, but he's just a high-spirited lad. So are most of the Blues."

Felix observed gruffly he would differ with that characterization, based on the Blues who had crossed his path.

Viator bridled. "If you're talking about the riots, there's many a citizen who says that Quaestor Proclus is behind all this strife in the streets. Ask around, and you'll soon see I'm telling the truth."

John, thinking that few citizens would admit to any such thought when questioned by men under the feared Gourd's command, asked the importer why Proclus would foment strife.

"Why? Because the manufacture of scapegoats is a profitable business. Especially if the profit someone seeks is the furtherance of his own ambition."

Viator caressed a marble slab displaying striking striations of white and pale green. "I tend my business and leave others to tend theirs. You see this piece of marble? It's for the tomb of a wealthy merchant whose fortune was made in vegetables. He was once a grocer's assistant, and before that he sold onions in the street. As you can see, the pattern in this slab resembles an onion. I rather anticipate that the tomb itself will be domed, again like an onion. As with myself, the merchant began humbly and rose through love of his wares. In his case, onions, in my case, stone and marble. There are those who wake up every day and check their account books. I prefer to visit my warehouse and admire the beauty it contains."

The importer of marble warmed to his theme.

"Yes," he went on, "I began as a common laborer in the building trade. After two or three years, the owner of the business gave me permission to take away unused concrete at the end of the day. After that, I worked for him during daylight hours and then at night I became an itinerant mender of concrete. I went around the city with an old bucket containing whatever had been left over. Naturally, I had to be persuasive, but it's surprising how often a steward or a tenement owner needs a small repair to a crack in a wall or a crumbling step."

Felix, interested in the tale despite himself, asked how Viator had moved into the marble business.

The importer smiled. "It happened that a shipment of marble intended for a job on which I was working for the business owner I mentioned was rejected as unfit for the purpose. Not the shade specified, or some such defect. Seizing my chance, I bought the marble and so began the rise to my present position. However, I was only able to purchase it because I had money earned by hauling those buckets of concrete about the city for years. There's a lesson in that for us all, as I have often pointed out my son."

"Speaking of jobs and marble, new emperors always love to refurbish the capital," observed Felix. "You must be looking forward to Justinian being crowned. It could well mean a lot of extra trade for you."

"Not at all," Viator said. "I wish Justin a long life. He's a man with dirt under his fingernails. Just the sort of man I admire, in fact. He too has humble origins. Besides which, I don't need any more business right now."

Felix expressed admiration for Viator's success.

The big man nodded happily. "Have you walked on the new flooring in the Baths of Zeuxippos? My marble was under your feet! I'm certain you've wagered on the races at the Hippodrome at some time or another. When you did, your backsides enjoyed new benches made from stone I imported. Or perhaps you've lingered in the shade of the new portico in the Forum Bovis? Its columns were born from marble shipped from this very warehouse."

"You're all over the city, it seems," Felix replied. "Rather like the Gourd himself."

Having complied with Felix's request to show them around his warehouse, Viator started back through the maze of artificial cliffs. At the front entrance, John's gaze fell on the open crate Viator had been examining when they arrived. The marble it held was black.

"Imported all the way from Greece," Viator explained. "It was ordered by a man of some influence. Let's say he's a senator who shall remain anonymous. It is intended for a private purpose. Some say he intends to build a shrine to a blasphemous deity whose name a Christian would not dare to whisper. As it happens, I know better. It's for a statue of the Nubian slave he keeps as a concubine."

"A fascinating trade indeed," replied Felix. "However, more to the point, where did your son go after he rushed in here?"

"I'm sorry, sir, I cannot tell you. He knows he is not to bother me when I'm busy and he could see that I had just opened this crate."

"Do you have any idea why he would have been at the Great Church?"

"Apart from worshipping there, you mean? Well, he said he wanted to see this work of art everyone's talking about."

"Interested in such things, is he?"

Viator puffed out his substantial chest. "No, not at all, but he was very proud that I was responsible for bringing in the material used for it. It was another special order. The purest white marble from Proconnesus, and I don't mind telling you it was an expensive affair. Naturally, I gave a little bit of a discount. It's very good for business to be connected with such a project. Word gets around, you know."

The importer continued at some length about the merits of the sculpture and the material from which it was made before John and Felix managed to escape.

Felix shook his head in consternation as he and John retraced their steps along the docks. "To listen to that man's boasting, you'd think he'd cut the marble from the quarry with his own hands, swum back to Constantinople with it tied on his back, and then chiseled the thing personally."

"It's not a bad thing to take pride in one's work," said John. "Although it strikes me that the longer he talked, the further away his son was able to get. I feel sorry for the father, but a murderer is a murderer. If it wasn't Victor who actually struck down Hypatius, he was certainly in the company of the culprit. I almost hate to say so, but now we should inform the Gourd we know the identity of the man I saw running from the Great Church."

Chapter Seventeen

"I've had men executed for such incompetence!"

The City Prefect stamped back and forth in the corridor outside his office, too angry to stand still. His misshapen forehead was coated with droplets of sweat, the poisonous distillation of his rage.

"You're telling me that you saw a man you personally identified as one of those murdering bastards and you allowed him to escape?" He came to a halt in front of Felix and stabbed a blunt finger at the excubitor's chest. "Why didn't the pair of you arrest him on the spot?"

"With respect, Prefect," Felix answered in even tones, "we have not been given authority to arrest anyone. We could only have interrogated him."

"A good excuse. You prize pair weren't about to pursue a fellow the size you describe. Or was it a case of bribery?" When the Gourd's big head swiveled toward John, the terrible asymmetry of his skull was obvious. Someone who didn't know better might have said the man had suffered a horrific injury, one sure to prove fatal.

The Prefect wiped his dripping forehead with a rough shirtsleeve. "We're not senators or courtiers. We don't have time to lounge about and debate philosophy while the city burns. Take as many men as you need and arrest father and son immediately. We'll have the truth out of them before the sun rises again."

❅ ❅ ❅

It was nearly dark by the time they had gathered the required force and tramped back to Viator's warehouse.

"We're lucky we escaped with our heads," growled Felix. He was still clearly angry.

"Our heads are currently protected by both the emperor and Justinian," John pointed out.

"What makes you think that would stop the Gourd? I knew I was in for trouble as soon as I found out I'd been yoked to a eunuch. When you're in a fight you want a man to protect your back."

"If you hadn't been so stupid as to shout at the Blue and warn him off we would've had hold of him before he even noticed us!"

"Why didn't you grab his cloak when you had the chance? Afraid to grapple with him, I suppose. We'll be lucky to come out of this alive." Now Felix sounded mournful.

"If we don't cooperate better we certainly won't."

Felix grunted. He had realized the truth of what John said and had also noticed the smirks on the faces of those men near enough to overhear their heated argument.

A search of Viator's warehouse revealed it was deserted.

"Not even a rat," said Felix in disgust. "But that's not surprising. If I were a rat I wouldn't take up residence in this pile of rocks with all the granaries I could wish to live in so close to hand."

A score of the Gourd's men had been clattering up and down the narrow lanes between the stacked marble and stone shouting to one another for some time before an old man with a lantern in one hand and a staff in the other limped through the main doorway. His pointed chin reminded John of a rat, after Felix's mention of that verminous creature.

"What are you doing here, grandfather?" Felix asked brusquely.

The man blinked and his features twitched. He shuffled a step forward, leaning heavily on his staff. "I am the night watchman, sir. I've just come on duty."

"You?" Felix said.

"I am the only watchman Viator needs in the warehouse," the old man said in an unperturbed but loud voice that led John to deduce he was probably half deaf as well as lame. "No thief is going to grab one of these pretty blocks of marble and run off with it under his cloak."

"What if they show up with a cart?" Felix asked.

"There's another man on watch for carts all night long. His perch is just in front of Viator's house. Since the master's dwelling overlooks this very warehouse, the master is able to keep half an eye on things himself most of the time as well. As you can see, everything is perfectly secure."

❋ ❋ ❋

They climbed the stairs down which they had chased Victor that afternoon, turned, and made their way along a stretch of street paralleling the seawall. Viator's house was easy to pick out, even before they read the plaque beside its door. The boxlike structure was festooned with a variety of marble decorations. Columns, lintels, cornices, decorative panels, and bas-reliefs jostled each other on its bricks walls. The building resembled a warehouse in the middle of a magickal transformation into a temple or vice versa.

"No one's home," Felix concluded after pounding at the door for some time. "Not that I expected it. After our visit they probably found urgent business in the country."

"Or another country."

A flagstoned space boasting a fountain and several benches sat between Viator's house and the seawall. The man who supposedly used this vantage point to keep a watch on the warehouse, whose tiled roof John could glimpse below, was nowhere in sight.

"The servants must have been told to make themselves scarce," Felix remarked. "I suppose we'll have to knock the door down, to be certain."

"Perhaps one of the neighbors observed something," John suggested. "In particular the fellow who's been almost falling out his window ever since we got here."

He pointed at the stolid and unadorned house next to Viator's. At the gesture a shadowed outline visible in the illuminated window ducked out of sight.

"You have sharp eyes. Let's hope we can get to him before he escapes too."

Felix's pessimism was unfounded. The observer suddenly emerged, and briskly greeted them.

"I am Theophylaktos, sirs. I happened to notice your fruitless pounding on my neighbor's door. I would be most pleased to assist if I can."

At closer range the man still had the look of a shadow cast by a guttering flame. He was bundled up in an overly bulky cloak and as he talked he continuously bobbed his head, first at Felix, then John, while rubbing his hands briskly together. His features never seemed entirely to emerge from shadow.

"We seek to interview Viator and his son," Felix said grimly.

"Indeed?" Theophylaktos drifted to the edge of the seawall and looked down over it. John and Felix followed.

"This is much the same view as from my windows, sirs. This afternoon one of my servants was wasting time staring down at the docks. 'What is so interesting that you're neglecting your duties?' I asked him. Then I saw Victor being chased into his father's warehouse and thought to myself, ahah, that boy is in real trouble now. And so after you left I kept watch just to see what happened next."

"I can understand your curiosity," Felix remarked.

"We get all sorts of ne'er-do-wells around here, being right next to the docks," their informant replied. "It's a good location for me, though, since I'm a ship owner. My vessel casts off for Egypt at dawn tomorrow. May the Lord send good weather."

"Your cargo on that particular ship wouldn't happen to include Viator and his son would it?"

The question sent Theophylaktos into a frenzy of hand wringing. "Certainly not," he said faintly.

"Do you have any information concerning the two men we're seeking?" John put in.

"I was getting to that. I apologize for rambling. Wasting your time, I know, sirs. That won't do. Time is short whenever official business is concerned. Even the candles burn faster. Yes, Viator and I are good friends."

"Have you seen either of them since late this afternoon?"

"Oh, yes! Indeed I have. That's what I was going to tell you. I happened to be looking out of my window at the very instant they came out of their house. They were carrying a couple of small bags. It was so soon after you departed, I'm surprised they didn't trip over your boot heels."

"They could have been going to buy something at the market," Felix suggested artfully.

"But what are servants for if not to go to the market? No, I believe they were going off on a trip. They were definitely dressed for travel."

"In addition to being observant, you are a man of logic," Felix said. "I couldn't argue with your reasoning, even if it were possible for me get a word in."

"Viator would not agree, I fear. He had no faith at all in anything I said, despite my own modest success in business. For example, I tried to warn him when he showed me a contract some while ago. It was with a senator, but I noticed it wasn't properly signed. I told him I thought this might raise problems later. He wouldn't listen. Said it was a favor for a friend. Then just as I predicted, an argument arose about the quality of the goods he supplied. The last I heard there was talk about a law suit."

John and Felix exchanged glances as the garrulous ship owner rattled on. "Now, I happen to know Viator is in financial straits right now. Taxes, for one thing. Then there was that shipment of marble that sank only last month. Some said it was no accident, yet how can a storm be conjured up at will? Then, too, he was worried about his son running wild. Very sad."

As Theophylaktos spoke his gaze wandered, from John to Felix, then to the warehouse below, from it to his ship. Even once or twice up toward the night sky.

"You say you're a friend of Viator's?" Felix asked

"Yes, and friends watch out for their friends. Especially given the current state of affairs. This reminds me, Viator told me he thought he was being followed around. I advised him that there are always hordes of people surging about the docks. He was uneasy. I think Hypatius' death was very much on his mind."

"Did he know Hypatius?" John asked with interest.

Theophylaktos rubbed his hands together so vigorously John could hear the palms rasp against each other. It reminded him of the rustling of dry leaves blown down a lane as summer died.

"Indeed he did! That was another example of his lack of business acumen. Hypatius was a very good friend of his. Or was, until he cheated Viator out of a great deal of money even though Hypatius knew Viator's finances were stretched. I'm not certain of the details. Now I suppose it will never be resolved."

He drew a breath and looked back toward his house, down at the roof of the warehouse, and then finally at John and Felix.

"So I suppose it was natural he got it into his head that he was suspected of Hypatius' murder. When you arrived this afternoon, well, you can see he would prefer to make himself scarce. That explains why his son has disappeared too. In the circumstances, you wouldn't want to leave any of your family behind either."

It was with some difficulty that John and Felix managed to separate themselves from the verbal clutches of the excessively helpful ship owner. The men recruited to apprehend the vanished fugitives lounged on the other side of the street, their impatience poorly concealed.

"I'm afraid Viator's neighbor is confused. It's the son who's suspected of murder, not the father," Felix remarked to John in an undertone.

"Unless Viator incited his son to do it. If the son really is the culprit."

"Either way, unfortunately, we have to return to the Gourd with empty hands."

"I must say I am not looking forward to that."

Felix laughed mirthlessly. "Then I suggest that you contemplate instead the wine which we will doubtless require to revive ourselves immediately afterward."

Chapter Eighteen

"You know you're welcome here, Felix, no matter what the hour! However, since you'll be venturing back onto dark streets I insist you partake a little bit less of my hospitality than you did last time."

Isis gave the excubitor a stern look. Nevertheless she refilled his wine cup. Turning to John, seated on a low stool by her couch, she continued. "Felix has a good heart. He once saved one of my girls from—"

"We don't need to talk about that, Isis," Felix interrupted. "Your kindness since, and the kindness of your girls, has more than repaid me!"

Isis said no more, but gave Felix a fond pat on his knee.

"There's something going on that we don't know about," Felix complained. "But what?"

"Is that why you're here? To discuss business?" Isis began to pare an apple with a dainty silver knife.

"Actually, yes, Isis. I certainly don't want to discuss this in the barracks. The streets are far too cold and the prospect of sitting whispering in a corner of a tavern doesn't appeal to me."

Isis lowered kohl-blackened eyelids thoughtfully. "There's a service I hadn't considered selling before. Offering gentlemen a discreet meeting place to discuss delicate matters." She popped a sliver of apple into her mouth. "In this city there's a market for everything. Why, a fellow approached me today wanting to supply my establishment with young boys. A lucrative trade, no doubt, but one I refuse to engage in."

The single lamp on the ivory inlaid table between the couches on which Isis and Felix reclined cast a pool of light that glinted off a silver bowl, gold embroidery on a pillow, and the varnished panther feet of the couches.

"You have done very well for yourself, without resorting to such things," remarked John.

Isis smiled. "Constantinople is a city where even the humblest can rise to great glory. "

"That's true," said Felix. "Look at Justin for a start."

"And Theodora," Isis reminded him. "From actress to empress."

"She's not empress quite yet and there are those who seek to prevent it happening," Felix pointed out. "A common whore, they call her. Not fit to be Justinian's wife."

Isis looked offended. "I've heard that as well. It's an ignorant opinion. Theodora was never a common whore. She was an actress and a mime. She didn't cavort among the audience. She performed on stage. Her favors weren't for sale to the common rabble, but only by special arrangement with men of refinement." She waved her silver fruit knife for emphasis. "Now take Euphemia, or rather Lupicina. There's a whore's name if I ever heard one. She was one of those untalented little girls who work sweaty crowds. Why do you think she hated Theodora so much?"

"Constantinople is certainly a city of endless opportunity," said John. "One day you're fighting with a mongrel in the gutter for a bone, the next you're supping on peacock with the Patriarch."

"Not when you fail at even a simple task such as we have been set," replied Felix dolefully.

"I'm certain even Justinian has failed at something, some time or other," Isis observed.

"And whether we've truly failed depends on what we're really meant to accomplish." John hesitated, uncertain whether he should discuss such matters in front of an Egyptian madam he had met only on one previous occasion.

"Go on," Felix told him. "Isis is absolutely trustworthy. You can rely on her discretion."

"I should think so," Isis retorted. "It's vital in my profession!"

"Very well," John said. "In short, a one-eyed man can see we've been planted as spies in the Gourd's office. Deliberately obvious spies."

"That's right!" Felix responded. "What use are our investigations? Why should these powerful men we've been interviewing tell us anything? They deny anything inconvenient and meantime must be finding it very humorous to send us off to bark at some rival or other. Doubtless they think it's a wonderful jest. No, what I'm certain our masters really want is for us to keep an eye on the Gourd."

"And they want the Gourd to be aware we're keeping an eye on him. Not only that, since we had specific instructions to continue our usual duties, in my case tutoring Lady Anna, I expect to be grilled about the senator's household in due course."

"Not to mention we are also supposed to be keeping an eye on each other." Felix grinned.

Isis dropped her knife onto the table and made a show of throwing up her plump hands. "I'm glad I'm not in your business. At least I have a pretty good notion of what my patrons are after! Your suspicions are probably correct, though. Justinian has always been fond of informers. It was an informer of his who introduced him to Theodora. Macedonia, a dancer for the Blues. Normally Macedonia would pass on to Justinian names of those who might pose a threat to him. Remarkable how loose men's tongues can be when they're seeking to impress a woman. She met Theodora in Antioch, or so the story goes."

"Why would this Macedonia have introduced Theodora to Justinian?" Felix wondered.

"Perhaps Macedonia thought Theodora would make a good informer herself. Or maybe it was because Theodora was such a strong supporter of the Blues, like Justinian. Or maybe it was because of that dream Theodora had."

"What dream is that, Isis? Excubitors don't hear all the gossip you do."

"Theodora told Macedonia she dreamt she journeyed to Constantinople. There she met the Lord of the Demons who took her to his bed and subsequently showered her with endless wealth."

"I see." Felix frowned. "I never have these portentous dreams, myself."

Isis chuckled. "Maybe you're not destined for greatness. What sort of dreams do you have, John?"

"None that I remember when I awake, Isis."

Felix stared down into his wine cup. "At any rate, I can't say we're doing very well as informers. We've learned nothing useful about the Gourd. He doesn't seem to be taking much warning from our presence, either. Look at that magick business the other night."

Isis leaned forward, her eyes glittering with interest. "That little act of his has certainly been much talked about. One of my girls entertained a gentleman who was present at that dinner party. He was so amazed, he took longer to relate the tale than he did to conduct his business."

Felix looked uneasy. "I didn't see it myself, you understand, but John here has a keen eye for detail, I'll say that. What he described would certainly convince many that the Gourd is an adept. Doubtless they'd wonder what else he can do. Conjure up demons? Spirit men away in a whorl of mist? He'd like you to think he has eyes everywhere. It's excellent strategy, I admit. You can't fight that sort of fear."

"True enough," John said, "but I can tell you exactly how he worked his little trick."

Felix looked at him in amazement. "How would you know about magick?"

"Not magick," John corrected him. "A trick. I know because for a while I traveled with a group of entertainers and sometimes we worked with other adepts."

"You have some talent, then?" Isis asked.

John shook his head. "No, but travelers like that often band together. Passing through Egypt we were joined for a time by a man who went by the name of Baba. He would set up a table and do magick tricks before we put on our show. There were always a number of coins tossed his way. I don't know if people were paying for his entertainment or because they feared him. One of Baba's most spectacular feats was to plunge his arm into a vat of boiling pitch."

"Just like the Gourd did!" Felix exclaimed.

"Exactly. But the trick is that the pitch isn't actually boiling. Baba added vinegar and a particular type of soda. The mixture bubbles when it's warmed so it looks as if it's scalding hot. I am sure that's exactly how the Gourd fooled his aristocratic audience."

Felix looked at John in disbelief. "That's all it was? A handful or two of common ingredients has the whole city cowering?"

"For the time being perhaps. The Gourd may yet overreach himself, just as Baba did. He wasn't content with coins, you understand. He wanted to see people terrified, prostrating themselves in the dust. There's bronze coins to be had from boiling pitch, but there's gold in terror, he would say. So one night he decided to conjure up a fiery, airborne demon. It was really a bird soaked in a flammable mixture, set on fire and released by a troupe member he had bribed. The poor creature flew straight into a pile of straw and nearly burnt the village to the ground. So I wouldn't be at all surprised if the Gourd releases his own fiery demon in the wrong direction sooner or later."

Felix stood up. John was relieved to see the excubitor would be able to return to the barracks unaided.

"A fascinating story indeed, John," Felix said. "And I say let's hope Gourd sets fire to his own roof before he burns down the city."

❋❋❋

Theodotus peered over Theodora's shoulder toward the alcove at the rear of the smoky room and raised his voice. "I am Prefect of this city! By what authority do you prevent me from speaking to Justinian?"

"By what authority do you seek to impose on him?"

"The emperor suggested—"

"Justinian cannot entertain visitors this morning. He is too ill. But you know that, don't you?" In contrast to the Prefect's loud tones, Theodora's voice was soft. No louder than the whisper of a blade slipping from its scabbard.

"I must discuss the matter of this eunuch he's saddled me with! I've already complained to the emperor about his man, the German excubitor. The pair of them are interfering with my duties. Justin ordered me to talk to Justinian."

"Was it Justin who ordered you, or the quaestor Proclus?"

Theodotus clenched his fists. In the dimly illuminated room, he might have been a deformed demon, every bit the horror that more than one potential malefactor feared meeting in a dark alley.

Theodora took a step forward. "What is it you managed to slip to Justinian? How have you accomplished this filthy deed?"

"What do you mean?"

"Is that the real purpose of your visit? Did you hope for an opportunity to administer a new dose of poison?"

"Poison? Ridiculous! When could I have possibly poisoned Justinian?"

"A magician is capable of many things. Perhaps the poison was borne here on a spell. You showed yourself as quite an adept the other evening."

Theodotus shifted his feet. He had to restrain himself from pushing past the woman. "I thought you enjoyed my little display, Theodora."

"I did. It delighted me to see how convincing you were. It was a very nice act indeed."

"You should know about acting!"

Theodora gave a throaty laugh. "I do. I have a professional's keen eye and skepticism. However, you certainly convinced the rest of your guests, which is the important thing. You see, what you obviously overlooked in giving that little demonstration of yours is that they'll all be convinced that a man with such powers would have no trouble at all in poisoning a future emperor, no matter how many guards he keeps."

Chapter Nineteen

The sky was so clear it might have been blown glass, but the cold still kept most city residents off the streets. Those who lived on them, beggars huddled in sheltered corners along the Mese, didn't even extend grimy hands toward John and Anna as they passed.

Perhaps, John thought, the cold numbing their ill-clothed bodies also froze their spirits. When every day was much like another and each had to be devoted to struggling to survive, it made men old before their time. After a time, old men lost interest in life.

Perhaps Dorotheus had been right in his dismissal of freedom.

John glanced at two boys playing kick ball in a portico. Perhaps because they had not matured enough to realize what lay ahead, such children lived only for the day. With each sunrise came the renewed hope that they might be given a crust of bread, or find a largely unrotted cabbage in the gutter or contrive to steal a fish from a shop. John envied them their hope.

He pulled his cloak around himself more tightly. Chilly air still managed to get in and nestle next to his ribs.

The boys almost collided with a man emerging from a shop. Obviously a servant, he struggled to carry a huge covered basket. His face registered alarm. He must have thought he was about to be robbed. He sidestepped his supposed attackers too hastily. Suddenly he was down on his back, along with his basket. The portico was immediately bestrewn with hundreds of olives of every conceivable shape and shade of green, as well as light brown and dull black. They went spinning and rolling in all directions. More than one beggar materialized and began scooping up the unexpected bounty.

The servant struggled to his feet and shouted virulent abuse after the boys, who were heedlessly kicking their leather ball across the Mese. One of them turned and made a rude gesture, narrowly avoiding being knocked down by a curtained litter borne by four slaves. He made the same gesture at the slaves, who shouted even worse sentiments back at him.

Anna sighed. "It's remarkable that children like that live long enough to become adults. Where are their parents? Although I suppose people cannot always keep an eye on their offspring."

Recalling the young Anatolius' near fatal adventure, John agreed. He watched the boys as they picked up their ball and disappeared, squabbling noisily, between two buildings.

When he looked back at Anna he was shocked to see she had picked up a large black olive. She wiped it clean on her cloak and popped it into her mouth.

The servant, on his knees hopelessly trying to sweep up the ruined olives, gaped up at her.

"Oh, I do apologize," Anna told him. "That must have belonged to you. Here, allow me to pay for it." She produced enough coins to refill the basket twice and handed them to the stunned man.

John and Anna continued on for a short distance, past shops where John and Felix had conducted fruitless interviews. Several beggars, having observed her generosity, now proffered their own stolen olives for sale, but at a glance from John did not press the matter.

The pair walked until they reached the entrance to the Augustaion.

"Perhaps we should return home now, Lady Anna. I'm pleased your father relented and allowed you this little excursion. Might it be best not to worry him by being away too long?"

"Don't fret about father, John. He'll never know I was out of the house. In fact, I have a small errand to run. A friend is soon to be married and I've given her gift a great deal of thought. I've decided to give her a perfume flask engraved with a portrait of Venus. I shall have it filled with rose water."

"That sounds most appropriate."

They continued on and before long the incongruously sweet odor of flower gardens filled the cold air. Perfumers were welcome shopkeepers here in the Augustaion. When the wind was in the right quarter, their fragrances would drift into the grounds of the Great Palace.

"Tell me, John, did you ever buy perfume for a woman?"

"No, she was not very fond of perfume." He stopped abruptly. He had been taken by surprise and answered without thought.

"So there was a woman then?"

John nodded silently.

"I doubt I will ever marry." Anna sounded more determined than wistful at the prospect, not to mention seemingly unperturbed that she was over-stepping the proper boundaries between slave and mistress. "I try to avoid mentioning the subject since the prospect disappoints and distresses my father."

"Naturally he wishes your happiness."

"He sometimes appears to think I have no more sense than those unruly boys playing in the street. Dominica visited again yesterday and lectured me on how to conduct myself. She pretended we were having a conversation about art, but it kept return-ing to her business affairs. Not that she handles details since she employs a steward. But, as she pointed out, one must keep an eye on one's emplo-yees. On the other hand, she kept telling me I wouldn't need to face these problems because a good husband looks after such tiresome matters, leaving his wife free to pursue her learning and artistic interests."

Anna's lips tightened. "More than anything, father seems to fear that if he should die and leave me alone in the world I would be lost. Perhaps it's because he feels lost without mother. Do you think I would be lost, John?"

"No, Lady Anna," John replied uncomfortably.

"He insisted I attend a dinner party the other night with Trenico. That is intolerable, wouldn't you say?"

"It is not for me to venture an opinion."

Anna laid her hand on his arm. "Wait! Before we go into the perfumer's shop there's something I must tell you. The street is one of the few places we won't run the risk of being overheard."

She had moved close enough to speak in a whisper. John's mouth felt suddenly dry and heat rose in his face.

"I heard certain conversations about Justinian during that dinner party," Anna began. "Some claimed that not all the senators support him, as is commonly believed. What distresses me is that father's name was mentioned as one of those in opposition. I'm certain it was because he championed Vitalian, but then so did Justinian and the emperor. I have never heard father utter an ill word against Justinian and despite the wagging tongues, he doesn't hold secret meetings at home. The only thing he's plotting is my marriage."

"I am sure you don't have to worry about your father. He is a man of experience and will take the right course."

Anna drew away. "You're right, but it worries me to hear such slanders bandied about. There's always the chance they'll reach the wrong ears. But now we're here, let's choose that gift."

Filled with many clashing scents, the perfumer's shop reminded John of Isis' house more than a flower garden. Tall cupboards, their doors ajar, displayed alabastrons of assorted sizes, delicate glass flasks, and large bottles of perfume.

An immaculately dressed man with smooth cheeks and a faint hint of lilies about him greeted them in a soft voice.

"May I offer you a sample of our latest import? Our best violet perfume, very refreshing and a delicate scent most suitable for a lovely young woman like yourself. Made with the lightest grade of oil, needless to say. We use only the finest materials for our wares. Or perhaps you might care to try the lily water? It's very popular with certain ladies at the court."

Lady Anna declined politely and described her quest.

"A flask engraved with Venus filled with perfume made from her sacred flower? What a charming notion. As it happens, we have just received a shipment of beautiful blue glass flasks."

The flasks were exquisite, as Anna remarked.

The perfumer looked gratified. "Being situated so close to court we are patronized by many of high birth and we offer only the finest wares. We're well known, if I may say so, for just that reason."

"Business must flourish then?" Anna responded politely.

"Indeed it does, and that despite the riots and the new perfumery that's just opened a few doors down. Owned by a grocer, it seems." The man sniffed. "What would a grocer know about perfume? I wouldn't want to wear a scent bought from a seller of cooking oil!"

Anna tactfully agreed. After inspecting a fine array of flasks, she chose one that was elegantly tapered and gave instructions on its engraving. Then the proprietor bowed them out of his emporium with a promise to deliver her purchase as soon as it was engraved. "Filled with the finest rose perfume in the empire, that you can depend upon."

✻ ✻ ✻

The air outside was invigorating after the heavy atmosphere of the perfumer's shop. Too long in such a place, John thought, and his reason would begin to reel.

"We need to clear our heads!" Anna said with a slight smile. "Let's stroll up to the Strategion before we return home and let the sea breezes refresh us."

Little sign remained of the horrific spectacle John had recently witnessed at that location, only a scorched area on the base of the obelisk. The open air market, so recently a slaughterhouse, displayed its usual crowds. The visitors did not seem to linger as long as usual, haggling over their purchases, preferring rather to complete the transaction as soon as possible. Doubtless this was met with favor by those whose tables and stalls held colorful piles of merchandise, since their customers were by and large willing to pay the asking price.

John and Anna paused beside the Baths of Actaeon. Its side, facing away from the windswept seawall above the Golden Horn, sheltered several small stalls.

"Buy a beautiful chicken for your evening meal tonight," a rotund, fresh-faced woman coaxed as Anna looked at her pile of plump, dimple-skinned fowl. "Fresh from the country this very morning. Killed so recently, if they hadn't been plucked, they'd fly into your cooking pot! I can tell your lady wife would make a most tasty dish for you and afterward, who knows…?" She gave a knowing smile, holding up a particularly large bird enticingly.

Anna blushed. Ignoring the chicken seller's loud complaints about parsimonious husbands, they moved hastily away and escaped around the corner of the building.

The sight of the baths reminded Anna of her father's as yet unrepaired bath house. "It is very inconvenient, John. I fear I'm not used to patronizing the public baths and now going there requires three or four bodyguards besides. But the worst aspect of the difficulty is Trenico. He seems to spend half his life at the Baths of Zeuxippos and so insists on constantly giving me advice. Which shops are best, the most interesting lectures, a particular statue of amazing workmanship I must be sure to see, that sort of thing. And all the while staring at me as if he's seeing me in the baths clothed with nothing more than steam. It's all most improper."

But not nearly as improper as a lady addressing a slave in such a manner, John thought.

At the seawall they looked down over the docks where ships sat at anchor, each vessel attached to an inverted twin beneath it.

"Do you ever long to sail away and never return to Constantinople?" Anna suddenly asked. "If you could, I mean. The city must hold some very bad memories for you."

"Other places hold worse." John feared this was a prelude to another inappropriate conversation.

Instead, Anna asked, "Can chickens fly?"

John could do nothing but look at her in silence.

"The woman back there said the chickens might fly into our cooking pot, but I can't imagine a chicken would be much of a flier from what I've seen of their wings. That's after the cook has finished preparing them, I'll admit."

"They can fly a few wing-flaps if necessary. In order to escape a predator, for example."

"So they take to the air only from necessity?" Anna's tone was thoughtful. "Well, they are merely chickens, after all. And speaking of birds, I've just realized we're not far from the home of my friend Avis. He's the inventor I may have mentioned now and then. We'll go and visit him now. The wings he's working on strike me as vastly superior to any chicken's wings."

Shouting broke out on the docks below.

Intrigued, Anna leaned alarmingly out over the wall and stared down. "It's some of the Gourd's men. They're dragging someone by his legs along the dock." She was indignant. "Poor thing, I wonder what he did to incur their wrath? Nothing at all probably."

John stared down at the growing knot of dock workers who had abandoned their labors to stand around and gape at the scene.

Two men were hauling the unfortunate man over the back of a waiting mule. He hung limply, hands and feet brushing the ground. As the Prefect's men urged the animal toward the nearest stairway, it passed directly below John and Anna and John got a clear view of their captive.

It was Viator. At least he would not have to face the Gourd's wrath. He was dead.

✳ ✳ ✳

Lady Anna arrived home to find Trenico waiting in the atrium.

"Let me help you with your cloak, Anna," he said.

She shrugged away his outstretched hand. Whenever Trenico was near those perfectly manicured hands hovered around her constantly, returning no matter how many times she brushed them off, as insistently annoying as a pair of flies.

"It's all right, Trenico, thank you."

"I can tell you've been to a perfumer's. The scents cling to your hair. The perfumes I gave you don't please?" He displayed a theatrical frown.

"I was choosing a gift for a friend." She remained in the atrium, hoping Trenico would leave and go about his business yet knowing he would not since she was his real business. "You're here to see father?"

"And you. Yes, I just arrived. So, who is this friend of yours? A mutual acquaintance? What is the occasion?"

"You don't know her, Trenico. She's getting married soon. That's something I will never do, as I was just telling John. He's just gone back to the palace now I am safely home."

"Your tutor? I would hope you had more of an escort than that, Anna, considering what almost happened to your father the other day."

"To hear the way people go on about that, you would think it was father who died rather than poor Dorotheus," Anna snapped.

"I just don't like to think of you out on those dangerous streets with only a eunuch for protection. Your father told me he had forbidden you to go out unless you had at least three servants to guard you. I would have been happy to do so too if you wished." A hand alit for an instant on her arm then departed. "It's fortunate you didn't run into difficulties."

"We only saw a dead man."

"You're jesting?" He looked at her, seeking confirmation.

"No, Trenico. John and I observed a corpse being carried off the docks by the Gourd's men."

"The docks? You were at the docks? A lady, and without a proper bodyguard?" Trenico looked shocked.

"In fact, we observed from the seawall so we were not actually on the docks. As to the other matter, John is quite capable of protecting me and I feel perfectly safe with him, Trenico."

"Anna, I must disagree. Your attitude toward this slave is quite improper. He's become your pet, I realize that, but still…I'll buy you a dove. That would be much more suitable as a companion. Or if you want—"

Trenico broke off. Opimius had emerged from his office.

"Trenico," Opimius said. "There you are. I thought you were late for our discussion. I see you've just been detained by my daughter."

His fond smile at them made Anna feel resentful.

"Why don't you both join me in my office?" Opimius suggested. "I'll have some refreshments brought, something warming." He beamed.

Anna began to unclasp her cloak. "No, thank you, father. I'm sure you have business to transact." She fixed Trenico in her gaze. "Besides, I would prefer other company right now."

Chapter Twenty

John appeared at Senator Opimius' house next morning, prepared to continue with Lady Anna's instruction. She surprised him by hurrying out of the servants' entrance before he could rap on the door.

"John. There's someone I want you to meet. We'll go immediately." She was shrouded in a heavy cloak.

"At this early hour, Lady Anna?"

"Who knows when we'll have another chance? Now, you recall the man I mentioned yesterday, Avis? The inventor? I had intended for us to visit him then, but of course we were distracted by that poor, dead man on the docks. Avis is the person we're going to see."

When John queried her about the reason for the unexpected excursion, Anna grew mysterious. He finally had to remind himself that it was not a slave's place to question orders given by his mistress, however flighty her apparent whim.

Anna did however expound on Avis' eccentric living arrangements as she led the way north along a wide thoroughfare that opened into a plaza near the Prosphorion harbor. It was the time of morning when the stark cries of circling seabirds had not yet been overcome by the rush and roar of humanity.

A path, so narrow that it could not be called an alley, ran between two warehouses facing the plaza. It led to the dwelling of Avis.

The brick sides of the four-story, octagonal tower were blank for the first three levels. A row of enormous windows circled the final floor. When lamps were lit inside at night the conical-roofed structure resembled a lighthouse. Constantinople-born mariners, noting a more earthy resemblance, had given the tower an obscene nickname which Lady Anna thought best not to mention to her companion.

She repeated, instead, its less scurrilous name. "They call this Avis' lantern," she smiled. "It's said that local sailors do not consider themselves truly home unless they can see its light from their ships."

John observed that its owner must have an inexhaustible supply of lamp oil.

"I don't know about that, but Avis is a night bird. He tends to work until dawn, so his lamps are lit almost as dependably as those of a real lighthouse."

"Then surely he won't be up this early?"

Lady Anna smiled. "I am hoping we'll catch him before he retires for the day."

From the base of the tower a staircase snaked up and around its sides to a platform perched in front of a door. The sound of birds singing and whistling reached their ears.

"A tower seems a strange place to keep an aviary," John observed as they climbed the creaking, splintered, wooden stairs. An updraft of wind from the docks below the seawall carried his words away into the leaden sky.

"At first glance, perhaps." Anna rapped at the door, which was opened almost immediately by the owner of the tower and provider of illumination to mariners.

"My dear lady! Such a pleasant surprise! How delightful! If you could just get inside quickly." Avis waved a hand, gently shooing back a sparrow heading toward freedom.

John and Anna stepped quickly into a white-washed room and Avis closed the door against the wind and smell of the sea.

"Who is your handsome friend. Lady Anna?" Avis asked. "A man with some taste and imagination, no doubt."

Anna colored slightly and introduced the two men without alluding to John's lowly rank.

John gave a small bow and murmured a polite greeting. The man seemed oddly familiar. Perhaps he had glimpsed him at the palace.

While Anna and Avis exchanged pleasantries John surveyed the room. One corner had been partitioned off, but otherwise its large expanse was filled with birds.

Birds flew around the high-ccilinged space, perched along the branches of trees growing in barrels and tubs, fed from piles of grain or fruit, their bright colors airborne jewels with one or two somber, dark-plumed birds making a gloomy contrast among them. John noted that while the fruit and grain available to the feathered residents was in copious supply, Avis' tunic was threadbare.

The birds' excited chattering sounded loud in a space which was bright despite the dark clouds outside since such light as entered the rows of windows around its perimeter was reflected and magnified by bone-white walls.

Anna and Avis finished their exchange. Anna strolled among the room's swooping denizens, a delighted smile on her face, oblivious to the occasional splattering of white which joined similar droppings on the floor.

"Be careful," Avis cautioned. "My servants will be up later to clean, but it can become rather slippery. Step into my study."

Avis' study was a tiny, walled-off space with an artificial ceiling. A many-paned window, large as that in a real lighthouse, presented a vertiginous view of the Golden Horn.

John's gaze was drawn not to the view, but rather to a table on which a thin, marble slab held the bones of two large, fan-like wings. Laid out in an arrangement he imagined echoed their natural placement, the bones were obviously in the final stages of being reattached to each other with thin, bronze wires. Several scalpels and probes lay between the slab and a platter holding a similar sized wing. The rest of their former owner was nowhere to be seen.

Most of the remaining space on the table was taken up by piles of codices and sheets of parchment scribbled with diagrams and calculations, onto which birds had dropped their own comments. Several empty cages and a small wooden carving of a raven sat below one window, next to a pair of boots and a chest.

"I see you find my scientific efforts of some interest." Avis sounded eager. "Do you know anything about our avian friends?"

John admitted that he did not.

"Except, perhaps, for enjoying a chicken for your evening meal now and then?" Avis chuckled. "Did you ever notice how remarkably tough their sinews can be? If only I could find something as strong."

Anna laid her hand affectionately on the man's arm. "How go your labors since I last visited? I see you have almost accomplished wiring the raven's wing together."

Their host nodded rapidly. "As you say. Once I have it entire again I think I shall be able to calculate how it bears such a large bird aloft. From there, who knows?" His voice trailed off wistfully.

Anna patted his arm reassuringly, but said nothing.

Avis insisted his unexpected visitors examine his drawings. They consisted mainly of minute renderings of wing articulations of various types of birds, doubtless drawn from life or, more accurately, from death. As sheet after sheet was displayed for their admiration and astonishment, John wondered if the man allowed his birds to die natural deaths, or if he hastened their ends as needed.

Avis opened the chest. "Here is something you haven't seen, Anna."

"How beautiful!" she exclaimed as he set a tiny, silver stork on his worktable.

"It belonged to my son." Avis caressed the bird's head tenderly. "It was a gift for his first birthday."

The world of sadness in the man's voice and eyes told John that the boy was gone from his father. Departed to seek his fortunes or gone forever? Anna's murmured condolences provided the answer.

Wiping tears from his faded blue eyes, Avis returned the bird to the chest. He walked over to a corner where a rough linen cloth concealed some object nearly the height of a man. "The last time you visited me, I believe I mentioned I had made a working model. I haven't tested it yet." Avis' voice wavered. "Although it is my intent to do so as soon as I have gone over all the calculations and measurements one more time."

Avis waved away a raven that had just found its way into the study, and then pulled the cloth off to reveal what was unmistakably a set of artificial wings. They were crude compared to the bones he had been wiring together. Closer examination revealed that they were constructed of thin, wooden slats, their joints held together with twists of wire. Silk, stretched taut, covered the upper surface. On the undersides, at the length of an arm, were two loops.

Avis proceeded to describe the mechanics of his invention, his face beaming. John heard little of it. He suddenly remembered where he had seen Avis.

He was the man with whom he had collided while pursuing Victor into Viator's warehouse.

❋ ❋ ❋

"It's a terribly sad story, John," Anna said when she and John had left the tower. "Avis told me he once lived on the coast not far from the city. He was quite well-to-do then and owned more than one villa. That was many, many amphorae of lamp oil ago, as he put it."

"He had a son, one now dead?" John inquired.

"Yes. This son was a scholar and very interested in the old mythologies. Harmless enough in itself, but unfortunately it seems that eventually he took the notion to fly."

"Like Icarus?"

"Like Icarus," Anna confirmed. "So he constructed some sort of device, perhaps with wax and feathers as is related in the ancient story, and jumped off the cliffs near his father's estate. He paid for his attempt with his life. After that, his father took the name of Avis and has devoted most of his wealth and all of his time to studying birds and their method of flight. His quest has taken over four decades now."

She sighed. "Avis persists, not because he wants to be the first man to soar into the sky, but rather because it was a passion with his son. By carrying on with the work he keeps his son's memory alive and the boy close to him. Besides, he says, he would prefer to think the boy had not died in vain."

They had come to a spot where a gap in the warehouses allowed a view across the Golden Horn. Anna leaned on the seawall and gazed toward the tiny buildings and trees visible on the far shore.

John stood beside her. "To give up one's life to achieve what anyone can see is impossible seems a useless death, Lady Anna."

"Is a thing impossible just because all the world insists it is?"

He observed that surely flying was the province of birds.

"You think we are not the equals of those gulls circling over the water?" She paused. "Beyond that, what would Avis be without his quest?" she went on. "Just another self-indulgent, wealthy man. One of the sort who spend their lives scrambling over one another for money or power, like quarreling dogs. And whichever wins out, what is accomplished? The victor is still just a dog."

John made no reply.

Anna glanced up at him. "Is there any work of man which did not begin as nothing more than an idea? How can someone who dreams of flying be of lesser worth than one who has no dreams? I try to believe all things are possible."

John looked away from her solemn gaze. Clearly Lady Anna had intended the visit to Avis to be instructional or inspirational. Just as clearly, a slave could not throw off his shackles any more easily than a free citizen could jump into the air and take flight. Anna's inappropriate interest in him was a danger to both of them.

"Do you believe Avis will ever try out that contraption he showed us?" John finally asked.

"Yes, I do, John," Anna replied softly. "When Avis is ready to go to join his son, then he will strap on his wings."

Chapter Twenty-One

John found Felix lounging on a bench set under a stand of pines overlooking the palace's seawall. Afternoon sunlight glittered on the restless water.

Felix looked around at the sound of approaching boot steps. "Am I late for our meeting? Or is there yet more trouble brewing? It's bad enough Viator managed to escape us."

"I'm early," John replied. "I asked at the barracks where I might find you. Senator Opimius just relieved me of my tutoring duties."

Felix scratched the stubble on his jaw. It had not grown enough to conceal the cut and the angry bruise where the snowball had hit. The jaw was obviously too tender to withstand the ministrations of a razor. "That will be trouble for both of us once Justinian finds out. You won't make much of a spy, peering in through the senator's windows.

What did you do to bring this calamity down on us? Who did you hit?"

"Nobody."

"Then why did Opimius dismiss you?"

"He somehow got the notion I was in the habit of escorting Anna on tours of the docks. From that he deduced I probably took her around various seedy tenements and dark alleyways."

"Somehow?" Felix spit over the seawall. "You mean someone's been putting poison in his ears!"

John was surprised at his reluctant partner's genuine anger.

As soon as John and Anna had returned from visiting Avis that morning he'd sensed something was awry. No one looked in his direction or offered the usual greetings as they passed through the kitchen.

Opimius was pacing the atrium. The senator's features were livid with anger, but he did not speak until Anna had gone into her study.

"John," he said without preamble. "I will no longer require your attendance here. You will leave my house immediately. Furthermore, do not ever attempt to return or to contact my daughter again."

"Senator Opimius...What...?" Had Opimius deduced that Justinian might have sent John to spy on him? Was his anger because he had something to conceal? Those had been John's first confused thoughts. Then Opimius, unable to contain his rage, began thundering at him about his gross negligence.

"You put my daughter in harm's way! Didn't you hear me when I told her she was no longer to go about the streets with you? And taking her to the docks. The docks! Wasn't there some handy den of cutthroats you could have introduced her to while you were at it? Or a riot? You should know how she romanticizes everything! Trying to impress her, were you? Oh, I'm sure she thought it was a great adventure. Where's your sense? I'd have said you were thinking with your gonads if you had any! Don't even bother trying to deny it! Trenico told me everything."

John had said nothing. How could he defend himself? Call the senator's friend Trenico a liar? A slave's word against that of an aristocrat? It would only have made the situation worse.

Felix was staring out to sea. "Do you ever think of Greece?"

It struck John as a strange question. "I try not to."

"It's been a long time since I was in Germania. Sometimes I wonder if I'll ever see it again. Perhaps we were barbaric, but at least we didn't grow villains as thick on the ground as they are here. If you ask me there are as many dangers at court as in the city streets. I wouldn't have chosen to work with you, but I know you wouldn't subject the Lady Anna to danger."

John stared out over the dancing swells with less enthusiasm than his companion. He did not care for deep water.

Felix looked pensive. He fingered his jaw. He was almost able to grasp the stubble growing there. "It's good for thinking, tugging at whiskers. Perhaps I'll keep them."

"What is it you're thinking about?"

Felix heaved himself off the bench. "Viator. Now that he's dead we can catch up to him. Gaius once told me that those who die in the streets or on the docks are usually taken to the hospice."

❋ ❋ ❋

The Hospice of Samsun was even more crowded than on their initial visit. Extra pallets were crammed into each of its already cramped rooms. Without exception the staff looked ill themselves. Wan and harried, they scurried along corridors rendered nearly impassable by patients lying on the soiled floor. The stench of urine burned the nostrils.

Inquiries for Gaius led them to a room where the odor of herbs emanating from shelves that occupied one wall masked the general stink. The physician reclined in a corner, which might have seemed inexplicable except for the presence of the wine jug next to him.

Felix muttered a curse. "He's drunk!" He tapped Gaius' side with the dirty toe of his boot.

Gaius awoke and muttered groggily. "Yes, yes, right away. Is the baby's head visible yet?" Blood-shot eyes peered up at them. "Just taking a little break. I need one every now and then. Haven't been out of this place in a week."

"Gaius, we must talk to you," Felix said loudly.

The stout physician winced and sat up.

"Be good enough to talk more quietly, Felix," he muttered. "The Furies are fighting a battle in my head and I can scarcely see straight. I've got to deliver a beggar's baby any instant."

"You'll need steady hands for that," John observed, helping him up.

"And probably plenty of opiate as well. The mother's just a child. We're starting to run out, but what can you expect?" Gaius picked up his wine jug and shook his head ruefully over its emptiness.

"We're here to ask about a man named Viator," Felix began. "He's dead already, not one of your patients. He was found at the docks so I'm betting he was brought here." He described the man briefly.

Gaius let out a morbid chuckle. "Ah, that's Viator, is it? Yes, he's here. Who could forget someone that size? The Gourd's men didn't tell me who he was, only that their master wanted to know what killed him. They also ordered that anyone who came to claim the body should be detained."

Gaius led them along the corridor, treading unsteadily between the arms and legs splayed in their path. They descended two flights of stairs, ducked through a low brick archway, and then into a cavernous room. Gaius clumsily struck a light to the lamp sitting on a sweating stone ledge beside its door.

Felix let out a grunt of surprise. The icy place was a barracks for the dead. A score of bodies reposed on marble slabs. Only a few were decently covered.

"We're still hosting some of the guests sent here by the Gourd after that business at the Strategion," Gaius said. Evidently the freezing air had somewhat revived him.

He patted the closest chunk of stone. "These were part of a defective shipment, donated to us by none other than Viator. That's why I was chuckling. I wager he never thought he'd end up laid out on one of them. Apparently the marble was destined for a private bath house at the palace. Now it serves a humbler class."

He drew a sheet back from the face of an enormous mound.

"That's him," Felix said. "What did the Gourd's men say?"

"Nothing much. They'd dragged him out of the water. Mind you, he wasn't drowned, but stabbed in the back. I can understand that. Who'd attack a man this size from the front? I'd say it was a robbery. He's well known and reputed to be wealthy."

"His son hasn't claimed the body?" John put in.

"No. If he has a son, he had better hurry up, otherwise his father will be buried by strangers tomorrow. I don't expect to see him. He would be here by now if he were going to come at all."

Back upstairs they were greeted by the wail of a child. The thin sound crept into the higher register and then ended abruptly.

"Could that be the infant you're supposed to be delivering?" Felix inquired.

Gaius shook his head. "No. It's a little girl brought in this morning. An accident. Dislocated shoulder. One of my assistants has been trying to manipulate it back into place. Let's hope she's lost consciousness this time so he can get the job done properly. Now I must go and see how my pregnant patient is doing. You're reporting back to the Gourd, I imagine. Tell him I will send him an official report on the matter of Viator as soon as I run out of patients to treat."

❋ ❋ ❋

The Prefect's offices were located in the drab, seemingly endless administrative warrens that formed as much a part of the Great Palace complex as its lavish dining and reception halls, gardens, and luxurious private residences. Anyone traversing its anonymous hallways might be traveling to any of a hundred destinations on the palace grounds. As it happened, John and Felix caught sight of Trenico just as he emerged from the Prefect's office.

The aristocrat turned smartly on his heel and veered away down the corridor. From his quick glimpse, John thought Trenico looked exceptionally startled.

A strapping guard eyed them coldly as they entered the outer office until a brief order from Felix in the name of the emperor led to an announcement of their presence.

The doorway leading into the Prefect's inner chambers was open and the man stamped out, wiping his hands on his shirt. He was in a foul mood, which turned fouler still after he impatiently heard their information concerning the cause of Viator's death.

"Now you've told me, I expect Gaius won't bother putting kalamos to parchment," he rumbled. "I agree with him. It was obviously a robbery, but that won't stop fools from wagging their tongues about it. Let me catch them at it and I'll see they have the wag yanked out of them on the spot."

John wondered why the Gourd would care if the death of Viator were laid at his door. Wouldn't such rumors enhance the ruthless reputation he cultivated so assiduously?

"If you hadn't blundered at apprehending the man when he was right within your grasp," Theodotus went on, "he would have told us everything by now, including where Hypatius' murderer is hiding."

"Even though the man suspected is his son?" Felix said.

The Prefect laughed. "Believe me, he would have revealed all we wanted to know, son or not. However, since you are here and I have been instructed to make use of your services. I have a new task for you. One of my informants tells me that some Blues are planning to make trouble in the Augustaion tonight. They never learn their lesson, do they? But I have a little surprise for them. My men will be hidden around the area to grab them as soon as they start assembling, before they even know what's happening. Find yourselves a good hiding place near the Augustaion. One of those foul alleys would be ideal. Just make certain you don't get into conversation with any of those kind-hearted ladies who inhabit so many of them." His leer was most unpleasant.

"What exactly will be our role?" Felix's tone was crisp.

Theodotus tilted his misshapen head to one side and looked at Felix with undisguised contempt. "Your role? Why, simply to wait. When the time comes, fight and, if need be, help capture any stragglers who attempt to escape. You can manage that, can't you? Yes, I'm sure you can. This is an assignment even you two can't fail at."

Chapter Twenty-Two

Anna stood in the garden behind her father's house, munching a fig as she talked to Trenico.

"Epic poetry is generally much more to my taste than the romantic vapidities of certain of our current poets," she said firmly.

Trenico frowned. "I am sorry indeed to hear that, Anna, since some of their writings are most beautiful. Often carnal in nature, I admit, but is not that part of romantic love?"

Anna looked at him keenly. "True enough, but whining about it won't get you what you want, will it? Wouldn't you prefer to win love rather than pity?"

"Perhaps we should go inside? It's chilly out here this morning. Surely you've had more than enough fresh air by now?"

"Don't you find it invigorating? Look how the ice shines on that poor Cupid on the fountain! Isn't it beautiful?"

"Your manner toward me has been even icier, Anna, and frankly I do not find that beautiful at all."

Anna looked around the garden. It was crammed with statuary and flagstone paths, with a tiny bath house fronted by two small columns half hidden behind a screen of pruned bushes. The garden was sizeable, especially considering the value of land in the crowded capital.

"The other morning I saw a stork standing in the fountain," she mused. "Imagine, all those thousands of storks we saw flying along the Bosporos a few months ago, yet this one somehow lost its way. Or perhaps it just chose not to follow the others."

Trenico fumbled inside his cloak. "If you insist on remaining out here, then please allow me to give you this small gift of affection before I leave. Perhaps you'll feel warmer toward me."

He held out a delicate golden chain from which hung a gold pendant.

Anna tossed the remains of her fig into a flowerbed filled with withered brown stalks and took the necklace.

"I see that the pendant is engraved with a rose. Interesting! That is Venus' sacred flower as well as my own favorite bloom. Well, well, I'm surprised at you. Was this intended as a love charm by any chance?"

Trenico looked surprised. "How did you...?"

Anna handed back the necklace. "One of the servants has the same charm. It's caused many heated arguments in the kitchen between her and her rival for the fellow's affections."

"One of your servants has an identical necklace?"

"It's essentially the same except that the pendant is pottery and hangs on a leather thong rather than a gold chain."

"But that's impossible! Where did she get it from?"

"Apparently it was sold to her by one of the Gourd's servants. As to what she paid for it, I didn't ask the price. Why?"

Trenico's voice shook with rage and mortification. "The Prefect assured me that he had commissioned this necklace especially for me. Given the speed with which it was created, he charged me extra!"

"I'm flattered you would go to such trouble," Anna replied calmly.

"I must apologize, Anna," Trenico said. "I don't put much faith in magick, but he assured me...and you can see how, when you insist on rejecting my protestations...I was thinking just a gentle nudge in the direction we all wish to go and which even you, certainly—"

"As I said, I'm flattered, but I meant it when I told you I have no romantic interest in you, Trenico. I trust you will forgive my bluntness."

Trenico was silent. His expression boded ill for his next discussion with the Gourd.

"It's interesting that you should mention magick," Anna said, breaking the ensuing awkward silence. "One way or another lately I've been hearing quite a lot about the Gourd's expertise. I also hear rumors that his interest in the topic extends in directions beyond demonstrating magick or assisting the romantically frustrated."

Trenico sullenly asked for details.

"According to the servant I mentioned, when she went to buy the necklace she was admitted into the Gourd's study."

"This is monstrous!" Trenico burst out. "I must inform him immediately that his servants are allowing strangers into his house!"

Anna smiled slightly, gazing dreamily toward the Cupid whose ice-glazed wings were beginning to drip as sunlight slanted into the garden, warming the air. "Your necklace closely resembles Harmonia's! Yes, the Gourd's servant got it out of a large, locked cupboard. Naturally he knew where the key was, and while its door was open, she saw a number of pots and flasks on the shelves. Some were glass, she said, so she could see they contained potions. Magick potions, no doubt. Some held different colored powders and unguents, that sort of thing. And beyond that, she says she's heard that the Gourd can provide poisons."

"A common slander," Trenico broke in uncomfortably. "And if it comes to it, anyone can find someone selling poison if they're really determined. So they say—I have no personal experience of it myself."

"Fortuna has certainly smiled on you then, since you spend so much time at court. Luckily, there are usually antidotes if one acts swiftly enough. On the other hand, there's no antidote to a well-placed sharp blade, is there?"

Trenico had grown visibly angrier during her comments and now threw caution to the winds. "Anna, it would be best if you were more cautious in your speech. Rumors swirl around the court like seagulls at the fish seller's stall. I worry sometimes that someone will put a nasty word or two about your father into Justinian's ear. You don't want to inadvertently help bring official disfavor on him, or even official attention."

"Nonsense, Trenico. My father has no grievance with Justinian."

"Look upon it as good advice, Anna. And let me add that for his sake it might also be wise for you to become more, shall we say, inclined to consider my petitions."

"If I wanted your advice, I would ask for it," Anna snapped. "As to your last remark, kindly explain what you mean or leave. Blackmail is despicable, however you disguise it."

"Anna, please. Consider what I have said of my affection for you." He offered the necklace again.

"I'm not influenced by your love charm, Trenico, but you need not take it as a personal affront. As I explained, I am one who will never marry. Perhaps I'm like that stork I saw in the fountain, destined not to follow the flock."

Trenico closed his fist over his spurned gift. "Destined to freeze to death alone, you mean."

Chapter Twenty-Three

"I've kept watch at the ends of the empire, in forests and deserts. I've never been as uncomfortable as I am right now," Felix grumbled.

He and John squatted just inside the mouth of an alley not far from the Augustaion in accordance with the City Prefect's instructions. They had found a place of concealment behind a heap of broken statuary spilling out into the street. In the darkness, their own shadowy forms merged with broken limbs and disembodied heads jutting from the marble debris.

John shivered. He knew if there were sufficient light he would see his fingers to be as pallid as those of the marble hand partially blocking his view of the Mese. Felix was right. The foul smelling man-made ravine they had chosen for their watch was more unpleasant than any outpost he'd known as a mercenary.

Out on the Mese, little stirred but the flames of torches set in front of businesses, their flickering light a feeble competitor to the sharp-edged moonlight flooding the wide thoroughfare. An occasional wail of a baby or the howl of a dog cut through the night air. Now and then a cart rumbled by, but otherwise the street was deserted.

A hideous yowl startled both men. They leapt to their feet, blades out.

It was merely a couple of feral cats confronting each other. A large, flabby, black cat enthroned on a marble head raised its paw menacingly at a scrawny, striped adversary before launching itself to the attack. The cats rolled down the marble pile in a mewling ball of fury before abandoning the argument and racing away in opposite directions.

Felix muttered an oath or two as he took a few paces up and down the alley. "Were those the rioters we're expecting? Perhaps the real ones have suddenly found their senses and decided to stay home to drink wine and plan glorious feats of arms instead."

"That's a notion that holds a great deal of attraction right now." John shifted his position to one less punishing to his lean flanks and found himself staring momentarily into the empty eyes of a discarded philosopher.

Felix peered out into the moonlit thoroughfare. "I don't like this. It makes the hair on my neck feel strange. Something peculiar is going on." He glanced over his shoulder at the pile of shattered marble bodies. "This hiding place doesn't help much either. They say that the Gourd can conjure up demons."

It wasn't the first time Felix had mentioned demons. "The Gourd's demons are no more real than that fraudulent boiling pitch, and I've explained the trick behind that." John slapped the hilt of the sword he had been given for the night's watch. "If any so-called demons appear this will prove the lie, you'll see."

"Big words from a—" Felix hesitated "—a tutor. I wish I could be as confident as you are in the military skills you claim."

A window creaked open above them and an irate voice demanded to know why they were disturbing honest workers at that time of night.

John remained silent. Felix's talk of demons was nonsense, yet he had to admit to himself he could not quite shake off the feeling that they were being observed. Perhaps one of the denizens of the tenement building towering above them was peering down through a cracked shutter.

The night passed, as sleepless nights do, in stretches of dark tedium when it was impossible to gauge whether time was flying or crawling by. Then, when it seemed dawn must still be hours away, the sky suddenly lit to gray and John wondered if he had dozed at his post.

As the city began to stir, ox carts rumbled down the Mese. The shouts of their drivers echoed loudly enough to wake late sleepers. Shop owners unshuttered their premises and swept their porticoes, adding to drifts of refuse already in evidence in the gutters. Beggars, whose arrival always preceded shoppers, searched for their breakfasts among the scraps.

"It looks as if the Gourd's demons decided to stay home after all. So have the Blues." Felix rubbed tired eyes. "Or else his informants are singularly ill informed. This must have been the quietest night we've had for weeks. Let's turn our report in and then get something to eat. After that, I think I'll visit the baths and soak some warmth back into my bones."

They emerged into growing daylight.

And were confronted by two men with drawn swords.

Their clothing and hairstyles proclaimed their affiliation with the Blues. But why, John wondered, would Blues choose to attack men carrying weapons in a street filled with shopkeepers wielding brooms? He glanced at Felix and the excubitor gave a slight nod. Both men leapt forward and sideways.

The tallest of their assailants pivoted on his heel as he brought his weapon up sharply, slicing through John's cloak and drawing blood. A splotch of red blossomed on John's tunic. He stepped inside the other man's reach, stabbing straight forward.

The tall Blue was taken by surprise. He must have expected his victim to draw back. A man who isn't used to fighting will always recoil at the first appearance of blood.

John's blade sank into flesh. The man shrieked.

Several beggars crowded in a nearby doorway shouted gleeful encouragement. This was entertainment superior to any ordinary street-players' antics.

John heard one of the beggars shout, "My boots on the Blue!"

Drawing on a well of black rage, John stabbed again. This time he was careless. This time his opponent recognized he was up against a fighter and counter-attacked. Fire blazed across John's chest once more. Now he could feel blood running down over his stomach in hot rivulets. He welcomed the pain, as he welcomed the fight. This was something with which he could come to grips.

His opponent stepped backward to gain more room to maneuver. The move brought him too close to the beggars. One of the ragged wagerers reached out a skinny arm and gave the Blue a shove in the back. Caught off guard, the man stumbled forward. John kicked his feet out from beneath him.

John's attacker fell face down and there he died.

The beggar who had just lost his boots grumbled obscenely at Fortuna to the raucous laughter of his fellow wagerers.

John looked around, seeking Felix. The excubitor was gazing down at the body of his own opponent. His glum expression was not that of a man who has just saved his own life.

"That was a mistake, John," he said. "We should have kept one alive. I'd like to know whose men these are and whose orders they were trying to carry out. They weren't street thugs. They fought like military men, or trained assassins. So why were they dressed like Blues?" He raised his gaze from the body to give John an appraising look. "My guess is they planned to dispatch you quickly and then team up to kill me. I would've done the same. I caught just a glimpse. You stab straight ahead. The proper technique—"

"Mithra!" John's sudden exclamation cut him short.

Two more Blues had appeared, seemingly from nowhere.

John whirled away from the blow directed at him by one of the onrushing figures. The blade missed, but the attacker's shoulder slammed into him and John toppled onto his back into a half frozen, muddy puddle. His head hit the ground.

Through a hazy mist, he saw a grinning figure approaching, sword raised. He told himself to move, but his body might have been made of stone.

Dimly he became aware of a sound. A cart, grinding to a halt. The wheel stopped less than an arm's breadth from his head.

As the sword descended John finally forced himself to roll sideways under the cart. The blade smacked harmlessly against a wooden wheel.

As John's head cleared he saw that the cart driver had leapt down from his seat and was thrusting a long-handled pitchfork at John's attacker.

The driver's act of goodwill would certainly have been suicidal were it not that several shopkeepers, perhaps remembering the Christian story of the Good Samaritan, had joined in the fray. They were better armed than the driver, for there wasn't a merchant in the city who didn't keep a weapon close to hand. It was obvious that they relished the opportunity to strike back. Even the cautious shop assistant they had recently interviewed abandoned his duties in the grocer's emporium across the Mese to join in, vigorously wielding a large club.

Unfortunately the battle originally begun against the newly arrived Blues was now degenerating into a senseless melee as several beggars took their opportunity to pilfer items from the deserted shops. When challenged, they fought back. A few wielded strange weapons, marble limbs snatched from the heap in the alley, so that here one swung a length of arm, and there another used a large foot and ankle as a club.

John looked around for the second pair of Blues, but did not see them. He forced his way though the growing mob to Felix.

"The bastards got away!" Felix shouted. He glared around, taking in the strangely armed beggars. "Well, I've heard of hand to hand combat before, but never seen it quite so literally."

"Sirs! Sirs! Please! Over here!"

It took John an instant to locate the source of the cries. A gray-headed man knelt beside the bleeding cart driver.

"He's badly wounded!" The man was so distressed he was in tears.

One glance and John could see the driver was doomed by a stomach wound too deep for any hope of survival.

Felix bent down to the cart driver. "You helped save us," he told him. "Now you're off to the hospice. They'll take care of you."

The carter's hands groped toward his horrific injury. John blocked them gently. The man's eyes were bright with fear. He must have sensed he would not be driving home again.

A couple of men lifted him onto his cart and another jumped up onto its seat. As he was driven away the carter shook his fist feebly and began to shriek at the sky.

"What reward is this for a Christian act?" he cried in a fading voice, going on to ask why He paid no attention to His loyal servants. For that matter, what about his family, why must they too suffer because he had tried to act as a decent Christian should?

The man who had been attempting to aid the carter shook his head sadly without a word. The grocer's assistant, heeding the call of commerce and apparently reluctant to lose a customer, took the man's arm and escorted him back to the shop as the crowd dispersed and drifted away.

"It's true enough from that carter's point of view," Felix muttered. He dolefully examined his knuckles, which were bleeding profusely. "Let's hope our earthly ruler is a bit more attentive to the welfare of us loyal servants."

Chapter Twenty-Four

"I hear that Senator Opimius has relieved you of your duties, John." Justinian was sitting up in his bed. Theodora perched on its edge.

The stuffy sick room was so hot a sheen of sweat had formed on the backs of John's hands as soon as he entered.

"That is so, Excellency," John replied.

"You weren't neglecting your duties on my account?"

"I was accused of placing Lady Anna in danger, something I would never do."

"Who leveled this charge?"

"It was a misunderstanding."

Theodora pushed a strand of hair away from Justinian's forehead. The man so often spoken of as the future emperor looked as if his future might be too short to include an ascent to the throne. There was no animation in his puffy face and his hands lay motionless on the sheet, suggesting they were too heavy to lift. "Do you believe this was the real reason you were asked to leave the household?"

"I was given no other reason."

"I see. You noticed nothing unusual at the senator's house these last few days?"

John shook his head.

"What visitors did Opimius have?" Theodora put in.

"I happened to see Trenico and Senator Aurelius. I only spent a few hours there each day. I didn't see everyone who visited."

"And what of Hypatius' murder?" asked Justinian. "That is why I summoned you here. Is there any progress to report?"

John described the investigations he and Felix had made.

"You have certainly been working diligently," Justinian observed.

"But have learnt nothing," Theodora pointed out.

"The culprit might well have been the large Blue Felix and I pursued. The man's father, as I reported, has just been killed."

Justinian closed his eyes and exhaled raggedly.

Theodora glared at John. "Our enemies seek to tie Justinian to these murdering Blues. You have discovered nothing to contradict their claims. Clearly, if the son is the murderer, he was paid by someone. Once he is apprehended he will tell us his employer's name. Then there will be no way to sully Justinian by linking him to Hypatius' death."

John wondered how Theodora could be so certain, but said nothing.

Nevertheless, Theodora answered the unspoken question. "Why was his father murdered? It is my opinion that, just as you were misled by their similar size, so the assassin mistook the older man for his son. Whoever hired the son would wish to be certain he is not captured and forced to talk. Obviously he confused one for the other."

Theodora wiped Justinian's damp forehead with a corner of his coverlet. The sick man's eyes remained shut. John thought he had lapsed into sleep until his lips moved and he spoke again in a voice barely above a whisper. "With every passing day these conspirators gain new allies. You must learn the truth before they strike out at me publicly with their lies."

"Yes, Excellency."

Did Justinian's hand stir? Was John being dismissed?

"One last matter I must report," John went on quickly. "Felix and I were attacked by men who appeared to be Blues, but, I believe, were in reality professional assassins. If so, it is proof that someone is using the faction to carry out or cover up their own misdeeds."

Justinian made no reply. It appeared he really had fallen into sleep or unconsciousness.

Theodora indicated that the audience had ended. John bowed and began to back away toward the door.

"Wait, slave! You have forgotten to pay your respects. Justinian may be careless about these matters of etiquette, but I am not."

For an instant John was not certain what she meant. Then he recalled his initial audience with the pair. As his face grew hot, he prostrated himself in a perfunctory manner, hardly touching the floor before he began to rise.

He felt the toe of Theodora's slipper on his shoulder.

"Don't be in such a hurry," she murmured. The smell of her heavy perfume did not quite mask the more common smell of sweat. "Slaves who are required to speak to their superiors sometimes forget their proper place. That can be dangerous."

The slipper left John's shoulder, moved roughly along his cheek, and came to rest on the carpet directly in front of his face. It was as small as a child's slipper, purple and decorated by tiny flowers formed of gold stitchery with amethyst centers.

"Why are you hesitating?" Theodora asked. "I should think the lips of a eunuch would rejoice to touch any part of a woman."

※ ※ ※

John welcomed the clean, cold air of the garden outside the Hormisdas Palace. He tried to calm his rage by concentrating on the task facing him. He wished now that he were working for Justin or for that matter anyone other than the insolent actress who appeared destined to be empress. For it seemed to him he was working for her as much as for Justinian.

He forced his mind away from his recent humiliation, toward the knotty puzzle with which he was wrestling. Was Victor indeed the murderer, and if he was, had he been hired to carry out the job? He had fled with his father and so, John thought, it was likely he had died with his father, but his body had yet to be recovered.

John was still pondering as he arrived at his quarters.

There he spotted something lying on his pallet. His fists clenched as he remembered the incident of the crown.

Then he saw it was a scrap of neatly folded parchment. The well-formed, bold writing declaring him to be the recipient was recognizable at five paces as that of Lady Anna.

She had written the note in Persian, perhaps to protect the contents from curious eyes. Trenico, she stated, had been insinuating that it would be best for both her and her father if she acceded to his marriage requests. Furthermore, she deduced from a comment that her father had let drop, that Trenico had been filling the senator's ears with slanders about John.

"If you need to see me," she concluded, "go to the servants' entrance and ask for the cook, whom I have instructed to bring me word should you appear."

John turned the parchment over. Not only had Anna written the note in a foreign language but she had also used a discarded exercise. A further precaution? To disguise its real function as a message of warning?

He glanced over it. It was a scribbled list of verbs and in one corner she had written out some brief verses.

Copied from a work John had not seen or were they of her own composition?

Beloved, the dark wells of your loving eyes
Haunt me in our bower by the fountain
Oh! That I might feel your breath upon my face
Sweet as honey, soft as moonlight, fragrant
    as roses

Beloved, I sicken as the waning moon
As is the lot of women, I weep, I mourn
Oh! That I might feel your heart on mine
Strong....

For a lady to send such a thing to a slave...it was unthinkable. He was afraid for her. What if it had fallen into the wrong hands? Worse, since she had had a word with the cook, by now every servant in Opimius' house knew about the arrangement. And Opimius? Perhaps not. The master was often the last to know what went on in the household.

John shredded the note.

He was angry with Anna for being so foolish. That was nothing compared to his blinding fury toward Trenico. It was Trenico, after all, who had forced her to write the ill-advised note by his threats and lies.

John stormed from the building. It wasn't long before he arrived at the Baths of Zeuxippos. Trenico seemed to spend half his time there, Anna had said. He would confront him immediately.

Confront?

What could he say?

He could not think clearly.

Perhaps he would simply kill the man, hold that sneering face under the water in the caldarium until his lying breath had stopped forever and could no longer poison the air. Soldiers died to win a field at the empire's edge, some muddy, rock-strewn stretch of land an emperor wouldn't consider fit for gracing with a latrine for his servants. Would it be so senseless to sacrifice his own life to save a lady from being forced to submit to a man like Trenico?

As John strode through the entrance to the baths he was aware that people, looking alarmed, ducked out of his path. The attendant cringed as he took John's admission fee. John realized his face had settled into the rictus of the battlefield, the terrible snarl that so much resembled the grimaces on the frozen faces of the dead.

He stopped in the courtyard and tried to compose himself. From a nearby lecture hall a monotonous voice recited what sounded like a homily from John Chrysostum, he of the golden tongue. Unfortunately, this particular speaker had a tongue of lead.

John resumed walking. He passed by shops selling oils for the limbs, and then the baths' library. Its attendant, John knew, fought an endless battle to prevent his scrolls and codices being ruined by bathers' damp hands. He did not see many people. There seemed to be as many statues in the building's hallways as patrons.

He had managed to bring his temper under control by the time he turned down a wide corridor lined with arched doorways from which issued clouds of steam. These were the private baths. Anyone who saw him would have thought he was merely a servant, here to assist his master.

John was no longer certain why he had come here. He continued walking, glancing through the archways toward circular baths in which bathers sat or stood, in steamy waist-high water, sluicing themselves, laughing, talking.

He stopped abruptly and moved closer to the nearest opening.

A shaft of light dropped through the roiling steam from a window in the dome, providing illumination. On the steps up to the bath, a few busts and the sculptured figure of a nymph sat on pedestals, partly obscuring the bathers. John recognized one.

Trenico.

There were six men in all, three of whom John did not know. Two others, however, were familiar to him. One was Senator Opimius. Joking with him was the merchant he and Felix had interviewed—Tryphon, who had only recently told his interrogators that he was unacquainted with Opimius.

Chapter Twenty-Five

"I wouldn't be quick to draw conclusions," said Felix. "Why should a rich man like Tryphon be truthful with the likes of us, anyway? I would be more surprised if there were two rich and powerful men in this city who never met at the baths."

"You're right," John replied. "Yet it still makes me uneasy."

At John's suggestion they had returned to the Hospice of Samsun. Victor had not claimed his father's body. John was not surprised. Now he and Felix followed Gaius, allowing him to clear a path through the teeming corridors.

"Those assassins the Gourd sent after us, John, they're what should make you uneasy," Felix said quietly as they trailed some distance behind Gaius.

"I agree, but I'm not so certain they were the Gourd's men."

"Isn't it obvious? He's tired of having us strapped to his back. We may just be in his way, but, then again, he might have designs on the throne. He might be formulating a plan to take over, at the appropriate time. He's popular with many. He has a force of men in the city. He wouldn't want either Justin or Justinian to know."

"Consider this," John countered. "Justinian learned that Opimius had dismissed me before I told him."

"Is that surprising? But what are you saying? You think Justinian wants to do away with you because you're of no real use anymore? Or perhaps because Opimius suspects you were a spy?"

"Was I a spy?"

Felix laughed bitterly. "Who can say for certain? We're actors in someone else's play. We're reading our lines, but we haven't yet seen the last page. Let's hope it isn't a tragedy."

Gaius interrupted. "There he is."

The doorkeeper they sought was spooning porridge into the toothless mouth of another patient, a being so ancient and withered it appeared as sexless as an infant.

"Demetrios is leaving this afternoon." Gaius gestured for the doorkeeper to join them in the corridor. "He's as tough as an old leather boot. He wanted to help out for a while before he left."

"And happy to do so," Demetrios said. "My own small contribution to the hospice. I wish I could do more."

"So do I," muttered Gaius, who hurried away, as overworked as ever. At least on this day, John noticed, he looked steady on his feet.

"Perhaps you can assist us also." Felix looked sternly at Demetrios.

"I'll try, sir, but I don't think I have anything more to tell you even though I've thought about it a fair bit since we spoke."

"If you could describe once more exactly what happened before Hypatius' murder?"

The man obliged, relating again the scene he had witnessed in the Great Church, the screaming and confusion, how the Blues had rushed out, wounding him on their way. In the end, he added nothing useful to what he had said during their previous conversation.

They were turning to leave when Demetrios laid a skeletal hand on John's arm.

"Sir, I have offered prayers that those murderers are brought to justice, but I begin to wonder if they will ever pay for their crime. After my stay here, ashamed as I am to admit it, I have begun to question whether there is justice in this life at all."

John observed that while the thought might be shocking it was perfectly understandable. "Yet isn't the justice we all seek more likely to be found in the next life rather than this one?"

"Spoken like a good Christian, sir. No, it isn't for us to question the ways of the Lord and yet.... Did the physician mention that poor cart driver? Isaakios? He helped to rescue a couple of courtiers, so it's said. What men from the palace were doing out on the streets at dawn...something unmentionable I suppose. He was stabbed for his pains, so he was, and died only this morning."

"I am sorry to hear that." John glanced at Felix, who muttered something under his breath.

"And," continued Demetrios, "I must tell you that the man's last words were for his family. He was afraid his cart would not be given to them and they would starve in the streets. If you could—"

"I will ask Gaius to make certain that it is sent to them immediately, if it has not already gone," John promised. It struck him that when the Lord was not quick enough to grant the wishes of His followers they were quick to turn their eyes to anyone from the palace. "You seem to have spent a lot of time talking to people during your stay here, Demetrios."

"Not talking. Listening. It is a skill I have learned in my regular work. A doorkeeper's job is not boring at all if he learns to listen well."

The man stopped abruptly, then blurted out, "There's evil abroad in this city. Pure evil. This Isaakios was a regular worshipper at the Great Church. A humble cart driver, but generous in his way. When Hypatius presented the church with his gift, it was Isaakios who hauled it from the sculptor's studio to the church free of charge. As a charitable gesture, you understand, even though he was one who could ill afford to give his labor for nothing, what with a large family to support. The family he has left behind. You will see about his cart?"

John reassured Demetrios that he would do so, but his thoughts were elsewhere.

"Thank you, sirs. I was hoping that you would help. Those from the palace wield much more power than the common person. They say that even the slaves there eat from gold plates."

John thanked the old man absently.

On the way out of the hospice he remained silent. At Felix's suggestion they stopped at the first tavern they saw. When the two had settled themselves at a table set against the back wall, the owner ladled wine into their cups from one of the open vats set in the counter.

"What is it, John?" Felix asked. "What are you thinking?"

John's gaze was directed toward the mosaic on the wall, a succession of triumphant gladiators and charioteers. His thoughts were elsewhere. "We have approached this investigation the wrong way."

"What? You mean tramping all over the city interviewing beggars too frightened of us to talk? You don't think that's a useful approach? Or do you mean our appearing in the doorways of aristocrats too contemptuous of us to cooperate?"

John ignored the excubitor's sarcasm. "The doorkeeper said that the cart driver who died had delivered that statue to the church. Doesn't it seem strange to you?"

"He was a carter, John. That was his living. What's strange about it?"

"I mean this. Hypatius commissioned the sculpture, Viator imported the marble to be used. Now we learn that the cart driver delivered the finished work to the church. All three are dead."

"The driver was fatally injured in a street brawl, we saw that ourselves. Viator was likely robbed. Hypatius, it is true, was murdered for a reason we have not yet been able to discover."

"Certainly it would appear they all died for different reasons, but perhaps the fact that they are all dead is more important than the apparent causes."

"Why would anyone commit murder over a work of art anyway? As for myself, I prefer looking at some of those detailed Aphrodites one runs across in the palace gardens, but to kill someone over a chunk of stone, however it's been shaped, it just doesn't seem likely."

"At times we see the connections before we can discern the meaning."

"Or you do." Felix rubbed at his stubbled jaw. "You overlook the obvious, John. I've been thinking this over myself. Remember that Viator and Hypatius were friends who had fallen out over financial matters. How do you know Viator's son was not responsible for Hypatius' death? Mark you, not necessarily with Viator's knowledge. Or if it comes to it, what if Viator was responsible? You mistook father for son, even if briefly, remember?"

"True," John admitted. "But then how to explain Viator's death? Hypatius had no sons to avenge him, at least not so far as we know. No, I am convinced we have been going about this the wrong way. I'm not even sure exactly how I know."

"We've just been wasting our time?"

"Not necessarily. We may know more than we think. We just haven't realized the significance of what we've learned. Because we haven't been looking at the matter from the proper perspective."

Felix's stool creaked as he shifted uncomfortably. "If the emperor suspected one of his bodyguards was taking suggestions from a slave.... I don't find this new theory very convincing. But I'm tired enough barking down blind alleys and at the gates of mansions to try something different. For a day. I'm not going to explain to Justin that we abandoned a reasonable investigation because you had a vague feeling we were on the wrong track. But what next? We don't have a list of people connected to this sculpture."

"We know of at least one other person close to the work. The man who chiseled it. And remember, Theodora mentioned that Hypatius was only one of a number of patrons who paid for it. That didn't seem to have any bearing on the murder before. No doubt Archdeacon Palamos would know the names of the others."

※ ※ ※

Palamos was still at his temporary post in the Great Church. A boy, indistinguishable from the child they had watched lighting lamps during their previous visit with the archdeacon, ran to fetch the man.

Felix strolled around the base of the marble Christ, shaking his head. "No, this is not to my taste at all. When I first arrived in Constantinople, it made me uncomfortable, having the eyes of this man upon me everywhere. Hanging on every wall, looming over me as I came and went from the palace."

Palamos emerged into the vestibule. A fond pat from his pudgy hand sent the boy who had found him back to work.

Felix watched the child race away. "You've got more urchins in here than there are on the street."

"The church is a safer place for them. We try to employ as many as possible. It brings tears to my eyes to see all the beautiful little boys living off scraps, shivering in rags, freezing to death in corners."

Felix stated their business.

Palamos' pallid features tightened into a frown. "There were two other patrons who, unlike Hypatius, wished to remain anonymous. Please don't misunderstand. I am not faulting Hypatius for proclaiming his generosity. There are those who take undue pride in humility. But you can understand my difficulty."

Felix produced a handful of coins. "Perhaps there are boys here who need new shoes?"

Palamos accepted the donation without hesitation. "How gratifying to see a military man concerned with things other than killing! I suppose I can tell you, in the strictest confidence, that one of the other patrons was Fortunatus. Another great philanthropist. He recently gave all his wealth to the church and retired to the monastery next door."

"And the second?" John inquired.

"A pious widow named Dominica." Palamos noticed the surprise on John's face. "You're acquainted with Dominica?"

"She is an acquaintance of an employer."

Palamos told them where Dominica lived. "If you're still interested in why so many oppose Theodora, ask Dominica. She can certainly tell you tales. I've heard a few myself. Did you know that Theodora's old actress friends, common whores the lot of them, are welcome at the Hormisdas at any hour? She arranges abortions for them. It's something upon which she is an authority, having had considerable experience of them herself. If Justinian expects a successor out of that one, he will be sadly disappointed. She's as worn out as a crone."

Palamos stopped abruptly and glanced around. "I should not be talking about such things with small ears around. The Lord willing, our boys will avoid these filthy entanglements. That would be a blessing indeed."

Felix gave a curt nod and thanked Palamos. Outside, he growled to John, "I think Palamos is much too fond of his boys. Where should we go now? There's the monastery, practically in front of us. I suppose we should speak to this Fortunatus first."

"If you don't mind, let's seek out Dominica. I find walking a useful aid in the contemplation of problems."

Felix said nothing, but accompanied John across the Augustaion. He came to a halt suddenly, jerked his head around and scanned the square. John followed his gaze, but saw only the usual array of citizens hurrying to shops or churches or homes.

Felix resumed walking. "I keep feeling eyes on my back."

"After being ambushed I'm not—"

"No. I'm not imagining things. Someone's watching us, following us."

As if to confirm his words, as the two men turned to enter the Mese, a young man in a bright red cloak, hardly suitable for street wear, came running toward them. Felix's hand went to his sword and then dropped away when he saw the youngster's heavily powdered and painted face. It was one of the pages who served as palace decorations, or in other capacities required by members of the court.

"They said you'd probably be lurking around here," gasped the page, thoroughly out of breath from his burst of exertion.

"You were almost right," John remarked to his companion. "Someone was looking for us."

The page looked from John to Felix. "What a pair! A soldier and a eunuch! You, excubitor. The emperor wants to see you. Immediately. Follow me."

"If Justin orders it, I shall attend," replied Felix. "However, I can find my own way to the palace." The black glare he directed at the page sent the youngster off at a trot.

"Trouble?" John wondered.

"We'll see. I'd go back to the palace if I were you, John. I'm certain we were being followed."

"I don't want to delay visiting these patrons," John replied reluctantly.

"Be careful then. At least I now know you can handle yourself in a fight!"

John watched as Felix turned back toward the palace, and then resumed walking. Now he felt as if someone were watching him. He cursed Felix for putting the idea into his head.

Chapter Twenty-Six

John's unease dogged him, abating only as he neared Dominica's house. His shadower, if there indeed was one, remained as invisible as John's fears.

The approach to the house he sought might have been just another narrow way cutting between brick boxes, apartment buildings which housed many of the administrative ant-like army that marched into palace offices every morning only to march back out each afternoon, the problems of the empire still largely unconquered.

The mansion was an eccentric affair, a two-story hexagonal structure with a series of porches. Hardly in keeping with the practical, unimaginative personality Anna had described. On the other hand, it had almost certainly been built by Dominica's deceased husband.

John was halfway across the courtyard when a shout sounded from behind.

"You! Stop!"

He whirled. Several men rushed at him, brandishing weapons.

Dominica's guards.

"I am here to see your mistress," he called out hastily, fumbling for the Gourd's letter of introduction. Further conversation was halted by the arrival of a curtained litter borne by six sturdy servants outfitted in matching red and yellow tunics. The litter was painted red and fitted with yellow curtains. Doubtless it had been accompanied by the guards who had just challenged him.

At a muffled command from within, the bearers set the litter down gently a few paces away. One of the guards snatched the letter from John's hand and pushed it between the curtains.

John ruefully watched the official talisman vanish inside. He wondered if the Gourd's magick charms were more efficacious than his seal. So far, the letter of introduction, while having the power to make aristocratic lips move, could not compel them to reveal anything useful.

As he waited, he studied the garishly painted carvings on the litter. Rows of crosses ran around the top, and a large cross was affixed to the front of the litter, tilted forward, pointing the way like the prow of a ship. Upon each yellow curtain had been painted an image of Christ and beneath it a short Biblical verse in Greek.

Before John could finish reading them, there was another murmur from within the litter and the guard drew its curtain partly open.

John stooped to see into the interior. Even in the suffused golden light seeping through the curtains, the widowed Dominica was a woman of stern visage. No makeup softened her wrinkles and her gray hair had been pulled back into a tightly coiled bun.

She gave John a keen look. "If the Prefect wants me to answer your questions, I will have to do so."

"If you would be so kind," John responded with a bow.

The interior of the litter was half-filled with blankets and pillows. Its front wall bore a shelf holding a trio of miniature busts of aristocratic mien. John recalled hearing that Dominica had survived three husbands.

"Are you going to question me or just stand there gaping? Senator Opimius told me about your grilling his colleague Aurelius. I think he rather enjoyed the spectacle. I never thought that I would be next on the skewer, especially since Opimius tells me you have been dismissed from tutoring his daughter."

"A regrettable matter, but I assure you—"

"I don't take reassurance from slaves. Lady Anna also spoke to me about you. In fact, she has spoken entirely over much about you. She should keep her attention on the aristocratic suitors she insists on driving off. All this talk about her being too plain for anyone to want to marry is nonsense. There are plenty of men who prefer intelligence to beauty, and even more are attracted to wealth. After all, you can rent beauty very cheaply. No, that is just her excuse. What does she think she will do when her father's gone without someone to look after her? She's an intelligent young woman, certainly, but not at all worldly. To go about accompanied by only one slave! Such madness!"

"You have not encountered any problems moving around the city?"

"Problems?"

"You have not been approached?"

"What do you mean? Attacked?"

"Yes. Or followed?"

"Certainly not! Besides, as you see, I am well guarded when I venture abroad. However, I don't believe you sought me out to inquire about my safety. Get on with it!"

John proceeded. Dominica had little to say about Hypatius, although her tone of voice indicated disdain for the departed pillar of the community. She had even less to impart about any connections existing between the dead man and the several names John mentioned, including Trenico's.

"They may have had business dealings, I don't know. My steward takes care of the details," she concluded. "Naturally I look over the account books now and then. When my husband was alive, that was his task. Even so, it is not a bad plan for women to inform themselves about their husbands' business affairs, if not about the other sort." A wintry smile lightened her face briefly.

Then she made the sign of her religion. "Lord forgive me," she murmured. "I have been blessed with fine and faithful husbands, left the most wealthy of women. I do my best to honor their memory and order my life as they would have done."

"Indeed," John said. "I had hoped that perhaps you could cast some light on this matter, particularly given your interest in the Christ adorning the Great Church."

"Co-sponsoring it, you mean? I merely sent a certain sum to Hypatius. Many have said that the work is impious or that it is intended to celebrate the talent of the artist, not the glory of the subject. Yet our talents are granted us by the Lord. If He had not meant for Dio to display his talent, He would not have blessed him with it. If people want to complain about impiety they should be bitterly complaining about this planned marriage of Justinian's."

John observed that he had heard numerous comments.

"And impious it is! I am not referring to Theodora's past, you understand. What I meant is that while Justinian is, thankfully, orthodox in his beliefs, Theodora is a monophysite. How can there possibly be any harmony in such a marriage? More importantly, it bodes ill for both sets of believers. Theodora has such influence with Justinian that their union will doubtless lead to monophysites flooding the church. Justinian can refuse her nothing. It's well known at court. Most unnatural, I do believe, for is it not the woman's place to serve the man?"

"Is it wise to speak out publicly against Theodora?"

Dominica sniffed disdainfully. "Do you mean is it wise for me, or for people generally? Some of my acquaintances are already afraid of Theodora. She has a long memory and recalls every slight she's received at the hands of the aristocracy. No doubt in due course it will suit her on occasion to remember slights she has fabricated. I should however like to see her try to implicate a pious widow such as myself in plotting against the empire, or any such nonsense!"

John, thinking that Dominica would be a worthy foe for many, even Theodora, smiled politely.

"You find me comical, then?"

John said he did not.

The widow looked up at him from her nest of pillows. "You think I don't know everything I say to you will go straight to your master? You're nothing but a wax tablet on which I write words for your masters to read. They are much more likely to dispose of their tablet than to harm me."

"That is probably so."

"You've realized why Hypatius visited the sculpture in the church so often, haven't you?"

John looked nonplussed and Dominica laughed. "Have you learned nothing about him? After it was installed, he spent part of every day at the church. He liked to watch people admiring his donation, you see. He would often engage them in conversation about its merits. Yes, he was a man who did a great deal of good and he liked to take his reward for it in this world. I certainly hope the Patriarch decides to permit the Christ to remain there. Whatever turns the minds of common folk toward heaven is commendable."

John murmured agreement.

"There are those who find the admonitions on the curtains of my litter in poor taste," Dominica went on. "But I guarantee they're the only spiritual works many in the street will ever read. Provided they can read, that is."

Dominica paused. John thought she'd decided her wax tablet had been filled until she leaned forward and spoke again.

"Pay attention to what I have told you, particularly about Lady Anna. Consider what a wax tablet looks like when it has been tossed into the fire."

Chapter Twenty-Seven

"Felicitations." The white-haired Fortunatus scarcely glanced at the now dog-eared letter of introduction presented to him.

He waved his visitor to a stool beside a long table arrayed with an impressive selection of sacred artifacts. "As you see, even one as old as I can still carry out good works, in this case polishing the monastery's silver. Yes," he ran on without giving John time to respond, "we must keep the silver polished and our animals penned and the floor swept clean and all in order in our corner so that chaos, not to mention the Persians, does not engulf us."

The workshop beneath the monastery had once been a cistern and could still serve the purpose were the city to come under siege, as had happened in the past. Three rows of columns with scavenged capitals displaying a hodgepodge of styles supported a vaulted ceiling. There were other tables scattered around the huge space, which smelled of torch smoke and freshly cut wood.

Lowering himself onto the stool John found himself almost at eye level with the dark stain around the nearest column. He thought uncomfortably that a hundred years ago he would have been up to his nose in water.

He leaned forward and carefully picked up a burnished chalice, turning it this way and that to examine the bands of engraved Greek lettering around its lip and foot. His labors in the office of the Keeper of the Plate had given him some knowledge of the quality of silver. This was a particularly fine specimen. Wondering who had presented it to the monastery, he set it carefully down and broached the matter on which he had come to question the man.

Fortunatus waved the paten he was polishing at John as if shooing away a horse fly. "This is one of several beautiful pieces given to the monastery by the widow Dominica. Do you see the scene engraved upon it?"

John expressed puzzlement.

"I fear, my friend, you are not attending." The man who had once been a very wealthy merchant now wore shapeless robes of rough, unbleached wool. His hands and face matched his clothing, almost without color, while his nose and cheeks and even his brows had begun to droop like a melting candle. His eyes, John noted, were the sharp blue of shadows on snow.

"Look," Fortunatus went on, "is this fine work not decorated with the raising of Lazarus?"

"Yes, but what—"

"Consider this. If you had been Lazarus, dead for four days but then called back from that dark journey, would you really wish to return? After all, who knows what you might find when you arrived home. Your children running screaming at the sight of your shroud and who knows what old friend of your wife being entertained in your bed?"

John found himself debating whether the man had reached that age where he had begun wandering in places unseen by others that were nonetheless real to him.

"I have no wife," he said carefully, "and am still alive so you will have to explain your point further, I fear." He couldn't help recalling the reception when he himself had arisen Lazarus-like from Justin's dungeon.

The old man began to work his polishing cloth more vigorously. "Not one for parables? I will be plainer. When a man is dead is it fruitful to dig him up again by going about asking impertinent questions? Especially someone as respected as Hypatius?"

"Is he respected in this particular religious community?"

"Certainly. He was exceedingly generous. Ostentatiously generous, to be honest. Before I retired and entered this foundation, I knew him as a businessman first and foremost, one with whom I often crossed swords. Usually he got the better of me."

"Could it have been financial wounds from those battles which brought you to this place?"

"No single wound, my friend. I never wanted to be a rich man. Accumulating wealth is an unpleasant task and retaining it is even worse. Yet what choice does one have? Either a man is rich or he has a foot in the gutter. It doesn't take long after that to tumble head first into it. So I did what was necessary. You might say wealth was the cross I had to bear."

Fortunatus sighed again. "And the worst of it was the lying. Look at this old face. White as a shade's, and why? Because the sun never touched it through the mask I had to wear all my life. Smiling and lying to all the other masks with whom I dealt."

"So what was it, finally, that brought you here?"

"It was when I had to ask some children playing in the street why the Forum Constantine had disappeared. It had become most annoying. I would venture out and my house would move while I was gone. I could cope with that, but when the forum picked up and wandered off just because I'd gone to the baths, well, I decided to take up the monastic life. I will be happy if I never have to go out into the streets again. Although I did have a fascinating conversation with Emperor Justin once. He was out in Forum Bovis searching for his reception hall."

Fortunatus did not smile as he spoke, even though, John thought, he must be joking. "Perhaps it's best to stay off the streets," John said. "They grow more dangerous all the time. This place is a safe haven, I imagine. You have not been threatened here, have you?"

"Only by the cook's unspiced offerings."

John looked around the enormous underground room. "Don't you ever wish for more comfortable surroundings?"

"At first I did. When Hypatius visited me to discuss the statue, he tried to convince me to resume my former life—at least until he found out I'd donated all my lands to the church. There was nothing left to swindle me out of even if I did reemerge into the world." He laughed.

"You find it humorous that the man was more or less a thief?"

"Not a thief, a businessman. Besides, I can laugh because who's sitting in a comfortable and warm place polishing silver and waiting for the evening meal and who is underground, never to taste a good roasted fowl or a cup of Falernian wine again or sample the delights of an obliging young lady? Not that I am suggesting that we sample young ladies here, you understand."

Was the man incompetent, John wondered, or merely playing at it, turning it to his advantage? Did he know something, some shred of information, that put together with other scraps would make a collection of tesserae that would somehow assemble themselves and turn into a coherent mosaic?

"You have been living here very long?"

"A year or so. It is very different. Noisier for a start. That's to be expected with being so close to the palace and the Great Church. The food may not be so varied or lavish as that prepared by my personal cook in the old days, but it is nourishing and there's plenty of it. Last summer I helped with the kitchen garden. My herbs were much praised. It's a simple life. It suits me more and more as I get older. Also, when I lose my way, there is always someone at hand to help me find my room."

He flourished his cloth. "Yes, I'm thankful to be here. Besides, although we live behind a wall, we can scarcely avoid hearing news of the goings-on in the city. Now and then, I even learn of interesting developments concerning some of my former business acquaintances. Not all of them do well, alas." The relish with which he made his final comment revealed his enjoyment of this sad state of affairs.

John observed that such occasional tidbits of news would certainly be of interest to one who had once fought on the fields of commerce.

"Yes." Fortunatus' blue eyes glittered under his bristling white brows. "It's surprising how so often they overreach themselves or invest foolishly, even recklessly. Some are extremely clever. Take Hypatius, the dead man who so interests you. He stole a choice estate right out from under my nose a couple of years ago. Persuaded the heir to sell it to him for less than he and I had already agreed."

John expressed his condolences.

"That wasn't as bad as the time he publicly challenged the purity of the wine I was selling. I admit it turned out not to be the exact vintage the importer had held it out to be. It was terribly unfortunate that that particular shipment was destined for the imperial kitchens. That was just before I decided to retire and enter the monastery."

"I suppose you don't have much opportunity to discuss such worldly matters here."

Fortunatus agreed dolefully that this was the case.

It was becoming obvious that the man relished such discussions and did not hesitate to use the safe shelter of the monastery to make comments he might not have dared to utter outside, especially about his former commercial enemies.

"I have heard similar tales of Hypatius' business dealings," John said. "Yet you joined him and Dominica in donating the sculpture despite your disputes?"

Fortunatus plied his cloth over a silver and gilt box with a lid that bore a border depicting the rout of the money changers from the Temple in Jerusalem. "I did not like the man. Neither did I dislike him. No, it was because Dominica requested it. I knew her late husband. That is to say, her last late husband."

"An impressive woman."

Fortunatus set the box down and John saw it was a reliquary. "Impressive. That's the word for Dominica, yes. At any rate, she had seen the work of this immensely talented young sculptor by the name of Dio. I was happy to contribute although I paid my portion of the cost directly to Dio just in case Hypatius suddenly developed honey-covered fingers when passing along my money."

John asked why Hypatius had become involved with the project in the first place.

"He was ever a man for public good works. An art work of that sort is bound to receive attention. Of course, everyone has been talking about it for days, although not for the reason that Hypatius anticipated. I believe also that he thought it would buy him favor in heaven. When you've paid half the city officials to overlook this infraction or that, you don't hesitate to attempt to bribe the Lord, do you?"

"No doubt Hypatius has discovered if it has worked," John said dryly. "Although it is just as well that the emperor apparently didn't know about his bribes. I've heard he is inexorable when it comes to public corruption."

"Justin doesn't seem to be aware of what is going on in his own palace these days. If you ask me, he would be far happier polishing silver here with me. It was the nephew, Justinian, who worried Hypatius. An avaricious man, Hypatius told me. He was completely opposed to Justinian's inheriting the throne."

"So despite your disputes, it seems you had a number of conversations of a private nature with Hypatius?"

"Oh, it's quite true. I used to attend dinner parties where confidences flowed freely as the wine. I could tell you statements several very prominent citizens made at such gatherings that would earn them stripes in public, if not worse. And they weren't all about Theodora, either!"

John ignored the comment. "Would you say this discontent was organized?"

"No. I took it to be your everyday grumbling fueled by overindulgence in the grape. Bribes costing too much, taxes too high, contracts being sold on the side. However, that was a year or two ago. Often dissatisfaction takes a long time to turn into action. It wouldn't surprise me if it did perhaps eventually come to something."

John said nothing, allowing the flow of words to continue.

Fortunatus snapped his cloth at the air. It might have been a gesture of disdain leveled at official-dom in all its guises. "If it's conspirators you want to talk about, interview Opimius. He seemed to know a large number of, let us say, malcontents who would just as soon Justinian did not become emperor. Why don't you ask him about it?"

"I don't think he would be very open with me."

"I suppose not. Well, let me be open then. I've had to spend my whole life behind a mask, mouthing lies of one sort or another, but I would not honor the Lord were I to take shelter in His house and continue lying, would I? It's been said that Justinian has purchased every senator, but it's not so. There are those who don't need his largesse and others who are not of the Christian persuasion, may the Lord have mercy on their souls. On the other hand, it's true that most of the Senate wants to officially request Justin to step aside. He is only a figurehead now, or was until this mysterious illness felled his nephew, who many suspect rules from the shadows. However, there are still a number of prominent citizens who oppose Justinian becoming emperor. Hypatius was one and Opimius is another. And I should mention two of Opimius' closest associates— landholders who fear Justinian's predations—Trenico and Tryphon are of the same thought."

He began to ramble about how he would advise the latter two to donate their land to the church before Justinian seized it and then retire to the monastery to help him polish silver rather than laying up further wealth.

John barely heard him. He had sought out Fortunatus, as he had Dominica, to pursue his new theory concerning Hypatius' death: that it stemmed from the donation of the sculpture rather than from political intrigue. Instead what he had found was unexpected confirmation of a possible conspiracy against Justinian.

Worse, it was not information Justinian would wish to hear for it could certainly be twisted to prove he would have had a reason to want Hypatius dead. Not to mention several others. There were many in the city who still believed Justinian responsible for Vitalian's death, even though the only evidence they could point to was that the death had benefited Justinian.

Beyond that, Anna's father clearly appeared to be involved with those who were opposed to Justinian ever ruling. It was not just coincidence that he had been talking with Trenico and Tryphon at the baths. The latter had denied acquaintanceship with Opimius for good reason.

Fortunatus talked on, but said nothing more of consequence. Still chattering, he finally escorted John to the monastery gate. Outside, passersby hurried along, bent about their own business. John glanced back at the low building they had just left. He would welcome the opportunity to sink into its peace, he thought, as he stepped out into the world again.

"One thing more," Fortunatus said as he held the gate open. "If you were thinking of interviewing Dio, there's no point in going straight to his studio. He visits a friend here now and then so I happen to know that he won't be back from Proconnesus until late today. He's been out there for the past few days choosing marble for his next commission."

"Do you happen to know what it is?"

"Hypatius had not begun building his final resting place, although he'd given Dio very detailed instructions for its design," was the surprising answer. "He greatly admired the tomb the young man created for Dominica's last husband."

Fortunatus gave John directions to Dio's studio. "Let's hope it doesn't decide to run away before you arrive," he concluded.

He began to swing the gate shut, but John stopped him. "You say Dio designed the tomb for Dominica's last husband?"

"Dio was the husband's bastard son. As for me, I tend to think he may be Dominica's offspring, but then I am just an old man who has fled the world, and glad to have left it behind."

The gate banged shut, leaving John alone with his thoughts—among them that Fortunatus had not left the world nearly so far behind as he claimed.

Chapter Twenty-Eight

When he was ushered into Emperor Justin's private apartment, Felix saw that the most powerful ruler in the civilized world was reclining on a couch. He was eating bread and cheese from an earthenware plate.

The homely sight heartened him. He could not help comparing the frugal fare to the culinary conceits offered at the Gourd's banquet. There was certainly something to the old saying that a man's nature was in his nourishment.

"Ah, my excubitor," Justin muttered around a mouthful of bread, without waiting for Felix to bow. He handed his crumb-dusted plate to the guard stationed behind his couch, who juggled with the dish one-handedly while contriving to retain his other hand on the pommel of his sword.

"Take that plate away," Justin instructed the man irritably.

"As you direct, Caesar." The guard eyed Felix suspiciously.

"He's one of my bodyguards, just like you, but one who doesn't balk at carrying out his orders," Justin snapped. "Leave."

Felix felt a glow of pride at the emperor's words. For an instant he forgot the chagrin that had been building inside him for the past few days as he talked endlessly to various people, never daring to say exactly what he meant, nodding politely at the palpable lies he was offered. It had made him feel as if he was an obsequious palace bureaucrat rather than a military man. He remembered now that however unpleasant his duty might be, the man he served had once been a soldier too.

When they were alone, Justin's voice fell to a tired whisper akin to parchment sheets rustling in a breeze. "What have you been doing, Felix? Do you have anything to report yet?" He made no effort to conceal a grimace of pain as he leaned back.

Felix outlined the investigations he and John had carried out. Put into words and presented to the emperor, their efforts sounded futile, even ludicrous.

Justin waved his prominently veined hand. "No, no. The words these people speak aren't worth a clod of dirt. I'm not interested in what they told you. What I want to know is what did you learn? What did you observe? What do you make of the situation?"

For a moment Felix could not speak. He could hardly believe that the emperor was asking for his opinion. Finally he said, "To begin with, Caesar, there are more axes to grind at court than there are in to be found in all the woodworkers' shops in the city."

"I have numerous axes myself. Mine are extremely sharp and very useful for removing heads from shoulders."

"As you say, Caesar. However, it would appear that the majority of those to whom we spoke were more intent on fomenting difficulties than in aiding our inquiries."

"This colleague of yours, Justinian's eunuch. Has he said anything about my nephew?"

"I regret that I'm not certain what you mean."

Justin shifted ponderously on the couch, his lips compressed into a tight line. A large crumb clung to the moist corner of his mouth. Felix had the fleeting impression that the man was not so much living within his big body as being crushed under its dead weight.

"Slaves always talk to each other. The palace is full of gossip. Do you think I don't know what is being whispered behind my back? What about this notion Justinian's got into his head, that I'm planning to accuse him of having a hand in the murder of Hypatius?"

"Justinian's man watches me, I watch him. He has revealed no more to me about his master than I have revealed to him about you."

"Oh, nicely said! Proclus should recruit you to work in his office. Very well. What are they saying about me in the streets? That's what really matters, as Euphemia advises me."

Felix felt sweat trickling down his back. A shade had just walked into the room.

Justin fixed him with a rheumy glare. "I asked you a question. Why are you looking like that?"

Felix cleared his throat. His gaze was drawn to the crumb hanging from the emperor's lip. He forced himself to look away. "I have heard nothing unusual."

"The mob isn't whispering against me? That's how it always begins. In the streets, in the forum. Like a festering wound down in the leg whose poison creeps nearer to the heart with every passing day. Blood flows in some stinking alley and before long armed men are breaking into the emperor's bedchamber to murder him."

"You are much respected, Caesar," Felix assured him.

"However, the Gourd has contained the unrest," Justin went on, ignoring his comment. "A good man at his work. Proclus recommended him to me. Yes, he knows how to handle my nephew's precious Blues. Personally, I'd like to set him loose on the actress."

"There are many who oppose Theodora, both on the streets and at court," Felix offered truthfully, happy to be able to tell Justin at least one thing he might want to hear.

Justin scowled. "My dearest Euphemia detests her and refuses to remain in the same room if their paths should cross by accident. Whatever can Justinian find to love in Theodora, the world's whore? But young men tend to be ruled by their loins, not logic, and she has certainly had plenty of practice in the art of seduction."

As Justin spoke he turned his head slowly until he was staring directly at the door. Felix was struck by an irrational fear that it was about to open to admit the dead Empress Euphemia.

"Caesar, about my mission. It is always a good plan when going into battle to be armed with detailed orders and—"

"But you have had your orders! Investigate the murder of Hypatius. Watch the eunuch while he works. Keep your eyes open, and your ears."

Felix made a bow.

"Now, hold that pot for me."

Felix looked at Justin in confusion.

The emperor gestured weakly at the plain ceramic vessel sitting on the floor at the side of his couch.

"My night soil pot. I wish to relieve myself. Yes, you could tell the time by me. I drip like a water clock."

"Caesar, I—"

"You're embarrassed for your emperor. Understandably." Justin grimaced. "I don't need a physician, Felix. What I need is a plumber."

※ ※ ※

John sat on the edge of his pallet and tried to organize his thoughts. He had been certain Hypatius' death was somehow connected with the sculpture. Not that there had been any obvious reason. It was simply a feeling he had, that bits of information were about to fall together to form a coherent whole.

He tended to take sudden leaps into the darkness of doubt. Usually he found what he half expected. This time, though, he had, perhaps, jumped in the wrong direction. Fortunatus' words, coupled with the group of men John had seen at the baths, clearly damned Opimius as one of the political intriguers Justinian feared. And what did that mean for Anna?

Should he warn her? Use the servants' entrance as she'd suggested? Perhaps he should see if the sculptor Dio had returned. Even if that avenue of investigation seemed fruitless, it would get his feet moving. As soon as his feet stopped his thoughts seemed to come to a halt.

He was just about to leave when Felix appeared. "I hoped you'd be here, John."

The excubitor looked pensive. John inquired about his meeting with the emperor.

Felix summarized the conversation. "I think the hardest fate for a military man like Justin is dying by degrees far from the battlefield. I hope neither of us suffers that fate. Tell me, John, what is your favorite tree?"

John said nothing. He expected to detect the reek of wine about the excubitor, but there was none. "You've come here to ask me about trees?"

"Well, if you understand...but if you don't...."

John realized what he was really being asked. He offered Felix a thin smile. "I suppose I would have to say the fig."

Felix visibly relaxed. "It is said the fig is sacred to certain proscribed deities."

"To Mithra, you mean?"

"To Mithra, yes. You called upon Him when we were attacked, my friend. You mention any number of deities and personages when you become angry, and in most unflattering terms. You speak Egyptian well, don't you?"

John looked at Felix, bemusement in his expression.

"Then I suggest you curse people in Egyptian henceforth, at least in public. It might be safer for you. For now, come with me."

***

The shadowy mithraeum the two men entered was familiar to John, even though he had never set boot into this hidden underground temple situated on the palace grounds. He had seen several mithraea in his time, the first one in far-off, misty Bretania. This place of worship could have been any of them.

To reach it, he and Felix had passed through a doorway set deep inside the armory behind the excubitors' barracks and then progressed through a series of subterranean corridors that reminded John uncomfortably of the path he had taken from the imperial dungeons to light and air only a few days before.

Finally they reached a stout door. An armed excubitor swung it open and they stepped into the mithraeum.

Felix kept his hand on his sword and a close watch on John. Passing between the statues of Mithra's twin torchbearers, Cautes and Cautopates, flanking the entrance, John bowed his head to the bas-relief set at the far end of the low-ceilinged room. It was illuminated by the shifting light of a small fire on the altar before it.

A man wearing the dark mask of a raven stepped forward to greet them.

"Welcome, brothers in Mithra," he said.

"This is John, a fellow adept," Felix replied.

"I am accepted as such?"

Felix grinned. "Had you not given homage to Lord Mithra, you would not have lived long enough to tell anyone about it," he said. Turning to their raven-headed companion, he added, "The ceremony will begin soon?"

"As soon as the Father and the initiate arrive."

John glanced around the narrow space. A dozen or so men, some wearing the masks of their Mithraic rank, stood talking. Torchlight threw strange shadows across the walls, flickering across the sacred scene behind the altar where Mithra, cloak flying in an eternal wind, had plunged His dagger into the Great Bull, releasing its blood to gush forth to create animals and vegetation.

The new arrivals sat down at the end of the low bench running along the right-hand wall as their fellow worshippers took their seats both beside them and on the bench against the opposite wall. A hush settled over the cave-like temple, the only sounds the crackling of the sacred fire and the torches set in brackets.

John gazed at the holy figure of Lord Mithra. He had found praying to his god calmed his mind when it persisted in twisting and turning in on itself, the Furies raging back and forth inside his head until he felt it would split open.

The familiar scene depicted Mithra, Lord of Light, and to him he prayed nightly for acceptance of the terrible fate his rashness had brought upon him.

There was a clash of cymbals and those assembled stood as the Father entered the mithraeum. Behind him walked the man to be initiated, naked, his eyes covered in a red cloth tied tightly at the back of his head, his hands bound around with entrails and stout rope. His two burly escorts, wearing masks whose flowing manes identified them as adepts holding the rank of Lion, guided him to the altar where the Father waited.

The Lions pushed the initiate down on his knees and stepped a few paces back as the Father raised his hands in prayer.

"Lord of Light," he intoned, "we assemble tonight to admit a new follower, Petros, to Thy service and to honor Thee, Slayer of the Bull and Guardian of all who serve Thee."

One of the Lions who had escorted the initiate to the altar stepped forward, drawing his sword with a whisper of oiled metal. The blindfolded man turned his head toward the sound and then back toward the altar, coughing in smoke drifting from its fire.

Looking down, the Father addressed the kneeling initiate.

"You are a soldier and have fought for the empire and seen the aftermath of battle, when Mithra's ravens come to cleanse the field and escort the souls of the faithful up His seven-runged ladder. Those who know not the mysteries of Mithra call His sacred bird carrion, but if you complete the ordeal then you will become a member of the first rank, a Corax, named for that very bird."

Petros nodded silently.

"It is difficult indeed to live the life that Lord Mithra demands of His followers," the Father went on, "for He demands all those He accepts to be honorable, chaste and obedient. Therefore, the adept guards his honor, does not defile himself or others, and never refuses aid to another follower. Above all, he loves the Lord of Light."

The Father paused and turned his head in the direction of the Lion with the drawn sword as he continued sternly, "Acceptance is not easily gained. First, you must die."

As he spoke, the Lion's sword sliced down and laid open the initiate's shoulder. The man swayed, but remained kneeling. He made no sound although his fists clenched the slippery entrails tied around them more firmly, their dark drippings running down onto his bare knees. A second sweep down of the sword and blood was running down his back.

Still he made no sound.

"It is well done," the Father said approvingly. "But mark this well, Petros. If you betray your brothers in Mithra, your end will bring only oblivion, for you will be forever barred from climbing Mithra's ladder to live with Him in heaven."

Turning to the altar, he picked up a small bowl set beside the sacred fire.

"Remember too that in all things a Mithran is discreet and speaks not of his knowledge to anyone but Mithrans," he instructed Petros.

The Lion bent forward and forced open the initiate's mouth with the bloodstained point of his sword, cutting Petros' tongue.

"And as the blood flowing from you symbolizes both the death of your old life and your rebirth, not of woman but into the care of the Lord of Light, then so too this...." The Father dipped a spoon of honey from the bowl and placed into the man's mouth. Most of it dribbled out, mixed with bloody saliva. Sufficient remained for Petros to swallow as the Father completed the initiation ritual, by pouring another spoonful of honey onto Petros' head as he continued, "...anoints you to silence and sweetens your soul, purifying it so that it is acceptable to Lord Mithra."

John, as all the adepts present, recalled the salty-sweet taste of honey and blood when he, too, had undergone the ordeal of initiation.

"Take off the blindfold!" the Father ordered.

Blinking rapidly, Petros looked around when the blindfold was removed. After a quick glance down at his shoulder, he looked up at the Father, who now displayed the bloodied sword to him.

"This was the instrument of your death," the Father said, "and now you cast off your old life—" a quick, dexterous slice of the sword removed entrails and rope from the new Raven's hands "—along with these, the entanglements of the old life. You are now reborn to serve Lord Mithra in the rank of Raven."

The new Mithran stood and was embraced by the Father. A cheer rang out as Petros was formally presented to the assembly, who now began to sing exultantly, praise rising to mingle with the smell of smoke in a heady mixture that intoxicated without wine.

John raised his voice with the rest, joyous to be able to worship his god in proper fashion for the first time in several years.

> Lord of Light, we worship Thee
> Thou art our strength, our life, our god
> Protect us on the battlefield
> Take us to Thee when we die
>
> Lord of Light, we honor Thee
> Thou art our hope, our shield, our sun
> May we serve Thee long and well
> Bring us to Thee when we die
>
> Lord of Light, we follow Thee
> Thou art our father, ruler, friend
> And when our earthly race is o'er
> Raise us to Thee when we die

Petros was handed a tunic and, having clothed himself and wiped blood from his chin, seated himself near the altar as the Lions distributed jugs of wine and platters of bread.

A short while later, Felix, passing a wine jug to John, asked, "So you were a military man?"

"For a short time," John admitted, "I was a mercenary."

"Explains your prowess with the blade, for a start," Felix said, around a mouthful of bread. "Not to mention how you handled that business with the boy. I was in the army myself before I joined the excubitors. Everyone in my company was a Mithran. That's how I came to be an adept." He stopped and looked at John expectantly.

"And you, John," he asked, when his companion said nothing, "how did you find Lord Mithra?"

"It was another man who found Mithra, really." John looked into his wine. He could not make out the bottom of his cup through the dark liquid.

"A friend of mine, a fellow mercenary, was a Mithran," he went on. "He spoke to me about it. I was initiated. Then he died. Drowned in a swollen stream. That was in Bretania."

John took a gulp of wine. He did not like to talk about the past and the person he had been. "There was some comfort," he continued, "in our belief that we go on to another life after this one ends, but I really began to think about Mithra only after the young mercenary that I was had also died."

"You have found some comfort then?"

"Comfort? Every morning, because I open my eyes again, I believe Lord Mithra has ordered me to continue living, and so I do. But as to you, Felix. Have you been long at court?"

"Not that long," Felix replied. "It's still a bit strange, to say the least. After years spent campaigning, guarding an emperor is quite different from chasing barbarians along the frontier. For one thing, here enemies are not hiding behind trees or in thickly wooded gullies. In Constantinople you're far more likely to see them out in broad daylight, walking in procession and covered in silks and jewels."

John, thinking of Theodora, agreed.

"It's all too subtle for a simple man like me," Felix continued. "Intrigues and plots and poisons and loyalties shifting every time the wind changes. Just think, John, in their own way, half the city wear masks of one sort or another. For most, including lowly folk like us, there are enemies everywhere."

"Especially for a slave?" John asked.

"Especially for a slave that someone in a position of power decides knows too much or asks too many awkward questions."

Chapter Twenty-Nine

John slipped away from the Great Palace just after dawn as a bronze sun climbed through the forest of crosses covering the rooftops of the city. He left long before he was scheduled to meet Felix to discuss their next step, for he guessed that the excubitor would not approve of his desire to warn Anna of the danger in which her father was placing himself—and her.

Ironically, now that they shared the bond of Mithran brotherhood it appeared less likely than ever that John and Felix would be able to cooperate effectively. When John had related his conversations with Dominica and Fortunatus, Felix had immediately dismissed John's theory about the work of art's connection to Hypatius' murder.

"As you just admitted, John," Felix had said, "neither Dominica nor Fortunatus has suffered for their involvement. So now you have investigated the matter and that's the end of it."

"Neither has been attacked, but we still have had three deaths."

"Three unrelated deaths of people from totally different classes," Felix pointed out.

"But linked by their involvement with the project," John persisted.

"Consider, John," Felix had replied. "How many people can you contrive to connect to that wretched statue? Let's see, there's the carter who transported it. What about the owner of the ship that carried the marble here, or the ship's captain? What of all those brawny fellows on Proconnesus who hauled the marble to the ship or cut it out of the earth, for that matter. What of the men of law who drew up the agreement to buy the marble? We mustn't overlook all the ecclesiastical officials who approved its placement in the Great Church! Would they include Palamos? The Patriarch? For that matter, what about—"

John had held up his hand. "Enough. I see your point. You think it is just coincidence."

"Exactly. This conspiracy against Justinian, though, now there's something concrete, if not marble. We must venture down that avenue."

John had all but reached the same conclusion. From what Fortunatus had told him about Opimius it appeared, even to John, that the murder could have political ramifications, just as Justinian feared. He was still not prepared to accept that it had been politically motivated, or did not have something to do with the sculpture. The connection between the dead and the Christ figure continued to tug at his mind. He should at least speak to Dio.

Whoever the murderer might be, Senator Opimius' intrigues had definitely placed his daughter in danger, he thought. A cloud of gulls rose noisily from the almost deserted street, leaving a few feathers drifting in his path. No, Felix would not have accompanied him to Opimius' house. He doubtless would have said it was both reckless and foolish and ordered him to abandon the notion.

By the time John arrived at his destination he had concluded that Felix would have been right. After all, what would Anna be able to do if she were alerted to the danger? If she took any action at all it might be one that was rash. And a visit from him would not remain a secret from Opimius for very long.

Anna's safety lay in finding the murderer. Her father was not the villain, of that John was certain.

From the street Opimius' mansion gave no hint of the luxury within or of the spacious garden lying behind. The building appeared nothing more than a nondescript box masked by a heavy, metal-banded street door. A few narrow windows interrupted its second story.

Was there movement behind one of those windows?

John suddenly feared that Lady Anna might see him and run out to meet him.

He ducked down the alley beside the house.

If Opimius noticed him lurking around he'd almost certainly send for the Gourd's men. Stamping down the narrow way John muttered a rich variety of curses, mostly called down on the thick head of Opimius. As he emerged into the next street he realized that he had been declaring his opinion of the senator to the world. It was fortunate that here at least there seemed to be only a few seabirds to hear his tirade.

Perhaps, on reflection, Felix's odd suggestion that if he must curse in public he should do so in Egyptian was a better one that he had originally thought. Yes, John decided, he should certainly practice doing so. Given his opinions of everyone from Justin downward it would turn out to be more sparing to delicate ears, not to mention saving his neck from the murderous caress of a sharp axe.

He considered returning to the palace. Felix had made it plain he wanted to continue their original line of investigation. While John had to admit it seemed the most sensible course at present, nevertheless he could not shake the strong feeling that the three deaths were connected.

This indecision was unusual for him. His mind was in a turmoil and at a time when it was most important he should think clearly. He willed himself to reason things out.

What should he do next? As it happened he was as close to the address Fortunatus had given him for the sculptor's studio as he was to the palace. That decided it, then. He should visit Dio.

***

The sculptor's residence nestled within an enclave behind the Domninus, north of where that colonnaded thoroughfare intersected the Mese, in an area populated by bakers, metal workers, and artisans.

An archway leading from the Domninus admitted John to a courtyard around which stood tiny shops selling glassware, jewelry, dyed goods and furniture. The sound of hammering, the thud of mallet on chisel, and the smell of sawdust, all gave evidence of workshops behind the shop fronts. Blankets, draped to air at open windows punctuating the upper story of the enclosure, disclosed the presence of residences.

John noticed several premises displaying marble pieces at their doors, but his eye was drawn to one emporium. Over its entrance loomed a huge, carved lintel. The doorway itself was surrounded by small squares and rectangles of marble, wood, metals, painted plaster, and mosaic chips, each repeating in miniature form the single word chiseled deeply into the lintel: Signs.

Curiously, however, the sign-maker's sign did not announce his name to prospective clients.

The proprietor, a red-faced man, appeared in the doorway and smiled expectantly as John approached.

"Good morning, sir," he said jovially. "What can I do to help you? Do you seek a sign for your business premises? A plaque announcing your name and profession?"

John wondered what he would do with a bronze plaque engraved with "John, Slave." Perhaps, he thought ruefully, he could wear it around his neck.

"Let me guess what you will want emblazoned on your sign." The man turned his head to one side and squinted hard at John. "I can always tell the professions of my clients. Tall fellow, aren't you? Little trace of calluses on your hands, I see. By your looks Greek perhaps? And you have the bearing of an aristocrat, sir. Definitely from the palace."

The maker of signs bobbed his head enthusiastically. "Yet there is something hardened in your features," he went on. "Military almost. And... hmmmm...there's that look...." The man straightened his head and chuckled. "Well, sir, I give up. All I can think to classify you as is a philosopher!"

"I regret to say I'm not here to buy a sign," John replied politely, "but rather seeking a sculptor named Dio."

The red-faced man looked disappointed. "Dio? Naturally. He has all the luck!" He pointed across the courtyard to one of the larger shops.

"He has all the luck, you say?"

"One big commission after another. Why, customers pour in over there and the way they're dressed, you'd think his door was the entrance to the emperor's reception hall. He's barely more than a youth. Granted, he has some talent."

John thanked the man. "By the way," he added, "you are quite correct about me, at least if you count as a philosopher someone who studied for a time at Plato's Academy."

The man brightened. "There it is. I do have a knack for reading people, sir. Very helpful in my trade, as you might surmise."

John strode over to Dio's shop. He guessed the sign-maker would soon be regaling everyone in earshot with how he'd identified a philosopher from the palace. Doubtless the tale of such a person visiting his emporium would be worth more to him as publicity for his wares than whatever he might have earned from a commission for a sign.

The sculptor's shop was deserted except for a few bits of carved marble populating a table. They were chiefly smaller versions of the sculpture in the Great Church but there was also a woman's head, startlingly realistic and thus none too flattering, depicting as it did every wrinkle and several prominent moles. A rejected commission perhaps?

John walked through the shop and into the studio behind.

The space was larger than he'd anticipated, two stories in height, with a packed dirt floor. Worktables covered with tools and partly shaped chunks of marble and granite lined unfinished masonry walls. Light poured down from tall, narrow windows.

Dio was nowhere to be seen.

At the far wall of the studio a dozen rectangular chunks of marble, all taller than a man, stood close together. Their grouping reminded John of the mysterious clusters of weather-eroded standing stones he'd seen in Bretania.

In front of them lay a chisel whose edge glistened moistly red.

A dark trickle curved from it into the marble grove. John followed its trail.

Spatters of blood had sprayed a tall marble slab set against the studio wall. A body sprawled at its foot, face upward.

Dio?

John realized he had no description.

Not that it would have assisted identification. Whoever had killed the man had applied the chisel to the victim's face. The white patches glistening up through its scarlet ruin were not marble, but bone.

Voices sounded in the shop.

Had the sign-maker followed him?

He peered cautiously out from the cluster of marble monoliths.

Armed men entered the studio. Not excubitors. Sent by the Gourd, then. Had someone already found the body and alerted the authorities?

But if so, why hadn't the sign-maker known Dio was dead? It was hardly the sort of thing whoever discovered the body would have kept secret.

Something else caused him to hesitate about revealing his presence. Perhaps it was a certain wariness in the way the men moved. A caution they would not have displayed if they were expecting to confront nothing more dangerous than a dead man.

Besides, he reasoned rapidly, why send so many men to look after one corpse?

"...tall and thin...a eunuch..." one of the men said.

It was John they sought. But why? The answer was as obvious as the murdered man at his feet. He was supposed to be caught at the scene.

Venturing another glance, John noted that two of the armed men were now blocking the door leading to the shop.

One of the others pointed toward his hiding place.

For an instant John considered surrendering himself. He was investigating a murder. Would it be so surprising that he might chance upon another victim?

Yet it was obvious that it had all been arranged. He was about to be wrongly accused. Or rather, first he would be murdered while supposedly resisting arrest. Then posthumously accused.

John made his decision.

Turning, he grasped the top of the slab against the studio wall and yanked himself upward.

Shouts rang out as he was spotted. By the time the first of the men reached the departed Dio, John had scrambled through the open window above the slab.

He found himself on the roof of a shed leaning against the back of the studio. Beyond rose a jumbled wilderness of buildings and tiled roofs.

He quickly crossed the shed, clambered onto the roof of the adjacent structure, and ran in the direction of the Domninus.

At the street, the tile roof came to an abrupt end. Here the buildings facing the Domninus were two stories tall, while the colonnade sheltering their shop entrances rose only to the height of a single story. Fortunately, the roof of the colonnade formed a serviceable route along and above the street. John lowered himself hastily onto it.

Looking down into the Domninus he saw several pursuers emerge from beneath the archway to the artisans' enclave. From behind him came the sound of pounding boots and shouted commands to stop.

He began to run past the windows of the apartments that looked out over the colonnade roof.

Passersby gaped up at him from the street. He glanced back over his shoulder. Three men had reached the roof of the colonnade. More ran down the street, paralleling his flight. A few urchins joined the pursuit, screaming with excitement as they raced ahead of the armed men.

John was dimly aware of pale ovals of faces behind the windows he passed as the curious looked out to see the cause of the commotion.

He almost missed the movement of a warped shutter opening into his path. He dodged, just in time, stumbled, but managed to keep running.

Behind him there was a crash and a string of oaths, as the shutter slammed into his closest pursuer and sent the man sliding off the edge of the roof and into the street.

Ahead the narrow ravine of the Domninus and its colonnade ran into a forum. The uneven tiles made running difficult. The men racing along the thoroughfare were staying even with John. It was obvious that if he tried to scramble down into the forum his pursuers would be upon him in an instant.

The next window he arrived at was closed. John kicked it in and plunged through.

He caught a glimpse of a young woman standing beside a brazier. The toddler at her feet looked up at John with immense, solemn eyes. Then his mouth fell open and he looked at his mother in bewilderment.

In an instant John was out the door and leaping down the steep wooden stairs beyond.

Reaching the hallway he turned away from the street. A door at the other end opened into an alley.

Unfortunately the alley was not connected to the maze of narrow ways in which John had been hoping to evade his pursuers. Instead it led straight into the forum.

John sprinted for the opening. As he burst out into it armed men began to arrive from the Domninus.

It was still early. There were few people abroad and thus no crowds in which to lose himself.

A seller of produce arranging his wares on a stall looked up as John rushed past.

Something slapped John's back. He didn't turn. Another hit, this time on the back of his thigh. Then a green and white projectile hurtled over his head and smacked into the ground in front of him.

A bunch of leeks.

The civic-minded produce seller was doing his part to assist the authorities.

Looking for concealment John dodged into a public latrine, past a mendicant who had already taken up a post beside the carved dolphins decorating its entrance, and into the long room beyond.

A door in the far wall led to a room filled with buckets of sponges on sticks, supplied for the personal hygiene of patrons. From there, another door revealed a concrete-floored corridor slanted downward and then John emerged into the light.

He found himself gazing out over the waist-high parapet of the northern seawall.

He started across the cobbled space between the seawall and the back of the latrine. Even this small area boasted one or two beggars, who stared sullenly at him as he passed.

A granary abutting the seawall on the opposite side of the open area blocked further progress in that direction.

Several of John's pursuers appeared, having made their way through the latrine, preventing any escape back along that path. The only other way out was a narrow opening between latrine and warehouse, but that led back to the forum.

John drew his sword.

He might be able to kill one or two, but he had no chance to against so many.

He leapt up onto the seawall.

Looking down, he did not see the roof of a warehouse so he could not put his faith in Mithra and leap as he had hoped. Only a sheer drop to the docks, much too far below. A jump would be fatal.

A stiff breeze brought with it a hint of seaspray.

John drew in a deep, painful breath, aware that he had come to a point where his remaining breaths could well be counted on his fingers.

His pursuers now moved forward warily, none of them wanting to be the first to feel the blade of a desperate, doomed man.

John was not afraid to die. If this were the death Mithra had chosen to grant him, he was thankful for it. It would be a soldier's death.

He tensed himself, preparing to attack.

But, crept in the treacherous thought, what if their orders were not to kill? What if he were, instead, to be captured and transported to the imperial dungeons?

To jump would mean a clean death.

He felt an urgent tug on his cloak and looked down as the withered hand of a beggar huddled at the base of the seawall tugged again.

"Excellency," the man croaked. "If you're going to throw yourself over, could I have this?"

John yanked the cloak from the man's grasp.

Furious, he nearly struck out at the beggar.

Then his quick glance in the man's direction revealed what he had not noticed before, something the angled side of the nearby warehouse hid from the view of anyone not actually perched where he now stood.

On the other side of the building the seawall bulged slightly outward, and above it rose the tower of Avis.

"Quick! Grab him!" someone shouted hoarsely.

John pivoted and began to run as best he could along the treacherously narrow wall. Where it hugged the warehouse there was barely room to place his feet. He prayed to Mithra he would not step on a piece of loose masonry or slippery moss, or that a sudden breeze would not gust in off the water and unbalance him.

The brick wall rising up to his right seemed suddenly to be leaning seaward, as if to force him over the edge. There were no windows or doors into the warehouse to offer him an escape. He had to continue running or fall.

Perhaps Avis would assist a friend of Lady Anna's, John thought rapidly, provided of course that he was not intercepted by armed men who doubtless would already be racing along on the other side of the warehouse to catch him when he emerged beyond it.

He came to the corner of the building, leapt from the wall and pounded up the tower's winding staircase, within sight of the first of his pursuers.

The door at the top swung open.

Avis began to smile a welcome. Then his eyes widened as he looked over John's shoulder and saw the small army now clattering up the splintered steps.

John made a show of shoving Avis out of the way, sending him stumbling down a few stairs. "You don't know me!" he whispered hastily. "I forced my way past you!"

There was no reason for Avis to die also.

John leapt into the whitewashed aviary. Startled birds took to the air, flapping up from feeding troughs and potted trees. Crows perched in the rafters croaked raucous warnings.

John slammed the door shut and shot its bolt as the first armed man toiled into view.

The door would not hold for long.

How could he possibly escape?

John found himself staring out of one of the enormous windows overlooking the Golden Horn.

The view was little different than from the sea-wall. How much extra span of life had his brief flight gained him? It didn't matter, because now he again faced the same dilemma, imminent capture or a fatal leap.

A distressed sparrow fluttered past him and perched on Avis' worktable.

John was struck by the irony. The sheer drop beyond the window was not a barrier to any of the feathered creatures in the tower. It presented one to him alone, who could only dream of flying.

A man who at least could dream about flying.

John grabbed the artificial wings set in the corner as the door burst open and his pursuers jostled into the tower.

A black shape dropped from the ceiling and flung itself at the first man's face, screeching like a demon.

A huge raven.

One of Mithra's sacred ravens.

Curses echoed off the walls. Blades flashed, swiped ineffectually at the black terror. The attacked man suddenly shrieked and clapped one hand to the side of his bleeding head.

The raven flapped away, part of an ear clutched in its razor beak.

By now John had grasped the loops on the undersides of the immense wings.

Leaping up on the wooden chest, he kicked at the window, once, twice. Fragments of glass exploded outward, sparkling in the harsh light that turned the water beyond the docks to molten bronze. As the glittering shards vanished downward, the small study was suddenly filled with a swarm of winged shapes.

For an instant John stood transfixed at the shattered window as the noisy cloud flowed around him and then outside, like multi-hued smoke.

Avis' winged captives had gained their freedom.

John did not expect to soar across the Golden Horn, but he had seen leaves drift placidly to the earth, moving lazily back and forth on unseen air currents.

It was a chance he had to take.

Offering a swift prayer to Mithra for escape or a quick death, he grasped the loops tighter and jumped.

He was never certain what saved him, whether it was the updraft from the docks supporting taut, silk-covered wings and belling out his tunic, or that one wing scraped against the side of the tower and slowed his fall, or perhaps a combination of both.

Whatever the reason, the dock rushed up to slam into him and a few heartbeats later, John lay amid the wreckage of Avis' wings, safe but almost senseless.

The Gourd's men would be after him immediately. He had to get up and run, he thought groggily as he got up on his hands and knees.

A hand clamped around his arm and dragged him to his feet. "Quick! Come with me!" shouted the huge man who hauled him up.

It was Victor, Viator's son.

"There's a door around the corner! Hurry up!" Victor pulled John roughly along and thrust him through the doorway as nearby workers pretended not to notice anything amiss.

That was always the best response to anything unusual.

John's head began to clear as the pair ran along a short corridor that was wet and slippery beneath their boots, and through a crude, stone doorway into yet another corridor, one that led to a narrow, dark tunnel that eventually branched into three even narrower ways. Without hesitation Victor plunged into the central passage.

John was already lost.

"My friends and I played in here when we were young," Victor explained breathlessly as they clattered further into the labyrinth. "Know them all like the back of my hand. The Gourd's men don't."

They turned aside into an arched tunnel, its noisome muck up to their ankles. There were more doors and passageways, and then without warning John was in a place he remembered.

Viator's warehouse.

"You probably wondered where I disappeared after you chased me in here," Victor said with a wry grin. "Now you know."

They flopped down on a pile of packing straw.

John looked down at the blood soaking through his tunic. A broken wooden slat from the wings must have scraped him, he thought vaguely. "Should I thank Fortuna you were on hand at the right time?"

"Not really," Victor replied. "I've been hiding around here for my own safety. When the Gourd's little army started thundering around so noisily I naturally took a look to see what was going on. And there you were, forcing your way into Avis' tower with a pack of armed men after you. Naturally that caught my attention, even before you came crashing out the window as gracefully as a marble Icarus."

John managed a smile at the imagery.

"Besides which, I wanted to see if the wings worked," Victor admitted. "I've been waiting years to see them tested. Avis visits quite often asking for what he calls a small monetary contribution to help defray the necessary expenses of his work. Naturally I've developed quite an interest in the project."

"Yes, I ran into him when we tried to arrest you, Victor," John said wearily. "However, I suspect there was some other reason involved. Why did you really help me just now?"

The big man shrugged. "I'm a Christian, I'm supposed to help people in need."

John was reminded of the cart driver who had tried to do the same thing and paid dearly for his effort, but found himself instead mentioning the doorkeeper who needed assistance after being stabbed as Victor and his friends escaped from the Great Church.

"I didn't stab the old man," Victor said. "I only found out about that later. However, I admit I do have a selfish motive for aiding you. I'm trying to find out who murdered my father."

John awkwardly offered his condolences.

"Thank you," Victor replied. "We tried to leave immediately after your visit, you see. We intended to sail on one of the ships father employed to transport marble, but as we made our way along the docks, a demon swooped down on us."

A dark wave passed in front of John's eyes. He blinked, but the dark mist remained. "A demon?"

"Oh, not a real demon, but it's a good description. It was a black shape that struck out of nowhere. We were taken by surprise. The beast got in a telling blow and father fell into the water."

Victor bowed his partially shaven head in sorrow, suddenly looking much younger. "I didn't know what to do. Needless to say, nobody came to our aid. I should have grabbed the miserable creature. Instead I dived into the sea to try to save father, but he was gone. You wouldn't think that such a big man could disappear like that. The water was so cold and dark. I couldn't find him. It was as if Hades had swallowed him up the instant he hit the water. If I could just have found him...."

The thought of the greedy, dark water made John shudder. The importer of marble had indeed been swallowed up by Hades or at least by John's idea of its antechamber.

"I saw your father when he was taken to the hospice, Victor, and he would have died whether you had rescued him or not. You acted bravely."

Victor raised his head. His eyes were full of tears. "So he has been recovered? Then I must trust to others to bury him and honor him when I can. In the meantime, we are both hunted men."

"The Gourd's men must know that the labyrinth we fled through leads eventually to the docks. Before long there will be dozens of them here, searching every ship and warehouse for us."

"We can leave by one of many exits."

John made a sudden decision. "Help me to my feet." His voice was fading.

Victor complied. "You're very pale. You need medical attention, and soon. But where can we go?"

John managed to move his lips and whispered the only sanctuary that came to mind.

"The house of Senator Opimius."

Chapter Thirty

"Why did you bring me here?" John demanded.

"You told me to," Victor replied. "I pretended I'd come to work on the bath house and asked for Lady Anna. Just as you instructed. Don't you remember?"

"No." John struggled to sit up and failed.

He lay at the bottom of Senator Opimius' private bath. The sunken room, usually filled waist deep with warm water, had been drained for repair. What little light seeped in wavered as a slight breeze stirred the vegetation half blocking the slitted windows. The rippling effect mimicked the missing water. John saw that not only was Victor present, but Felix and Gaius as well.

The physician, who had examined John, climbed to his feet with a grunt. "That's likely the result of smacking your head on the ground. It's made you groggy. Yes, there's a nasty bruise there. Despite all the blood, that new cut is nothing. But I see you have some more serious wounds just starting to heal. You should not exert yourself for a day or so. No violent exercise. I'll send achillea in case you start bleeding again. That's what you have to watch for. The stuff is wonderful for stanching blood. In fact, what I always say is, if it was good enough for Achilles, it will certainly suit my patients."

"That's all very well, Gaius," John said weakly, "but I have tasks to carry out. They can't wait. Besides, staying here puts the senator and his daughter in danger." Again John attempted to sit. This time he succeeded. He leaned back and shivered. The disused bath house was cold as a mausoleum. "I'd be surprised if everyone in the house doesn't know we're here by now."

"Everybody's in danger all the time in this city," Gaius replied. "I've given you my medical opinion. Make sure you heed it. Next time we meet, you can buy me a cup or two of wine. We'll consider that my professional fee."

"I'll take care of your fee, Gaius," Felix said. "Lady Anna's gone to get clothes for you, John. When you leave you'd draw attention in those bloody things and that's the last thing we need. You were lucky you had a place to hide. Even luckier to be alive. When Victor arrived at the barracks, the first thing I thought was you'd been killed."

"The second was that I intended to kill you next," Victor said. "You practically had your sword in me before I could hand over that letter from the Gourd."

"The Gourd's signature is certainly a potent charm. It got you into the palace and as far as the barracks."

"It didn't convince you that you didn't need to keep the point of your blade between my shoulder blades all the way here, though."

"How could I be certain you hadn't stolen the letter? You might have been leading me into a trap."

"I should return to the hospice," Gaius interrupted. "I'll wager there's been more than one unfortunate arrived since I left who really has been run through with someone's blade."

Felix agreed. "Victor, you'd better leave with Gaius. You'll be safer if you go back into hiding for the time being. As far as I'm concerned, you've cleared yourself of suspicion by assisting John. But the Gourd's men don't know that. Now if we just knew who set them on John…"

"They certainly had an excellent description of me from the little I overheard in Dio's studio."

"So it seems. We'll have to be careful, with eyes everywhere, but I think we can make it to Madam Isis' house. She'll hide us while we decide what to do next." Felix looked around the stark, echoing space. "Speaking of which, this place must have seen some trysts in its time, although those other goings-on would have been a lot more enjoyable than our little illicit gathering."

"You're probably right," came the reply in a woman's voice.

Anna stood in the doorway, neatly folded clothing in her arms.

"Lady Anna, I apologize for my crudeness," Felix said hastily.

"Do you suppose I don't know what the servants get up to? Lack of privacy is the bane of their existence."

As Gaius and Victor departed, Anna turned toward Felix. "If I could have a private word with John?"

Felix stepped outside and Anna descended the four steps into the dry bath. She sat on the lowest, facing John. She looked at him in thoughtful silence. It was the appraising look one might give a work of art, or a stranger.

"You appear more alive than when Victor brought you to the door," she finally said. "I feared you were mortally wounded when I first saw you."

"Lady Anna, I apologize, I wasn't thinking clearly when I asked Victor to bring me here. However, it does give me an opportunity to warn you. I will be blunt since there is no time to waste. Despite what you might think, your father is one of those who opposes Justinian's ascension. Worse, Justinian suspects."

Anna's only reaction was an almost imperceptible widening of her eyes. Her features remained frozen for several heartbeats. "How can you possibly believe such a slander?" she blurted out at last.

"I would not say it if I did not know it to be the truth. I observed your father at the baths with Trenico and Tryphon." John quickly explained Tryphon's lie and what he had heard from Fortunatus. Perhaps he was still not thinking clearly, not expressing himself well, because Anna merely shook her head.

"No, John. The very notion is impossible."

"Lady Anna..." John began desperately.

Anna put her face in her hands and her shoulders shook with sobs.

"Don't worry. Your father is a clever man. All you have to do is warn him. He will find a way to extricate himself."

"It isn't that," came the choked reply.

When Anna raised her face the aqueous light filtering into the bath house glistened on the tears streaking her cheeks. "It's because I can't see you again, John."

"Your father has banned me from the house. You must obey him."

Anna looked away. "I came in while you were still unconscious, when Gaius was examining you...."

"I understand."

"John, it isn't your condition. Not really. But actually seeing...it made me realize...and accept the truth. I have been deluding myself. About many things."

Anna slid off the step and knelt beside John. He was enveloped by the fragrance of the roses with which she seemed always surrounded. "I would like to ask a question. You mentioned there was once a woman."

John hesitated before speaking. "Yes. Cornelia." Emotion warmed his voice.

Anna smiled sadly. "I can tell you love her, by the way your lips shape her name."

"Can you? We met in Crete. I had been a mercenary, but she persuaded me there was much to be said for the domestic life. We lived together for some time, traveling around with a company of bull-leapers. We came to Constantinople. It was before I was captured and mutilated."

He paused for a while. When he managed to continue the raw pain in his voice lent it a rasp. "I was eventually brought back here in chains. The troupe had long since gone and with it my Cornelia. I have heard no word of her since."

Anna wiped her eyes. "What a tragic story. No wonder a dark look dwells in your eyes."

John laid his hand on hers, wondering at his own daring. Anna's warm fingers clasped his hand tightly.

"There is no need to grieve for me, Lady Anna," he said gently. "The man capable of loving a woman died long ago, and he died loving her. As he still does."

"No, John. He isn't dead." Anna pressed her lips against his forehead and then ascended to the door without further hesitation.

"Goodbye...Anna."

She did not respond and John was not certain she had heard. He was left only with a faint memory of roses.

Felix returned. "Let's get you on your feet," he said gruffly. "Can you do that?"

John nodded. The fog in his head was beginning to clear.

Felix took hold of an arm, unnecessarily it turned out, since John managed to stand without assistance. "Excellent!" Felix paused. "Now must ask you something, my friend. When Gaius was examining you—"

"How pleasing to hear yet again that while I was unable to protest I was stripped and put on display like an old Greek statue!"

"Yes, well...but...you claimed your captors had...."

"I was castrated, Felix. You have seen. Is that not sufficient? Can you imagine how many times I have been questioned about this matter? The very thing I most wish to avoid ever discussing with anyone, let alone the drunken louts who are always the most obscenely curious? So I long since decided to give the prying bastards an answer that would make them wish they hadn't asked." A brief smile crossed John's face. "Yes, they always regret hearing the details. I will not be giving Madam Isis any business. Now we had best be on our way to her house while I'm still able to walk."

Chapter Thirty-One

John and Felix took a circuitous route to their destination. They dodged in and out of narrow passages and cut across noisome and noisy courtyards to avoid better traveled thoroughfares. Once they were on their way, the chilly air revived John further and they were able to make steady progress.

Before long they entered a crooked finger of an alley pointed toward the Mese. Halfway down its dim and debris-strewn length they were startled by the sound of running feet.

Felix's hand went to his sword, but the noise was nothing more than a pair of filthy boys. The two urchins raced around the bend in the alley, straight toward John and Felix. Behind them limped a beggar, yelling promises of obscene punishments for some unspecified misdeed. From the way he hobbled, it was obvious he had no chance of catching the culprits.

In fact, the boys had time to stop and spit in the direction of John and Felix before disappearing from sight.

Felix reddened with rage, but allowed them to escape.

John, however, took several swift strides and grabbed the beggar's shoulder as he turned to limp back the way he had come. "You!" he shouted, viciously shaking the ragged man. "You're the one who bet his boots on our deaths! The cart driver came to our aid, but you were placing wagers we would die!"

"Not so, good sir!" Alarmed, the beggar took a couple of steps backward until the rough masonry wall of a tenement overlooking the alley brought his retreat to a halt.

Felix trotted over and looked the beggar up and down. "You do appear to have lost your footwear. Unless you consider rag wrappings to be adequate. I'm not surprised you couldn't catch those two. My advice would be to never wager what you can't afford to lose."

"No, no, you don't understand. It was those…er… children. They stole my boots while I was asleep." The beggar's voice was feeble. He held up a deformed hand as if to ward off a blow.

John shook the man even harder. "No!" he shouted. "It was you! Do you think I wouldn't remember your voice, making a wager like that? Furthermore," he looked at the grubby man more closely, "when was your miraculous cure?"

Felix gaped at John for an instant. Then understanding dawned. "It's the mute beggar we tried to question a few days ago!"

"Mute?" croaked the beggar. "Of course I'm not mute. As you can hear. There's the proof! You must be thinking of the...uh...the mute beggar who hangs about in the Mese. An easy enough mistake to make. He's my brother. People confuse us all the time."

John grabbed the man's dirty wrist and slammed his hand against the wall.

"I see you're also missing two fingers, just like this mute brother who so closely resembles you. What a remarkable coincidence."

Felix gripped the hilt of his sword. "You lying bastard! What are you hiding?"

"Nothing, nothing at all, good sirs," the man replied in a wheedling tone. "I admit it was me you spoke to. It was just that I didn't want to get involved with people in authority. Especially when they come around asking about someone dying. Can you blame me?"

Felix looked thunderous. "You're telling us you know something about the murder we're investigating and deliberately concealed it?"

The beggar's expression crumpled at the words and the threat they carried. John thought if the man could have turned around he would have begun leaping up the tenement wall like a trapped mouse in a futile attempt to escape.

"No," the beggar gasped. "I don't know anything about any murder. It was an accident!"

"A man gets a blade in the ribs and you call it an accident?" Felix growled. "How could anyone be careless enough to accidentally fall on someone's blade?"

"Stabbed? But I thought—"

"We were questioning you about the death of the man who was murdered in the Great Church," said John. "What did you think we were asking about?"

The beggar opened his mouth, but whatever lie might have been forming died on his tongue when he saw the fury in John's eyes. "When you said death, I thought you meant the death of the grocer's boy. Timothy's son. He was run over by a cart just the other day."

Mithra's light flared in John's mental darkness.

The bits of information he'd accumulated, like fragments of colored glass, until now glistening and tantalizing, but meaningless, had finally converged into an image.

"Such accidents are common enough," he replied. "Why didn't you want to talk about it? Were you involved?"

"It wasn't my fault, sir," the man whined. "It was those accursed boys. The ones who spat at you. They were friends of the grocer's son. The three of them were always tormenting me. My own personal Furies, they were. Then when I went after them that particular day, they ran away across the Mese. Right into the path of a cart. It ran the boy over and crashed into the column in front of his father's shop. They're still trying to repair it. But I had no part in his death! It was the carter's fault anyhow. It was a small cart. Far too small for that huge marble it was hauling."

"The sculpture of Christ, you mean? The very one Hypatius died in front of?"

"Why, indeed sir. That is true. You know everything."

"Yes, I think I do."

"His father's shop." Felix's tone was thoughtful. "That means the shopkeeper has a reminder of his son's death every time he looks out."

John did not reply. His thoughts were on the intricate mosaic that had formed in his mind's eye. He barely heard the beggar.

"And the boy was his only child," the ragged man was saying. "Thank the Lord Timothy does not know how it came about. I would fear for my safety if he did. Yet," he concluded sadly, "I would not blame him if his grief unhinged him. I had a son myself once, but I don't know where he is now, or even if he is still alive. At least until I know otherwise, I can believe he is living somewhere in the city and that I may see him again one day. Timothy does not have that comfort. Not in this life."

John was not listening. He had already begun to walk away in the direction of the Mese. Felix followed.

"John, what is it?"

"Fortuna has smiled on us, Felix, by bringing us here. She has allowed us to complete our interrupted investigation. We've found the final fact I'd hoped to find. Not that I had guessed exactly what it would be."

"I don't understand."

"Timothy the grocer's son is the final piece. Now the picture makes sense. We knew all the deaths were connected to the sculpture, but not why."

"Well, so the boy's death was connected to the sculpture too. The cart ran him over. You mean... the cart driver? He killed the boy and also...but Dio, wasn't he killed after—"

"The boy died first, Felix, as the marble was being delivered. It was his death that started it all. One might blame the cart driver, certainly. But then, if one were grief stricken, one might also blame the Christ figure itself."

"And everyone associated with it," murmured Felix. "We had better get to the grocer's shop at once."

❋ ❋ ❋

They were almost too late.

As John and Felix hurried across the Mese, a man bolted from Timothy's emporium, raced down the street, into the Augustaion, and headed toward the Great Church.

John and Felix gave pursuit. By the time they reached the church vestibule the man had scrambled up onto the high pedestal supporting the sculpture and was embracing Christ's legs. The man began to harangue the shocked onlookers.

"Don't put your faith in the Lord!" he screamed, his agonized tones echoing in the cavernous space. "For He is full of deceit! He did not allow me time enough to complete my task!"

"That's the gray-haired fellow who tried to help the carter the other day." Felix looked at John in confusion. "I thought we were after a murderous grocer. Why did this man run off when he saw us?"

The man heard him and shouted down, with a twisted smile. "Because I realized you were coming after me. I am the man you're seeking, fool! It was me, Timothy, who delivered the death blow!"

He tightened his grip on the figure of Christ. "Yes," he shouted even louder, "that carter often passed down the Mese in the course of his work. I had to watch him, the murderer of my son, drive past almost every day. Ah, but I was just waiting for my chance. When he gave it to me by coming to your aid, I stabbed him. In all the confusion no one noticed. You might say I helped him. Helped him on his way to Hell!"

A woman screamed and made the sign of her religion. Some men began shouting virulent curses at Timothy. Curious spectators were filling the vestibule, a number of them drawn from the church itself by the commotion. A group of Blues, sensing the anger in the air, appeared from the street to add their vulgar jeers.

John caught bits of panicked conversations.

"What is it? What's happening?"

"...dead. Murdered!"

"...treachery, so they say."

Suddenly several more Blues, obviously intoxicated, burst into the vestibule. "Beware the Gourd!" They surged unsteadily through the crowd to join their companions. "We're in for some sport now!"

"Justinian's dead!" one of the new arrivals screamed. His shrill, slurred cry cut through the clamor echoing in the vestibule.

"No!" another shouted even more loudly. "Justin was murdered! His bodyguards have all been executed! Justinian has proclaimed himself emperor!"

Archdeacon Palamos appeared from the body of the church, shooing away several small boys who sought to follow him. "Someone remove that blasphemer immediately!" he shouted in thunderous outrage, pointing at Timothy.

Felix grabbed the grocer's legs and got a boot in the face for his pains.

"Archdeacon," John said swiftly. "You must hear what this man has to say."

Palamos stared at Timothy in horror. Wild haired, his eyes glaring, the grocer resembled a demon.

"Yes, listen to me, archdeacon!" Timothy demanded. "I executed the cart driver and others too, all of them connected with this blasphemous

- 302 -

statue. I started with Hypatius, one of those who sponsored it. That was as quickly done as it was with the cart driver. Yes, I wept tears of joy over the carter. It's amazing what you can do in the middle of a rioting crowd without being noticed."

"Come down and speak to us privately," Palamos coaxed.

Timothy simply laughed and continued. "The sculptor, Dio, he was another."

"You were outside the monastery and overheard Fortunatus tell me where Dio could be found?" John guessed.

"You are clever, Excellency," Timothy said, "but not half as clever as I am. I already knew where Dio lived. Hadn't Hypatius bragged all over the city about the expensive sculptor he had employed? No, Dio would have died sooner had he not been away the day I first visited his studio. However, when I overheard Fortunatus say he would shortly be back, I was there first thing next morning to warm his homecoming."

"And to set the Prefect's men on me," John said.

"A marvelous stroke of good fortune, that was. I noticed you coming up the Domninus as I was leaving. I'd been keeping my eye on you as much as I could anyway, ever since my assistant told me you'd been asking about Hypatius. So I helpfully alerted the first of the Gourd's men I could find."

"You wouldn't have to look far," Felix growled. "They're everywhere. What's more, they're sure to be here soon to deal with this disturbance. John, we'd better grab him and make our escape while we can," he muttered in an undertone.

John shook his head. "We must make certain of the facts, my friend, while we have the archdeacon as a witness. Tell me about Viator, Timothy."

"Viator! Wasn't that a wonder? I asked for the Lord's help in finding all the people who were involved with this disgusting sculpture, and was granted heavenly aid! It was a true miracle! To begin with, at least. Even you and your friend were part of it," he said to John. "I hadn't yet been able to find out from whose warehouse the marble had come. Then you obligingly led me to it. Not only that, you also frightened the importer so badly that he ran away practically unguarded. I soon stopped his flight with a blade in the ribs!"

"So Dominica and Fortunatus were spared because they chose not to talk publicly about their co-sponsoring the sculpture with Hypatius?"

"Again you are wrong! I knew them for the murderers they were. I own a perfume shop too, you know. My wealthy clients tell me many things. They might have thought nobody knew, but their contributions were common knowledge among the high born."

Timothy's gloating grin turned into a sorrowful scowl. "The problem was they were too well protected. The widow never stirs without a small army of guards. As for Fortunatus, it's true he has a name of good omen, yet he does well to skulk in the monastery. I had planned to climb over the wall one night and see if I could catch him at his devotions."

Palamos shuddered. "I've heard enough. This man is Satan himself."

"You think I'm Satan?" screeched Timothy. "Think it then. I'm just doing the Lord's job since He wouldn't do it Himself."

"Satan walks among us all right," bellowed a nearby Blue, a young man with a spotty face. His voice was thickened by wine. "It's not the madman perched up there, though. It's the King of the Demons who's just mounted the throne, not to mention the new empress!"

A portly, middle-aged man with the look of a clerk in his stooped shoulders and pale face pointed an accusing finger at the younger man and yelled furiously at him.

"Whoever rules, the populace is going to suffer! You should be on your knees asking for forgiveness instead of stirring up trouble!"

The young man he addressed replied with an exaggerated low bow. "Such fine talk from one about to die!"

"Not at your hand, you idiotic fop!"

"Is that so?" The Blue drew his blade. "I think you are wrong!"

The Blue grabbed the man's throat, but before he could make another move a familiar voice cut through the tumult.

"No, my young friend. I believe he is right."

It was the Gourd. He strode through the crowd, which shrank away from him, clearing his path as if by magick.

"No indeed," he remarked in a conversational tone. "He's not going to die at your hand. In fact, it is you who will die at mine. But then, you already knew that, didn't you?" The Gourd hardly paused before casually running his blade through the Blue's stomach.

Felix stepped between John and the Gourd.

The Gourd nudged the lifeless body at his feet with the toe of his boot, then addressed the stunned and silent onlookers. He tilted his monstrous head toward a knot of Blues. "Quite a few of you may soon be joining this fellow in the afterlife. As I have warned, riots will be crushed without mercy. I do believe that one was brewing here."

Archdeacon Palamos stepped toward the Gourd. "More killing won't resolve anything. In the name of the Lord, I command you to leave this holy place immediately!"

Dozens of the Gourd's men poured into the vestibule, herding terrified people before them. Another contingent emerged from the nave, having entered through a side door.

The operation was well planned. It would not be long before troublemakers, real and imagined, would be hauled off to the dungeons. Nor would it be long before the Gourd's men, methodically examining the crowd, discovered the tall thin Greek whom their master wanted dead.

John glanced at Timothy. The grocer still embraced the marble figure. Though no longer the center of attention, he grinned with apparent delight at the incipient slaughter.

Then John turned his gaze on the Gourd and drew his sword. He could do some good before he was discovered.

Felix caught his wrist in a crushing grip and shook his head slightly.

The Gourd's men had closed their ring around the crowd, forcing it into a tight mass. The portly man cursed as he was crushed against the statue, and again as more men were forced against him by the tightening circle. A number of the crowd sought safety by clambering up onto the pedestal next to Timothy.

"The bastard's going to set his men loose," whispered Felix. "He wants a bloodbath. He'll call it a riot afterward and who'll contradict him?"

Even as Felix spoke, the Gourd began to raise his sword as a signal for the sort of slaughter John and Felix had witnessed near the Strategion.

Before the signal could be completed, the mass of men clinging to the looming sculpture unbalanced it.

The great Christ figure rocked backward and then toppled forward, shedding human barnacles as those who had sought its safety leapt away.

The sculpture hit the floor and shattered in a thunderous, echoing explosion. Chunks of marble went spinning and rolling across the vestibule.

An unearthly scream mounted into the shadowed vault overhead before trailing away in a chilling gurgle. For a heartbeat John thought of the death bellow of the Great Bull slain by Mithra.

Even the Gourd stood transfixed.

The Christ lay stretched out toward the church entrance like a toppled marble tree. The head lay in one corner. Here was a hand, there a part of the cross beam. One or two of the crowd lay moaning on the floor, but the only person seriously injured appeared to be Timothy.

John knelt beside him.

The grocer's eyes were closed. Blood flowed from his mouth, but his chest still moved in a shallow fashion.

Felix was at John's side instantly. "Hurry! We have to get out of here! You're sure to be spotted!"

"No, Felix. There's one last thing I have to know."

He shook Timothy's shoulder roughly. The grocer's eyes opened. His lips moved. Blood bubbled out. He spat and began to speak. "He was my son. My only child. He was playing in the street. Didn't the driver see him? Heaven should have blinded him for it. I have been faithful to the Lord all my life. Why did He take away my son? And do it with a cart carrying a likeness of His own son? Was it some horrible joke? What have I done to deserve this?"

John heard a choking sob. He glanced over his shoulder and saw Archdeacon Palamos standing a few paces behind him. He turned back to Timothy. "Yes, we understand that. But why did you attack Opimius?"

"I saw him talking to Hypatius here in the church...admiring that blasphemous piece...so I thought he must also be connected with it..."

"But in attacking Opimius you ended up killing a devout old servant trying to protect his master."

"A master so arrogant...he went about with only a tottering old slave...for a guard! He'd still be alive...if he hadn't fought so hard...I ran off and hid in my perfume shop after stabbing him...it's in the Augustaion...very close to the alley by Samsun's Hospice...." Timothy's voice was fading. "But the old man should not have died...I have prayed for the Lord's forgiveness..."

"You think your Lord will forgive you for snuffing out the lives of five people?" John said quietly.

"No, not five...I did not mean to kill the old man...so his death does not count." Timothy's eyes glistened. "I was only given time to kill four...four for a boy. Yet forty or four hundred...would not have been enough!" Anger made his voice stronger. "And there were others waiting to die too...that drunken physician at the hospice...said he could do nothing for my son...didn't even try..."

"His Lord may not be very ready to forgive," Felix observed quietly to John, "for it's always possible that Timothy will live to see the inside of the emperor's dungeons."

"And so will both of you."

John looked around. The Gourd loomed behind them, sword at the ready, several of his men at his back.

The Gourd inclined his massive head in John's direction. "Or will you survive? There's blood soaking through your tunic, I see, John. Been fighting, have you? What does heaven have in store for you, I wonder? I suppose heaven does as it pleases, but since we are not in heaven, what would please me most?"

"Halt!"

A man in full military regalia strode into the vestibule.

"Mithra," breathed Felix. "It's the captain of the excubitors!"

The captain, his face a mask of contempt, came to a stop before the Gourd. "By order of Justinian, I place you, Prefect Theodotus, under arrest!" he declared. "Arrest him, Felix!"

Felix grinned and clapped his big hand on the Gourd's shoulder. "With pleasure!"

Epilogue

John and Felix watched as workers finished unloading a cartload of marble busts and commemorative diptychs, and heaped them haphazardly under a portico before rumbling off.

Felix surveyed the large pile of castoff public monuments. "It looks as if Emperor Justin is thinking of doing some redecoration."

The obscure square they were crossing had been used for years as a repository for discarded statuary. An eerie crowd of motionless dignitaries surrounded them.

"Look." John paused to read an inscription chiseled next to the foot of a man dressed in military garb. "It's Vitalian."

Felix shivered. "Is this cold ever going to leave? Even the sun doesn't seem inclined to celebrate Justinian's sudden recovery."

"Unfortunately the weather doesn't pay much attention to what we'd like."

"Rather like Fortuna."

"She has been good to us on occasion." John looked toward the building forming one side of the square. Over its portico sat a statue of Hermes. A few bits of peeling gilt on the Hermes glinted in the thin light.

"Fortuna's ways are often strange, Felix. What if Timothy had not murdered Victor's father? If he hadn't, Victor wouldn't have been on hand to save my life. I owe my continued existence to another's untimely death."

"And if the Gourd's thugs had succeeded in killing you, who knows how many more victims Timothy would have dispatched before he was caught? I wonder who I would have been working with if you had died."

"The Gourd wanted both of us out of the way. Didn't he order both of us to wait out in the cold all night for a riot that was not going to happen, and then send those assassins to attack us when we were exhausted from lack of sleep?"

"You think that was why they waited until dawn? I thought perhaps they failed to notice us behind that pile of debris. Do you think the Gourd was planning to take over by force of arms when Justin died?"

"It's happened before, and it probably will again," John replied. "Come to think of it, we're fortunate the murderous grocer didn't put his blade in our backs since he followed us more than once. No wonder you kept thinking someone was watching us. Timothy was interested in us only because his assistant told him we'd been asking about Hypatius. If he had concluded we were connected with the sculpture in some way, I suspect one or both of us might not be here."

Felix scratched his chin. "John, I admit I couldn't understand why Justinian had chosen a—pardon me—a slave to undertake such a delicate investigation. Now I see he gave you the task because of your discretion and intelligence. Then, too, your tutoring Lady Anna in Persian presented a wonderful opportunity for him, since it meant that he already had someone in Opimius' household to act as a spy, however unwilling."

"We both better use our intelligence and be exceedingly discreet, Felix. It's been made very plain to me that any knowledge of this investigation reaching other ears will have swift and terrible repercussions not only for us, but also for Anna and her father. I was also informed that we shouldn't allow ourselves to think the services we rendered our masters will protect us in future either."

John looked at Vitalian's marble twin again. "Since Opimius is pagan," he went on, "I wonder if he thought it a wise move to align himself with Vitalian, a man known and admired for his orthodoxy?"

"It turned out to be a bad alliance," Felix observed. "But Opimius is nothing if not shrewd. I was on duty when that delegation of senators arrived to present their petition to Justin. It was signed by every single member of the Senate and Opimius and Aurelius formally presented it to the emperor. Justin understood right away when he saw those two advancing toward him together, practically arm in arm."

Felix scowled at the memory. "To formally petition an emperor to agree to share his throne with an impatient upstart, even if that upstart is his nephew... to demand that an emperor give up power...I wish

I hadn't been witness to such a spectacle. If those senators had had the courage to attempt a proper coup I would have enjoyed putting my sword in every one of them. Unfortunately, it was all legal."

His scowl grew more pronounced. "Yes," he went on, "Quaestor Proclus glanced over the petition and explained it to the emperor as if he already knew its contents, which I'd wager he did. It's a sorry thing to see men disgrace themselves, and none worse than Opimius. After all, he abandoned his principles, and in supporting Justinian has betrayed Justin, a man to whom he had proclaimed loyalty."

"I think Opimius was acting more out of loyalty toward his daughter," John replied. "He abandoned his principles rather than Anna. What would have become of her if her father had been arrested and executed for opposing Justinian? Everything the senator owned would no doubt have been forfeited. Anna would have been left not only fatherless, but destitute and homeless as well."

He paused. "And speaking of shrewd senators, when Senator Aurelius suggested in front of his friend Opimius that I interview Tryphon and Trenico, he was as much as anything giving Opimius a clear warning. I'm certain he had spoken about it to him privately, but perhaps he felt it would be more persuasive to place two of the other conspirators under direct suspicion. You know, Felix, I would not be at all surprised to discover that Aurelius were pagan also. That would explain the close friendship between him and Opimius, despite their political differences. Our faith binds us strongly together."

"You are back in Opimius' good graces, I suppose. Are you tutoring Lady Anna again?"

John shook his head. "It is best I not see her just yet. I did speak to the senator in private, but our conversation was brief since Aurelius and Anatolius arrived. Somehow the tale of my flight from Avis' tower has got around, and in its travels become much exaggerated. Apparently I was halfway up the Bosporos before I fell out of the sky."

Felix chuckled. "I'll wager young Anatolius was thrilled to hear that story."

"He looked very disappointed when I explained I'd left the wings in pieces on the docks. Then he asked his father to make certain that Avis had a few coins now and then to continue the project."

"That's not very likely to happen, is it?" Felix observed. "Aurelius must be thanking whatever gods he worships that it was you who first tried out those wings, and not his son."

"It is strange, Felix," said John. "Consider that here there were two sons, both of them only children. One would think Fortuna had bestowed enough favor on Anatolius, making his a prosperous family when so many others are destitute. Yet he was saved from certain death the night he decided to join the Blues, while that poor grocer's boy died playing in the gutter."

Felix said nothing. He glanced uneasily at the statue of Vitalian and then resumed walking.

"Lady Anna must have gone to her father immediately," he said. "Once she relayed the warning you gave her, he wasted no time in throwing his support into Justinian's camp. Now Justinian has recovered, and frankly I begin to wonder if he was half as ill as was reported. He's been just as swift in removing the Gourd from office. The question is will anyone believe Justinian's claims that the Gourd has been poisoning him? With all those guards around him, not to mention Theodora constantly at his side, how could the Gourd possibly have managed it?"

"True or not, the Gourd cut his own throat by persuading everyone he was able to perform magick," John observed with a wry smile. "You can do all sorts of impossible things with magick. Besides, Justinian's accusation is all the proof any court of law can afford to consider."

They had reached the building overseen by the leprous Hermes. Felix gazed back uneasily over the frozen throng populating the square. "There's something strange about seeing all those statues crowding about in public as if they're about to start rioting. Speaking of which, the superstitious are already spinning tales about how that statue of Christ miraculously punished Timothy."

He frowned and went on. "As to Justin, in the end he was rather relieved by the senators' suggestion that he and Justinian co-rule. It would certainly lift some of the burden from his shoulders, so he will be considering it, or so he was muttering to Euphemia this very morning. Yet still I feel I have somehow failed him. I don't know why."

"Justinian considers we have both aided him, and it's his opinion which matters now."

Felix looked thoughtful. "Do you realize Justinian has reason to be doubly grateful to you? First, you disarmed those opposing him by uncovering the real murderer of Hypatius and making it impossible for them to use his death against Justinian in some way or another. Then, on top of that, you were instrumental in persuading Opimius, the leader of the conspiracy, of the wisdom of publicly declaring himself one of Justinian's staunchest supporters for reasons we will never see made public."

A wry grin crossed the excubitor's face. "Not that Theodora will thank either of us for any of our efforts," he continued. "I have a strong suspicion she does not enjoy the notion of Justinian being grateful to anyone except her. If he was, such people might well have some influence with him and she's the sort who cannot tolerate even the thought of any such possibility. Still, aside from that, it's all been tied up very neatly."

"There is one matter still left unfinished."

Felix gave John a questioning look.

John's fist smashed into the excubitor's jaw, sending him to the ground. He looked up at John, his expression more bewildered than angry.

"Don't you recall what you said outside Isis' house?" John asked. "'Watch your tongue, slave, or I'll give you a thrashing you won't soon forget.' Those were your exact words. Were you too intoxicated to remember? A man can't allow himself to be insulted in such a manner, but a slave has no choice. A slave does not dare retaliate. There can be no real friendship between a man and a slave."

John extended his hand. Felix took it warily and allowed himself to be helped to his feet. He rubbed his jaw, frowning.

Then he grinned widely.

"I see you've guessed, my friend," John said. "As a reward for my services, Justinian has granted me my freedom."

Felix's shout of joy disturbed several seagulls rooting among the gutter debris. They rose, squawking with indignation, into the slate gray sky.

Afterword

The fate of Prefect Theodotus, nicknamed Colocynthius (Gourd), is related by the historian Procopius in his *Secret History*. As soon as Justinian regained his health he accused Theodotus of being a magician and poisoner, obtaining evidence against him by torturing the man's friends. Only Quaestor Proclus had the courage to protest publicly that Theodotus was innocent. Thanks to him, Theodotus was not executed, but instead was exiled to Jerusalem. When he later heard that men were being sent to assassinate him, he hid in a church and spent the rest of his life there.

Glossary

Glossary

NOTE: All dates are CE unless otherwise indicated.

ACHILLEA

Yarrow. Its botanical name, *Achillea millefolium*, is derived from the legend that Achilles employed it to stop his men's wounds bleeding. It has been thus used for centuries, earning it the alternative name of Soldier's Woundwort.

ALABASTRON

Glass or pottery flask for massage oil or perfume. The name is derived from the Greek *alabastros* meaning alabaster, from which early examples were made.

ATRIUM

Central area of a Roman house, open to the sky. An atrium not only provided light to rooms opening from it, but also held a shallow pool (impluvium) under the square or oblong opening in its roof in order to catch rain water both for household use and decorative purposes.

AUGUSTAION

Square between the GREAT PALACE and the GREAT CHURCH.

BATHS OF ACTAEON

According to legend, Actaeon was a hunter who accidentally saw Artemis, goddess of the chase, while she was bathing. He was transformed into a stag and subsequently torn to pieces by his own dogs.

BATHS OF ZEUXIPPOS
Public baths in Constantinople. They were named after a Thracian deity whose name combined Zeus and Hippos. Erected by order of Septimius Severus (146-211; r 193-211) and situated northeast of the HIPPODROME, they were generally considered the most luxurious of the city's public baths. They were famous for their classical statues, numbering between sixty and eighty.

BLUES
See FACTIONS.

CALDARIUM
Hottest room in the public baths.

CARYATID
Column formed in the shape of a female figure dressed in flowing garments. The best known caryatids are probably the six supporting the roof of the Porch of the Maidens of the Erechtheion, a temple on the Acropolis in Athens.

CAUTES AND CAUTOPATES
Statues of twin torchbearers Cautes and Cautopates were part of the sacred furnishings of a MITHRAEUM. Cautes always held his torch upright while Cautopates pointed his downward. The twins may represent the rising and setting of the sun. Other interpretations hold that they symbolize life and death or the twin emotions of despair and joy or perhaps that they are both MITHRA, depicted at different hours of the day.

CHALKE
Main entrance of the GREAT PALACE.

CHURCH OF EIRENE
Popular name for Hagia Eirene (Church of the Holy Peace), situated near the GREAT CHURCH.

CITY PREFECT
High ranking urban official whose main duty was to maintain public order.

CONCRETE
Roman concrete, consisting of wet lime, volcanic ash, and pieces of rock, was used in a wide range of structures from humble cisterns to the Pantheon in Rome, which has survived for nearly 2,000 years even without the steel reinforcing rods commonly used in modern concrete buildings. One of the oldest Roman concrete buildings still standing is the Temple of Vesta at Tivoli, Italy, built during the first century BC.

EXCUBITORS

The palace guard.

EUPHEMIA (d c 524)

Little is known about Euphemia, wife of JUSTIN I. She was originally called Lupicina, a name commonly associated with prostitutes. It is said that she was a slave whom JUSTIN I purchased, freed, and married, and that she had also been the mistress of her previous owner. She supported JUSTINIAN as her husband's successor, but was bitterly opposed to any suggestion of JUSTINIAN marrying THEODORA.

FACTIONS

Supporters of the BLUE or GREEN chariot teams, named for their racing colors. Great rivalry existed between the factions. Brawls between them were not uncommon and occasionally escalated into citywide riots.

FALERNIAN WINE

Considered one of the finest Roman wines.

FORUM BOVIS

See MESE.

FORUM CONSTANTINE

See MESE.

FROM EGGS TO APPLES

From beginning to end. The saying is based upon Roman dining practice. A modern version would be from hors d'oeuvres to dessert.

GREAT CHURCH

Popular name for the Hagia Sophia (Church of the Holy Wisdom). The first Great Church was built in 360 and burnt down in 404. The second was erected in 415, but destroyed during the Nika riots (532). It was replaced by the existing Hagia Sophia, constructed by order of JUSTINIAN I and consecrated in December 537.

GREAT PALACE

Lay in the southeastern part of Constantinople. It was not one building but many, set amid trees and gardens. The grounds included barracks for the EXCUBITORS, ceremonial rooms, meeting halls, the imperial family's living quarters, churches, and housing for court officials, ambassadors, and various other dignitaries.

GREENS

See FACTIONS.

HARMONIA'S NECKLACE

According to mythology, when Harmonia married Cadmus, one of her wedding presents was a necklace which later brought calamity on everyone who owned it. Proverbially it refers to a possession that brings misfortune.

HIPPODROME

U-shaped race track near the GREAT PALACE. The Hippodrome had tiered seating accommodating up to a hundred thousand spectators. It was also used for public celebrations and other civic events.

HORMISDAS PALACE

Home of JUSTINIAN and THEODORA before JUSTINIAN became emperor.

HYPOCAUST

Roman form of central heating, accomplished by distribution of hot air through flues under the flooring.

HEMSUT

Egyptian goddess of fate. Also known as Hemuset.

JOHN THE HUNCHBACK (known 490s)

Leader of an army sent by Anastasius I (c 430-518, r 491-518) to put down an Isaurian rebellion. JUSTIN I, then still serving in the ranks of the military, was one of John's subordinate commanders. Although they were defeated at the battle of Cotyaeum in Phrygia (491), it took several years to finally subdue the rebels.

JUSTIN I (c 450-527, r 518-527)

Born in the province of Dardania (part of present-day Macedonia), Justin and two friends journeyed to Constantinople to seek their fortunes. All three joined the EXCUBITORS and Justin eventually rose to hold the rank of commander. Justin was married to EUPHEMIA. He was declared emperor upon the death of Anastasius I (c 430-518, r 491-518). Justin's nephew JUSTINIAN I was crowned co-emperor in April 527, four months before Justin died.

JUSTINIAN I (483-565; r 527-565)

Nephew of JUSTIN I and his successor to the throne. Justinian's greatest ambition was to restore the Roman empire to its former glory. He succeeded in temporarily regaining North Africa, Italy, and southeastern Spain. He ordered the codification of Roman law and after the Nika Riots (532) rebuilt the GREAT CHURCH as well as many other buildings in Constantinople. He married THEODORA in 525.

KALAMOS

Reed pen.

KING THEODORIC (454-526; r Ostrogoths 471-526; r Italy 493-526)

Known as Theodoric the Great, he was educated in Constantinople, having been taken there as a diplomatic hostage at the age of eight. Ascending to the Ostrogothic throne on the death of his father Theodemir in 471, he eventually regained control of Italy from the barbarians who had won it from Rome almost twenty years before. During his reign he favored Roman methods of government and law.

KEEPER OF THE PLATE

Court official responsible for the care of palace plate, which included ceremonial items as well as imperial platters, ewers, goblets, and various types of dishes, often made of precious metals.

LUPICINA

See EUPHEMIA.

MASTER OF THE OFFICES

Oversaw the civil side of imperial administration within the palace.

MESE

Main thoroughfare of Constantinople. Enriched with columns, arches, statuary (depicting secular, military, imperial, and religious subjects), fountains, religious establishments, workshops, monuments, emporiums, public baths, and private dwellings, it was a perfect mirror of the heavily populated and densely built city it traversed. The Mese passed through several fora, including FORUM BOVIS and FORUM CONSTANTINE.

MIME

After the second century CE, mime supplanted classical Roman pantomime in popularity. Unlike performers of pantomime, mimes spoke and did not wear masks. Their presentations featured extreme violence and graphic licentiousness and were strongly condemned by the Christian church.

MITHRA

Persian sun god. It was said Mithra was born in a cave or from a rock, and that as soon as he emerged into the world he clothed himself with leaves from a fig tree and ate of its fruit. Mithra slew the Great (or Cosmic) Bull, from which all animal and vegetable life sprang. Mithra is usually shown wearing a tunic and Phrygian cap with his cloak flying out behind him and in the act of slaying the Great Bull. A depiction of this scene was in every MITHRAEUM. Mithra was also known as Mithras.

MITHRAEUM

Underground place of worship dedicated to MITHRA. Such places have been found on sites as far apart as northern England and what is now the Holy Land. See also CAUTES AND CAUTOPATES.

MITHRA'S FIG TREE

See MITHRA.

MITHRAISM

Of Persian origin, Mithraism spread throughout the Roman Empire via its followers in various branches of the military. It became one of the most popular Roman religions during the second and third centuries CE but declined thereafter. Mithrans were required to be chaste, obedient, and loyal. Parallels have been drawn between Mithraism and Christianity because of shared practices such as baptism and anticipation of resurrection as well as the belief that MITHRA, in common with many sun gods, was born on 25 December.

Mithrans advanced within their religion through seven degrees. In ascending order, these were Corax (Raven), Nymphus (Male Bride), Miles (Soldier), Leo (Lion), Peres (Persian), Heliodromus (Runner of the Sun), and Pater (Father). Women were excluded from Mithraism.

MONOPHYSITE

Adherent to a doctrine holding that Christ had only one nature (divine) although others declared this one nature to be a mixture of two (human and divine). Monophysites holding the former view were condemned by the Council of Chalcedon (451), but nevertheless the belief remained particularly strong in Syria and Egypt during the time of JUSTINIAN I.

NEREIDS

Mythological sea-nymphs. Fifty in number, they often aided sailors in peril. The Nereids were usually depicted riding marine denizens such as seahorses or dolphins.

NUMMUS (plural: nummi)

In the early Byzantine period the nummus was the smallest copper coin. Although the minting of nummi was suspended in 498, it was resumed in 512.

ORACLE OF TROPHONIUS

Trophonius and his brother Agamedes were legendary architects whose works were said to include Apollo's temple at Delphi. The oracle of Trophonius was at Lebadeia in central Greece. It was consulted by performing purification rites and sacrifices, and then descending a shaft to reach an extremely narrow passageway leading to a cave. After the supplicant returned, priests interpreted any revelations that had been granted. Since the former invariably emerged in a state of extremely low spirits after visiting the cave, the melancholy were commonly referred to as having "consulted the oracle of Trophonius."

OVID (43 BC-c l7 CE)

Roman poet best known for his erotic verse. Author of the *Art of Love* and also *The Metamorphoses*, a mythological-historical collection.

PATRIARCH

Head of a diocese or patriarchate.

PENDULIA

Small ornaments, often jeweled, hanging from a circlet or crown.

PLATO'S ACADEMY

Plato (?428-347 BC?) founded his academy in 387 BC. Situated on the northwestern side of Athens, its curriculum included natural science, mathematics, philosophy, and training for public service.

PLINY THE YOUNGER (?62-c 113 CE)

Orator, public official, and consul. He is famous for his letters, which provide a vivid picture of contemporary Roman life and are thought to have been written for publication rather than as individual communications.

PROCONNESUS

Island in the Sea of Marmara. It was famous for its white marble quarries.

PROSPHORION

Harbor situated on the northern side of Constantinople.

QUAESTOR

Public official who administered financial and legal matters.

SAMSUN'S HOSPICE

Founded by St Samsun (d 530), a physician and priest. Also known as Sampson or Samson the Hospitable, he is often referred to as the Father of the Poor because of his work among the destitute. His feast day is 27 June. The hospice was near the GREAT CHURCH.

SAUSAGES
Sausages were a popular Roman dish. The best were considered to be spicy Lucanian sausages, said to have been brought to Rome by soldiers returning from service in Lucania in southern Italy.

STRATEGION
Forum in north Constantinople, close to the Golden Horn.

TESSERAE (singular: tessera)
Small pieces of glass, stone, marble, etc., usually square and used to make mosaics.

THEODORA (c 497-548)
Wife of JUSTINIAN I. Before her marriage she was an actress and MIME as well as allegedly working as a prostitute. She exercised great influence upon her husband.

THUCYDIDES (c 460-400 BC)
Eminent Greek historian, author of the *History of the Peloponnesian War*.

VITALIAN (d 520)
Defended the orthodox faith against Anastasius I (c 430-518, r 491-518), who supported monophysitism (see MONOPHYSITE). Vitalian went into hiding after being defeated in 515. After his ascension to the throne, JUSTIN I invited Vitalian to Constantinople to honor him for his actions. Appointed consul in 520, Vitalian was murdered several months later at an imperial banquet. Popular rumor maintained that JUSTINIAN I was responsible for his assassination.